The World Entire continues the story of Ascher Lieb (from Jo Perry's critically acclaimed 2021 novel *Pure*).

Ascher returns in a fast-moving, intense, and layered mystery about a dog accused of murder and a violent group who are targeting the man Ascher loves.

Love, as we all know, is complicated —and in her efforts to save the dog, Ascher must find the real murderer, risking everything to fulfil an impossible and dangerous promise.

"Decidedly literary and unapologetically noir, this is a monster of a beautiful book. ...A triumph."

–Matt Phillips, author of A Good Rush of Blood and Know Me from Smoke

"A complete original. Everything happens–murder, mayhem, love and loss–to humans and pets alike. I loved this book."

–Steven Cooper, author of the Alex Mills and Gus Parker mysteries

"The World Entire perfectly captures LA's beauty, ugliness and energy. This finely observed and artfully crafted novel shows Perry to be the poet she was and ever will be."

–Josh Gidding, author of Failure: An Autobiography

"Powerful and propulsive, The World Entire is about murder, hatred and love's redemptive power. A hymn to L.A.'s frustrating and fabulous beauty, it deserves a place alongside Chandler, Ellroy and Mosely."

–Derek Farrell, author of The Danny Bird Mysteries

First published 2024 by Fahrenheit Press

ISBN: 978-1-914475-69-6

10 9 8 7 6 5 4 3 2 1

www.Fahrenheit–Press.com

F 4 E

Cover Design & Manuscript Typesetting by www.SkullStarStudio.com

The World Entire

By

Jo Perry

Fahrenheit Press

Also by Jo Perry

- *Dead is Better*
- *Dead is Best*
- *Dead Is Good*
- *Dead Is Beautiful*
- *Everything Happens*
- *Pure*

For Alix and Ian

"Whoever destroys a soul, it is considered as if he destroyed an entire world. And whoever saves a life, it is considered as if he saved an entire world."

– Mishna Sanhedrin 37-1

Part One

"Only what we have lost forever do we possess forever."

–Brother Theodore

1.

The white ambulance with the red shield emblem trundles east on Third Street, emergency lights extinguished, sirens silent. The yellow dwarf star that is our sun electrifies the ambulance driver's black beard and eyebrow hairs—then collapses behind the Beverly Center. An N95 mask is crumpled around his neck and a silver clip secures the black kippah he washes by hand and air-dries in a bowl to keep its shape. He wears the "MAKE BIG MONEY BEING A KOSHER CHEF" sweatshirt I gave him for Hanukkah. His permanent press, white button-down shirt, reflective vest, I.D. and medical bag are stashed behind the seat. Everything else is in the back of his truck.

Well, not his exactly.

The ambulance I'm slouching in belongs to L.A. Hatzalah, the volunteer EMS group the operator—Isaac Kahn—volunteers with when he's not running his catering business. The deal is that he keeps the ambulance at his place so he's available whenever he's needed.

I lean to the left and kiss Isaac below his right ear—a spot redolent of nutmeg and the opalescent Smart & Final liquid soap he buys in bulk.

"Thank you," Isaac says. "I owe you one."

"More than one."

We stop at the traffic light opposite the defunct, stately as in "lying in state before interment" K-Mart, soon to be razed for a new, mixed-use condo-tower thing with a macrobiotic market at the bottom. Two weeks ago, members of a fringe hate group strung up homemade banners with swastikas spray-painted over stars of David from the K-Mart roof—"Ye and Hitler are right about The Jew$" and, "Honk if You Know the Jew$ caused COVID and Control YOU."

Once he saw them, Isaac double-parked the ambulance, climbed a bent, rusty and rickety fire ladder to the roof and pulled them down.

Isaac—the muscles in his jaw working—glances at the roof, but doesn't mention the banner.

I don't, either.

I keep my eyes behind my sunglasses on a wheel-less CVS shopping cart spilling a blur of disintegrating objects before a huddle of tents at the bus stop.

The light turns green. Isaac looks straight ahead as a woman staring at her cell phone leads two dogs across the intersection. Despite their cotton-candy fur and matching bubblegum pink bandanas, these poodle-ish creatures lack the charisma and life-force of Freddie—my opinionated, epileptic, senior miniature pinscher with abandonment issues.

The woman and her canine tumbleweeds complete their transit. The ambulance advances, then drifts onto Fireside Avenue where the uniformed guard inside the Los Villas del Fairfax Village tiled-roofed kiosk waves him on and smiles the way most people smile at Isaac—as if they know him and like him.

"Why are we in Los Villas del Fairfax Village?" I prefer to call this historic complex of Mediterranean towers, Spanish-ish-style apartments, mature Jacarandas and green spaces "Los Villas del What the Fuck," but I can't be sarcastic about everything. "I thought we were getting those great tamales at the farmers' market on La Brea—the ones that always sell out right away."

"We are. But there's a slight detour." Isaac's face relaxes into a smile. "There's someone I want you to meet—just for a few minutes. I know you'll like her and Los Villas isn't really out of the way.

My cheeks warm and my spine straightens. This is not the first time Isaac has surprise-matched me with women he thinks will fill the empty spaces in my life. The sinkhole I fell into after my parents' fatal car accident became an abyss last year after my last close relative and favorite and only aunt died of COVID and other things she never told me about.

I know Isaac isn't looking for an aunt-replacement—he understands how impossible and unhelpful that would be. And I'm sure this Los Villas del What the Fuck person is perfectly wonderful—just like the other old ladies he's tried to fix me up with—or maybe tried to fix me with—smart, witty, wise, interesting, talented, white-haired painters or ceramicists who speak four languages or start sourdough and then bake it or who are retired environmental scientists who write short stories. People he meets through his EMS and food work and who strike him as being just the right void-pluggers for me—not aunt-like, but aunt-lite.

But Isaac should cut it out.

My aunt—Miss Evelyn Pauline Mandel—Paulie to her close friends—was a one-off—both prototype and archetype. Soon––yes, I'm counting—it will be three hundred and sixty-five days since she was forced into her favorite blue pantsuit, Zoom-funeraled, and buried under a deer- and coyote-frequented hill in a Jewish cemetery overlooking a cement flood channel, the 134 Freeway and the Warner Brothers and Disney studios.

I try to communicate telepathically through the side of Isaac's head that—though the dreaded *yahrzeit* of my aunt's death is stalking me, I don't require a stand-in or a substitute. The negative spaces that are my parents and my aunt have become an almost-companionable entourage. And though I haven't told Isaac this—there is only one Aunt Evelyn-type being I'd be willing to hang out with, and I've already had a surprise and not completely satisfactory meet-up with her—Evelyn Pauline Mandel's distracted, meandering ghost.

"I told her all about you while we were waiting for the paramedics after her fall. She can't wait to meet you." I can tell Isaac is pleased with the ambush he's contrived as he searches for a jumbo parking space along the narrow, Jacaranda blossom-festooned "Calles" of Los Villas del Nice Elderly Ladies.

"She was a social worker— a therapist for emotionally-disturbed kids or something—and she has a Masters from U.C.L.A. Her husband was a professor. And she was in a chevra kadisha, just like you. She hasn't been mobile since her fall, and it will be great for her to see a fresh and friendly face."

"My face isn't friendly or fresh." My face burns and I wonder if this lady's experience with emotionally disturbed children made Isaac think that she was an especially good candidate to be my friend.

"How perfect is this? She lives in number forty-nine, just a few doors down." Isaac noses the ambulance into a spot that miraculously opens just as we approach. The ambulance faces a turquoise door in a row of doors to two-story units painted hues from the Los Villas mid-century modern/Spanish mission mash-up palette. The turquoise door has a wooden plaque that says "LOVE IS LOVE" in rainbow letters hanging from the knocker.

"And you didn't tell her all about me—because if you had, she wouldn't want to meet me."

"Okay, Ascher. I didn't tell her everything—" Isaac crosses his arms over "CHEF," signifying that he will sit on his very nice ass in his shiny ambulance in this magical parking space until he gets an EMS call or I agree to schmooze with this destined-to-be my-bestie victim of gravity's malice. "But I told her enough––that you're smart, brave, kind, funny, beauti—"

"I'm not kind. I'm not brave and I'm not that other thing." I stare at the LOVE IS LOVE door decoration not sure why I am so pissed off and sad. Is it that Isaac made me blush? Or that he won't stop looking for a miracle cure for my orphanhood?
Isaac and I listen to whatever under the ambulance's hood is going tick, tick, tick. We watch the turquoise LOVE IS LOVE-adorned door open and eject a Los Fairfax 'What the Fuck Villager' in a billowing shirt though no wind jostles the violet haze that is the nearest Jacaranda tree.

The man carries a pair of long-bladed garden shears and passes the ambulance without looking at it—which is strange as I've learned from hanging out with Isaac that ninety-nine percent of passersby stare fish-eyed into the ambulance's interior as if there's a seriously wounded or very sick person sitting in the passenger seat.

The man stops before a tall shrub, looks it up and down, applies his shears to the hedge, then steps back a few paces to evaluate his work—a heart—symmetrical and plump—emerging from the mass of waxy, viridian leaves.

"Love is love," I say.

Isaac covers my hand with his and the shimmery spark of his skin meeting my skin tugs my gaze back to his infuriatingly sweet, effective, frank, hot and completely disarming smile.

2.

"Not too long with What's Her Name, okay? Can we agree to make this kind of snappy—" My aunt always said "make it snappy." "—or there won't be any tamales left."

"—L.S.," Isaac says. "Her name is Linda but she goes by L.S. Her last name is Rutledge." Isaac doesn't explain why this woman goes by two formidable-sounding initials instead of Linda Sue or Lavinia Sandra or Lily Shirley. He strides—straight and assertive as a bolded capital letter I—to a cinnamon red door and I follow him up the step. There's a patinaed mezuzah—the kind made in Israel and sold in Judaica shops—angled to the frame and hot orange geraniums in plastic pots. "Since when are you eager to eat tamales?"

"Since I got hungry." I leave out the new diet I invented that involves skipping breakfast and lunch and drinking tons of filling, decaf coffee. I have to pee and hope that I can use my new buddy's—L.S.'s—bathroom before our chitchat session begins. I stand behind Isaac—not next to him—on purpose. My height is exactly mid-percentile because I'm not the thin, tall reed I aspire to be. But because I'm almost short, L.S. Rutledge won't even see the surprise human lurking behind Isaac when she opens her door. L.S. Rutledge will only see some Mystery Hips sticking out on either side of Isaac's muscular narrowness despite the big plastic bag he holds that is filled with plastic containers of food he cooked for her and stashed in the back of the truck where I wouldn't see it.

I wish I had Isaac's gift for thoughtfulness and for schmoozing with strangers. I'm grateful the N95 Isaac gave me covers my not-smile and I'm embarrassed to be wearing my old black leggings, flip flops and Isaac's oversized Blue Matzo—-the name of his kosher New Mexican catering business—blue sweatshirt.

Is it too late to run?

"A few minutes with L.S. and you'll be wonderful friends, I know it," Isaac balances the food bag in one arm, pulls down his mask, kisses my forehead—his clairvoyant eyes bright—then turns to my soon-to-be soul-sister's door and knocks.

3.

The food bag flops against the potted geraniums. Isaac has had his left ear flat against L.S. Rutledge's door for what feels like a long time. He's already delivered three assertive, official-sounding knock-sequences to its ruddy surface which replied with expectant silences. He's already tried and failed to see inside the apartment through a slender opening between one bent and one straight vertical blind behind the window. And he's called L.S. Rutledge from his cell phone twice to say what he is saying again now.

"Mrs. Rutledge? It's Isaac Kahn. I'm here with my friend, Miss Lieb—Ascher—for the visit we talked about this morning."

"Maybe today isn't the day." I touch Isaac's shoulder. "Or maybe she forgot, or turned down her hearing aid, took a pain pill and zoned out on the couch." Having visited my aunt many times at her elder community, and having lived in her condo during the pandemic lockdown after she died—I know a little about senior dozing.

"Even if she did forget, she'd hear me. She's not hard of hearing and she can't use the stairs. Until her knee heals, she's stuck on the first floor with the knee scooter and she has nowhere to sleep except the living room couch."

What's a knee scooter? I think, but only say, "What about the bathroom?"

"Maybe. How long have we been here?"

"I don't know. Ten minutes?"

I push my hair away from my face and press my own ear against the door, hold my breath and listen. There's the non-sound that empty space or moving air makes, then something I can't identify. "I hear something, Isaac."

"What"

"I don't know." I close my eyes this time. After a few seconds the soft, almost-weightless, whoosh or waah resumes. "Maybe it's air conditioning. Or a humidifier. Or something brushing against the door. Or maybe I'm just hearing the blood vessels inside my own my own head or my own breathing. I can't tell."

"Something's wrong." Isaac jogs the few steps back to the ambulance, then lopes back to L.S. Rutledge's doorstep with his red medical bag and a long, narrow black duffle. He removes a vest, a pair of latex gloves, an I.D. lanyard from the medical bag, pulls the lanyard over his head, slips on the Day-Glo yellow vest with the L.A. Hatzalah shield and heartbeat insignia on the back, snaps on the gloves, unzips the long, black bag and lifts out some sort of hooked pole, a mallet, and from a zipper compartment, a key.

"What's that pole for?"

"It's called a Halligan tool. I may have to use it to force entry, Ascher. So please step back."

"You're going to break down her door?" I move closer. "Are you even allowed to? What if she's just taking a long shower? Before you scare the crap out of her, shouldn't you wait a little longer or call the apartment manager?"

"If she's unwell, I've waited too long already. And yes, I am allowed to force entry. I'm just going to try to bump the lock—don't worry." Isaac puts the pole down and holds up the key and the mallet as if doing that makes sense to me.

A man pushing a French plaid-vested-and-bow-tied corgi in a dog stroller stops to watch Isaac Kahn insert the key—it looks like ordinary-looking key with jagged teeth—into the lock, retract it slightly, then strike it almost soundlessly with the mallet.

"Is the woman who lives there okay? Is she your relative?"

I suffocate the impulse to tell the man that yes, the woman is not only a relative—she's my grandmother. But I put myself on a lying diet, too.

"She's a friend of my friend. When she didn't answer her phone or the door, he got worried. She hurt her knee and has to use a knee scooter." The man nods as if he's an expert on knee scooters. "So, he decided he should check on her."

Hitting the key with the mallet must have been the bump.

Isaac turns the key, removes it, and slips it into his pocket. "If she hasn't locked the deadbolt, I won't have to use the heavy tool."

4.

L.S. Rutledge didn't lock her deadbolt.

Though I have no business entering the apartment of a stranger I didn't want to meet, I follow Isaac from the light into her darkness.

"Mrs. Rutledge?" Isaac has become straighter and taller and–
–despite his mask—his voice is more resonant than it was outdoors.

We're in a tiny entry, but the silence and gloom swamp us. There's a dark staircase climbing the darkness on the left, a big box of darkness that must be the living room ahead of us, and a small, dim kitchen with the lights off and the blinds closed on my right. As my pupils widen, things materialize—a table with junk mail piled on it, a wide-brimmed sun hat on a hook and a paper shopping bag full of empty plastic water bottles on the floor.

"Please close the door, Ascher," Isaac says, "Then remain where you are."

After the door lock clicks, a greasy metallic odor defeats my mask.

Isaac points the heavy flashlight that he took out of his bag into the darkness ahead of us. Its phosphor beam reveals a high-contrast black and white tableau—a black T.V. console a lot like the one my aunt had, a tufted black couch, a glass-topped table with white photos arranged on it, a gray box with a tissue issuing from it like an ice-plume, an economy size Advil bottle, a bottle of hand sanitizer, an open flip cellphone—the kind they sell in the AARP magazine—and a remote control. Then Isaac Kahn redirects the cold light to the carpet. Gleaming jet blades of moon-grass glitter under the sweep of lunar light then—as the light moves—they glisten the color of barbecue sauce.

Isaac's light moves again, landing on something black pushed up against something else. "Mrs. Rutledge? L.S.?"

The black thing moves.

"Stay where you are, Ascher."

Why does Isaac Kahn imagine that what I most want to do is to go galumph up to whatever is moving in that living room?

But because I'm worried about Isaac, I unnail my flip flops from the floor and follow him as he takes deliberate steps toward the dark shape, then turns to me and—I can tell from the way his mask moves—speaks to me.

But an ocean of impenetrable silence and distance has engulfed Isaac—I cannot hear what Isaac is saying the way you can't hear what a free diver is saying when he's at maximum depth.

Isaac's volume has been turned all the way down to off.

I shake my head, then swallow to unplug my ears—but that doesn't help.

Isaac points his flashlight at some rusty splatter on the ceiling. Then his black eyes flash platinum as he points the light at a dark thing that—like origami in reverse—unfolds itself into something big streaking toward me.

Then all the darknesses in here—the black thing, the black room, Isaac Kahn, and the black haze of my own fear—dissolve into a black fog.

5.

Isaac's beard smells like copper. He flicks his warm tongue against the place where my forehead hurts, then over my closed eyelids, ears, and neck.

I must have had too much of his kosher wine.

I must be in his bed.

Freddie. Shit.

Freddie must be out of his mind waiting for me.

What if he's had a seizure?

"I have to go. Freddie needs his meds and food and a walk."

Isaac pushes his tongue in my ear again.

Maybe he didn't hear me. My lips feel the way they do after the dentist injects Novocain. I sound like I'm talking through a sock.

I force my eyes open and see a face hovering over mine—a Goth, Macy's Thanksgiving Day Parade balloon dog-head.

"Don't move. Don't fucking move!" The visage bares its stained teeth, then solidifies into a rubber dog mask.

"Why shouldn't I move?"

"Do what I say, Ascher. Stay still."

"Not until you tell me why a dog-thing that talks like you is pinning me down like this?"

"Just promise you won't move an eyelash and I'll tell you."

I flutter my sticky eyelashes.

"Don't be a smart ass, Ascher. Please. Promise me."

"Okay. I promise," I lie.

"You passed out, Ascher. You'll be fine if you remain absolutely still. Please. I'm serious."

My forehead and backhead throb. I have to get back to

Freddie right away. I really, really have to pee. Why is Isaac playing games with me?

"You passed out" doesn't cover whatever weirdness is going on or explain why I'm staring at this effigy of a dog.

I can't not move. I have to get out of here.

With both hands I shove the wet dog head so hard I feel the sharp occiput under the slick fur. Then I elbow myself halfway up and squint.

"I'm telling you, get down!" Isaac is losing it now.

I force myself to sit all the way up.

The dog—there's definitely a canine body attached to the canine head—a black lab or shepherd or something medium-sized—shrinks back, sits and pants—its eyes wide with dread.

I touch my lips and discover a damp mask. I rub my eyes and forehead and my fingertips bloom red. Isaac aims a horribly bright light at the dog's big, dipped-in-red paws, its coyote-narrow chest, red-splattered, angular face, and lingers on the two full mini-moons it has for eyes.

"Why did I faint? What happened?"

"That creature from hell is what happened, Ascher. So, make yourself small and keep still." Isaac shouts.

The dog thumps its tail against the floor, whines, then stares at me.

I look into the dog's glittery, interrogating mirror-orbs, then at Isaac.

He wears a white N95 and holds a fat, black flashlight raised like a weapon. The reflective edging of his EMS vest incandesces as he aims the flashlight beam at a dark chair floating in the blood-swamped carpet into which his black chef's clogs are sinking.

6.

Isaac commands the spattered, already-sitting dog to sit, sidles past the creature, puts his flashlight—aimed at the dog's forelegs—on the carpet, pulls me rockily to my feet and—keeping one solid arm around my waist—flicks on a light switch.

Isaac looks into my eyes. His forehead is pale and greasy with sweat. "No sign of trauma. You'll be fine."

I look at the carpet and I'm treated to a view of a mess of red and Isaac Kahn's red-slathered clogs. Then the memory of why Isaac brought me here zaps me with a shudder.

Seeing Isaac in his Hatzalah vest makes sense.

But not the red-stained black dog, or our shadows stretching across the maze of ketchup impressions pressed into the carpeting. Or the long chair supporting a mannikin the color Pantone would name Exsanguination Crimson.

Oh, God. Is this What's Her Name? The lady Isaac Kahn wanted me to meet? Sunny-side-up with the contents of her circulatory system gelling into a La-Z-Boy set to maximum recline? And what is the low-wheeled thing next to the chair in a slick roast-beef-colored puddle? Isaac keeps his eyes locked on the dog as if doing so will empower him to remotely control its movements. The dog whines, but stays down as Isaac again tells me to stay just where I am, calls 911 and Animal Services, then talks in Hebrew to someone at Hatzalah.

I evade the dog's stare and look at the chair and the body in profile—slashes in a cheek, short hairline-to-earlobe slices, a blood-flood spilled from neck to shoulder, a gashed freckled, chubby hand, a ribboned sleeve, and ripped socks that look like the white nylon anti-embolism socks my aunt wore—except that these are red below the polyester pantleg.

The dog gives up on me and looks at the recliner, too—the way Freddie looks at me when I'm leaving the apartment—heartbroken. Slack-mouthed.

"I told you. Stay!" Isaac actually interrupts his phone conversation to yell at the dog.

"He is staying," I say. "He's doing what you tell him to."

Isaac raises his eyebrows at me as the dog lets out a deep, soul-scorching sorrow-howl that rises through the ceiling, through the second-floor and the roof, through the purple-blossomed Los Villas Del What Just Happened? Jacaranda canopy, then wreathes itself into the tangled wails of approaching sirens.

7.

White flashing bursts behind the blinded windows of the murder apartment. A haze of voices dissolves into evening's cool indigo.

I'm in Isaac's ambulance, the only emergency vehicle without its engine running or its lights flashing among the vehicles crowding Calle de las Artes.

The screaming LAFD fire truck and ambulance arrived first––their station is close on 3rd Street. Then two Los Villas del Fairfax Village security guards with walkie talkies, batons and pepper spray canisters rattling on their belts hummed in on electric Los Villas del Fairfax golf carts. The LAPD cruisers sped in next, then the albino LAPD Crime Scene Investigation and L.A. County Coroner's vans.

When I close my eyes, this is what I see—a vermillion figure stiffening in a recliner chair, the anguished and bloodied dog, then Freddie—panicked, frightened, hungry, medication-deprived and having a seizure as he waits for me behind my apartment door.

When I open my eyes, these apparitions remain—thin mists, two brownish-black, the other red—veiling everything.

I couldn't talk to Isaac. After a police officer with a head like a concrete slab finished asking me questions, he suggested that Isaac escort his recently passed-out, unsteady-looking friend—me—to the ambulance. As soon as he'd led me past the potted plants and we'd descended the steps and passed the guards keeping concerned Los Villas villagers at a distance—the man with the bow-tied dog and the topiary guy and some other people including three women wearing huge curlers and bathrobes—

Isaac halted, looked at me the way he did when he was searching for signs of a traumatic brain injury and said "I love you, Ascher Lieb" through his N95 with emphasis on "you."

Isaac lowered his mask and kissed me. Then, as he walked me the rest of the way to his ambulance, he asked me not to do what he knew I wanted to do—call a Lyft and return to Freddie ASAP—and to please wait for him in the ambulance no matter how long it took because the first thing that was going to happen when he was free to go would be that we would haul ass—lights on and sirens screaming—to my apartment.

I said yes. I'd wait.

But though I think I do—I did not tell Isaac that yes, I love him back.

My heart was frozen and I couldn't stop shaking. I felt certain that my instant rejection of L.S. Rutledge—her knee, her knee scooter, her suitability as a friend—my friend—and my indifference to her isolation—had somehow contributed to her violent death, and that the sharp splinters of aloofness, mockery and unkindness that had my name on them were enough to have caused a homicidal surge in the already almost-full-to-the-brim store of human cruelty and selfishness.

Isaac never said what he said to me before—he's never come close.

Love? People—except my late aunt and my parents—don't find me lovable. If you don't believe me, ask Hans, my ex-boyfriend and Neil, my ex-boyfriend before Hans. Which is why I got angry when I realized that Isaac had over-promised his murdered friend.

I'm not brave, I'm not kind, and I'm not the b-word signifying pretty.

So, ignoring what Isaac said about loving me and never holding him to it—even if I have the urge to say something along the same lines to him—seems right, doesn't it?

Despite his emergency medical training and experience, Isaac was freaking out. The tastes good, cooks good, smells good, does good, tall, hairy in a good way, benevolent guy in the bloody chef shoes who uttered my first and last name and then said he loved me could not have been himself when he said that probably soon-to-be-horribly-embarrassing-for-him thing that must have been an involuntary response to death—an upswell of emotion and primal need for living human connection as unprofound and transitory as a fart.

So, I hereby declare that Isaac saying he loved me never happened.

8.

Its amber light-bar flashing, the freezer-white Los Angeles Animal Services truck sends tremors through the pristine floor of Isaac Kahn's ambulance and that penetrate my flip flops and the soles of my bare feet as it rolls a few doors past L.S. Rutledge's door and stops. Two men in black uniforms hop out, one opens one of the truck's side compartments and removes two long poles with nooses on the ends. One man carries the poles and the other follows as a police-officer waves them into Mrs. L.S. Rutledge's apartment.

I open the passenger door a little and listen. It's all radio crackles and blurred voices for a while, then muffled shouts and scraping. The apartment door opens and the two Animal Services officers accompanied by their enormous black shadows are not providing services to the frightened animal—they're dragging it down the steps.

Each man has his pole's noose fitted tightly around the black dog's neck. Its eyes bulge with terror and its open, drooling mouth produces a dry scream as one of the men hands his noose-pole to the other, opens a different door in the side of the truck and reveals a metal box with a few round air holes drilled into it. As the men tighten the cords around the dog's neck and force it inside the small compartment, the frantic animal manages to wrench its head and send a taser-jolt of anguish and fear through the ambulance's spotless windshield and into my thumping heart.

9.

I can hear Freddie before the elevator—which smells like lasagna—opens. Isaac holds the wilted bag of food containers pressed against his chest and follows me barefoot down the industrial-carpeted hallway. He left his bloody clogs with the Los Villas del Oh My God Jacaranda blossoms stuck to them in a plastic biohazard bag in the back of the ambulance.

Freddie loses it every time it's me in the hall. But I wonder if this time he's reacting to Isaac and the food he can smell through the Tupperware—or if he smells the other dog's fear in its saliva on my forehead, or the scent of the human blood that turned the white block letters on Isaac's hoodie the color of Dr. Pepper.

While researching a paper I plagiarized for money, I learned that dogs have three hundred million nasal smell-receptors and that almost half their brain-power goes to processing scent. Dogs can detect the odor of thousand-year-old skeleton-fragments, and can smell the difference between pre-seizure and post-seizure human sweat. So, it's not a stretch to assume that Freddie is sniffing out the unique olfactory signature of the dog among the mix of volatile organic compounds Isaac and I wear like invisible clouds.

I unlock my apartment door and Freddie is dancing and yipping.

Except for being hoarse and slightly missing the pee pad I'd put out for him, Freddie is okay. After he swallows the pills I rolled in cream cheese and scarfs down his canine pâté dinner, I kiss the tan dots above his eyes and tell him what a good old doggie he is and how much I love him and how sorry I am that he was alone for so long. But when I look at him, all I see is that other dog being drag-choked into the Animal Services truck.

I slide the halter over his head and attach his leash and Freddie wags his tail against the floor just as the dog in the apartment did when Isaac commanded him to sit.

Isaac pauses unpacking the food containers he'd prepared for R.S. Rutledge. "Do you need company?"

"We're just going to the park. What we need the now is a shower, food and coffee." That was the first thing Isaac said to me since our grim, astonished and wordless ride in the ambulance, and the first thing I said to him. Why are we so brittle?

Isaac opens the cupboard above the sink where I store some of his supplies. "True. I'll heat the food and make some lattes."

Isaac has his own kitchen stash because he's an observant Jew for reasons that involve his personal beliefs—yes to God, no to strict orthodoxy, yes to his wish to honor his family and the memory of a beloved grandfather, and a big fat yes to being a 3-D, twenty-four-seven, walking, breathing fuck you to antisemites.

So Isaac wears a kippah. He covers his shoulders with a prayer shawl and—Sunday through Friday he wraps the black leather straps attached to boxes containing handwritten Torah verses—*tefillin*—around his forearm and forehead before he prays—which he does in Hebrew three times a day. And he keeps kosher—which poses a dishes, cookware, utensils, food and cutlery problem when he's here that Isaac solves with meat and dairy cookware and tools and disposable cutlery, plates, plastic and insulated cups, kosher products and kosher coffee for the fancy espresso-latte maker he gave me for Hanukkah.

My stomach grumbles as Freddie and I descend in the fragrant, empty elevator and his nails click across the lobby flooring and onto the sidewalk where nothing is too small for God or him. As he investigates sidewalk flecks, blackened gum deposits, a discarded surgical mask, a lifeless scarab beetle and a Power Bar wrapper, I can't help wondering how Isaac could ever imagine he'd fallen in love with a not-slender atheist Jew who swears all the time, who used to numb herself with Valium, who didn't visit her beloved aunt often enough, who plagiarized for money and who—from the age of thirteen until last year—lied to herself and everyone else about everything that mattered.

How can someone as together, brave, effective and idealistic as Isaac love a flailing person who probably doesn't have what it takes to complete the courses required for the mortuary science degree and the career as a death-worker she thought was a great idea?

Freddie tugs me past the lantana bush snagged with trash and across the driveway to the below-ground parking lot and I realize with a brain-thud that my car is still at Isaac's place.

How could I forget my car?

Freddie scratches the gate as I enter my key-code, then skitters onto the slippery, faded-green plastic-turfed rhomboid the property management company calls a "Dog Park" and assumes the rapt expression that signifies he's about to take a shit.

I look away to give Freddie some privacy just as the moon—a veil-thin opal aligned with my home planet—climbs above the new condos across the street. Can Freddie smell the thundering tides or the mineral scent of the moon's pull?

One thing happens and then another happens that washes it away for all eternity. So, in this inescapable cycle of manifestation and obliteration what do people mean by God?

Taking too much Valium and sleeping through the emergency call from my aunt's assisted living place was all my fault—but the hideous fuck-up that was arriving after my aunt died of COVID and a cancer she never told me about felt as though it involved something bigger than my own frailty—maybe some sort of cosmic irony generator.

And something—whispering stones? —signaled my parents that it was time to depart Camp Whispering Stones exactly when they'd be cruising the fast lane opposite an approaching big rig and a panicked bird flapped into the open driver's window. Was what made this happen the same thing that made the moment L.S. Rutledge's dog decided to maul her to death different from all the moments that had come before?

Or if the dog didn't murder her—which I can't stop feeling is what happened—what pushed her human killer from malice to murder?

Freddie regards his turd as if it is a sentient alien freshly arrived from deep space and suspiciously observes me package it in a biodegradable bag from the Courtesy Dispenser, then relinquish it to the Courtesy Receptacle.

I open the gate and Freddie trots smartly ahead of me, then stops to check that I am still behind him holding the other end of his leash.

I am.

I'm not ducking out, dumping him or being anywhere except right here with him under this godless and degradable sky.

10.

Reclining in what has unofficially become his side of my queen-sized bed, Isaac does not wear his kippah, his spare jeans, t-shirt or the boxers he keeps in my dresser's bottom drawer. He sips a kosher latte from his kosher paper cup—flecks of nondairy froth attaching to his glistening kosher beard and moustache—and watches me turban my wet, atheist hair with one of my late aunt's towels. Freddie sleeps on the foot of my side of the bed on my aunt's white sweater—which, if you press it against your face—still delivers the fading scent of her Arpège perfume.

"How are you feeling, Ascher?" Isaac uses his concerned, but emotion-less EMS voice.

"Feeling how? Is there something wrong with me?"

"Not at all." Isaac smiles. "You seemed perfectly healthy just now."

The second humiliating blush of this shitty day rises from my breasts to my scalp.

"Sometimes confusion and memory loss—temporary, don't worry—can present after a bump to the head. And you fell pretty hard."

What are the symptoms of a blow to the spirit, I want to ask him—but I make a joke. "I know what day and year it is and who's President. And my skull is harder than a geode." I tap the top of my head to demonstrate. "I guess I should have told you, but I hadn't eaten before I drove to your place, so it was probably low blood sugar or too much coffee and terror that made me pass out."

I don't tell Isaac that I feel like I'm dissolving from the inside out. And I don't mention that I've been skipping breakfast and lunch for almost two weeks—but today was the only day when I lost consciousness.

Or that I've fainted once before and that other blackout also involved being close to a dead person.

Still, Isaac knows something's up with me. He looks me up and down if he is performing an x-ray-vision full mind-body scan, then runs his fingers through his beard—the tell that he's formulating his diagnosis.

"I think you should stay with me for the time being. It's not a good idea for you to be alone."

What does "time being" even mean? How long is "time being" in minutes, hours, days and weeks?

I unwrap the towel, shake out my generic-brown, fine hair so it will seem fuller than it is, slip under the sheets, slide close to Isaac and press my cheek against his warm, hairy chest. "But wouldn't I be alone when you're working? And don't you work pretty much all the time?"

Isaac strokes my damp hair so softly that I get chills—but he doesn't answer me. He inhales, then waits a long time before releasing the breath.

"I'm not alone," I chatter to fill the silence. "I live with Freddie and as you know, he doesn't handle change very well." I kiss Isaac's hairy sternum. "I appreciate that you care about me, but you can be with me any time you want. That's why I gave you a key."

Isaac gently lifts my head off his chest, kisses the top of my head, rolls off the bed and—his back to me—cycles through channels with the T.V. remote. "There is nothing in the Valley," Isaac declares, the screen outlining his nakedness in electric blue. "There's no reason for you to be here and not with me."

I know that Isaac's assertion contains others—that he can't move because his place provides the space and affordability he requires for catering and for the ambulance, that he must reside in the area he serves through Hatzalah, that mid-city offers a variety of great kosher food and is where most of his kosher catering clients live. And that his place is close to the storefront shul he attends sometimes on Shabbat, on holidays and whenever its elderly congregants need him to make a minyan.

And what Isaac says is true. His neighborhood is diverse. Alive. And delicious—the Milky Way Restaurant's silky blintzes are swoon-worthy. So are the crispy rice salmon cakes at the tiny kosher sushi place he takes me to and the just-charred-enough shawarma with fresh tahini, pomegranate arils and pistachios, and the hummus with a soft-boiled egg at his friend's restaurant. Also, the makes-you-sweat-spicy vegan kosher takeout ramen Isaac gets when he doesn't feel like cooking.

The Valley is cement sunlight boomeranging off gray strip malls, flat grids of faded pastel apartment buildings—The Oxnard Oaks, The Regal Terrace, and The Roberta —on streets without oaks, royals or terraces submerged in a general forlornness.

The Valley is four-story mausoleum-shaped, mixed-use people-containers with bicycle and car parking and E.V. charging below first-floor boba places and an environmentally- safe dry-cleaners. Containers with conceptual names like Vista 23 or River Sky Lofts spelled out in white neon Futura.

The four-story thing Freddie and I live in is called Life Space and offers its "stakeholders" single-occupancy cells, each with a pretend balcony with a view of a high injury network—a street with a high number of collisions, hit and runs and traffic fatalities—or of a section of flood channel littered with capsized shopping carts, confetti-ed trash, cushion-less couches and egrets taking flight over the homeless encampment.

I choose to live in this little Valley box within a bigger box that's walking-distance to a psychic, an Urgent Care, Val Surf, four Ralph's markets with pigeon-invaded parking lots, three Whole Foods—one contact-less—, a new Erewhon, a surfeit of non-kosher sushi restaurants, mattress and chandelier stores, medical/dental offices, Botox and nail "spas," doggy daycares with forlorn doggies in their windows where I'd never send Freddie, and boutiques selling flowing early Billie Eilish tops and size zero workout gear.

The Valley's generic blankness and complete obliviousness to its own weirdness makes me feel free.

But I only have one serious reason for staying—one I can't confess to Isaac—which is that the house I lived in with my parents before the accident is here.

"I almost walked right into the drummer in that band you like across from the Studio City Starbucks," I tell Isaac. "That proves the Valley isn't completely boring, doesn't it?"

Isaac addresses the T.V. "If you lived on the other side of the hill, you'd run into drummers all the time."

I hate this Why Does Ascher Live In The Valley? quarrel because it always takes us where we don't want to go and leaves us there. And because of what it always makes me say—and not say.

I don't tell Isaac that the drummer I stupidly bumped into was an asshole.

I don't explain that here on the wrong side of the hill in this studio with amenities, sustainable finishes, wood-like floors, impossible-to-keep-stainless stainless-steel appliances, a vertical washer-dryer combo, and "Dog Park," I feel close to the trace-after-presences of my parents emanating from the old house—and that I occasionally receive images—oversaturated fragments radioactive with grief—of the life I lived with them there—

My father flipping scorched Nathan's hot dogs on the grill—my grandfather's analog Movado on his wide wrist.

My mother tan and barefoot in her short, lime seersucker robe—it must have been August—holding a Froot Loops box and smoking a cigarette behind the sliding door.

The kitchen's knotty pine's cowlick whirls swirling like galaxies.

How do I explain to Isaac that the farther away from the house I am—the less real the people who once lived there—including me—become?

Will the phantasms evaporate if I am no longer close?

And if they disappear—what will happen to me?

I take a swig of the now cool decaf latte Isaac made and the foam deconstructing itself on my tongue is perfect. "Can we please change the subject?"

Isaac watches two big, lustrous suffocating fish writhe on

hooks while a pink, grinning man holds them aloft on the television screen. "Fine."

I watch the fish die, then speak. "Was Mrs. Rutledge your first murder?"

Isaac's shoulder blades contract. "I was with Mrs. Weskinski after her fall. I've had cardiac arrests, some really ugly fractures, serious burns, car accidents, a few elder abuse cases that became fatals—but I've never seen a human being completely savaged until today."

Isaac looks at Freddie snoring on the bed. "Mrs. Rutledge was my first homicide by dog."

11.

"What's wrong?" His Ikea bag neatly packed with rinsed food containers, Isaac slips on a pair of clean black jeans and a black t-shirt and secures his kippah to his head with the silver clip. "You look like you've seen a ghost."

"Sort of. On the T.V. just now. Can you go back to the beginning? I want you to see."

Isaac retrieves the remote, reverses the frames until in cloudy black and white an L.A. Animal Services officer drags a terrified, black dog with a noose attached to a long pole.

"Look. That's him. Mrs. Rutledge's dog."

Two more animal control officers enter the frame and with the first two force the dog—whose paws slip on loose gravel—into a stainless-steel outdoor kennel as "CANNIBAL CANINE LIKELY RABID" marches across the bottom of the screen.

Isaac unmutes the T.V. and an exaggeratedly basso voice warns, "What follows is not appropriate for small children or sensitive viewers. In a breaking KNXL exclusive, we can report that Mid-City police officers came upon the out-of-control canine eating its human victim late this morning in a Los Villas del Fairfax Village apartment. Animal service officials speaking off the record told KNXL News that despite the threat of protests from animal rights groups, Angelenos can expect the unchipped killer Dog Doe to be put down and its brain tested for rabies within the next forty-eight hours. The name of the dog's victim has not been released."

Isaac freezes the broadcast on the image of the blood-crusted, wild-eyed dog's face.

"How can they report all that as fact? A cannibal is a person who eats people. And you and I both saw that the dog wasn't eating anybody. And I'm sure he wasn't rabid, either. How can they euthanize him without investigating first?"

"How do you know what that dog was doing, Ascher? You were unconscious for part of it. And it's a fact that dogs sometimes kill and eat their owners."

"I read *People* too, Isaac. But I also did a lot of research when I was writing papers. Dogs eat people when they are literally starving—not right after a person dies. Was that dog starving? No. You saw him. And you saw how he licked my face. And he must have done the same thing to Mrs. Rutledge to try and rouse her. That must be how her blood got on him. Come on. You know that dog didn't kill anyone."

"I know what I saw. And what I see right now." Isaac looks at the T.V. screen. "That thing is something out of a nightmare and it needs to be put down."

"Are you for real? You told the dog to sit—he sat. You told him to stay—he stayed. And he wagged his tail. The dog was docile. Affectionate, even. He didn't rush the door when we entered the apartment. He didn't charge or bark. What he was doing was guarding your friend. And he tried to help me, too."

"Don't you ever get tired of pretending to know more than everybody else?" The muscles in Isaac's jaw work under his beard. "You know nothing about L.S. Rutledge or that dog. Inheriting your aunt's pain in the ass dog and writing papers for dishonest students doesn't make you an expert in anything."

Isaac Kahn does not use his neutral EMS voice or the musical voice he used to say he loved me—but a voice I've never heard him use before—the stony, wounding, male-condescension-voice that my ex-boyfriend Hans used until it was the only voice he had.

"I may not know when to shut up, Isaac. And I'm probably out of my depth a lot of the time. But I was there. I know what I felt and what I saw—" My heart accelerates inside my chest. "And you are wrong about that dog."

Isaac squeezes the remote until the T.V. goes black. "This has been a surreal, terrible day. Let's agree to disagree—okay?"

"No, I can't do that, Isaac. Because nothing's okay."

Isaac picks up the Ikea bag. "Are you coming to pick up your car or staying here?"

12.

I ignore Isaac ignoring me.

I gaze deeply into my phone screen as the ambulance rumbles over Laurel Canyon and down Fairfax— and scroll through the tweets proliferating under #LosVillasKillerDog, #DeathDog, #CannibalCanine and #DogDoeMustDie hashtags while Isaac Kahn looks through the windshield into an Ascher Lieb-free future.

The silence roils until I decide that I have to say something to the scowling, impatient man bristling when the light turns red. "Anything about L.S. Rutledge that you didn't tell me?"

A gaggle of skateboarders enters the intersection. "No. She was a widow. She had an advanced degree. She volunteered with a chevra kadisha years ago—before she and her husband moved to L.A. She was an intelligent, nice person. May her memory be a blessing."

A straggler attempts a jump over a cardboard box collapsed in the crosswalk and fails.

"She and her husband moved here from Albany, right? What about kids?"

"Yes. Albany. They had a daughter who died when she was three or four. Of Tay-Sachs, I think."

"That's very sad."

"Yeah."

"Any extended family?"

"She didn't mention any."

"Did she happen to tell you her maiden name?"

Isaac flushes. "Isn't after she's been murdered a little late to be interested in her life? I practically had to kidnap you to get you to her apartment."

"I was just wondering if she has people to take care of things before the funeral." I look out the window at the barefoot, shirtless, sunburned man in a kilt igniting a can of hair spray with a lighter in front of JustFoodForDogs and will my tears to stop.

"Everything is covered." Isaac runs his fingers through his beard as the skateboarder ollies the curb. "Before the surgery she said that she'd put her affairs in order and had made her burial and funeral arrangements. And if anything comes up, Shomrim and Hatzalah will take care of it."

"I know you don't understand—but I want to help if I can—and attend the funeral. Where will it be?"

"Hillside, maybe? Or Eternal Home of Peace—I have no idea when the medical examiner will release her." Isaac shakes his head. "You want to know why I don't know, Ascher? Because this is my first run-in with a killer dog."

13.

The security light above his door turns Isaac and the mezuzah on his doorpost sci-fi green as he carries the biohazard bag with his bloody clothes and clogs inside, then repeats the trip with the Ikea bag and his black EMS carry-all. Isaac leaves the door ajar for Elijah or maybe for his infuriating, exasperating girlfriend who is sweeping a shit load of Jacaranda flowers off the Lexus her clean-freak aunt left her and which she'd thoughtlessly parked under the tree.

A breeze flavored with exhaust dumps a fresh purple blossom-cloud on my car. I can't help wondering if Isaac didn't tell me everything he knew about L.S. Rutledge and her death-arrangements because he didn't want his argumentative, stubborn, atheist, Valley-girl girlfriend or soon-to-be-former or already-former girlfriend or just former friend to attend L.S. Rutledge's funeral with him because he is sick of her and also because she is not Jewish enough for his strictly observant Hatzalah and Shomrim colleagues and their girlfriends and wives.

Wouldn't the Hatzalah people I heard him talking to and who volunteered to sit with the body at the mortuary have some idea when her body will be released and know the mortuary's name?

Since the authorities are positive that L.S. Rutledge's cause of death was a dog-mauling and Isaac said that L.S. Rutledge had been a Jewish burial society volunteer—wouldn't she, when planning for her own funeral and burial, have requested that Jewish law—which forbids any physical alteration of the body—be observed? So maybe there won't be an autopsy.

The traffic on Fairfax fizzes and the glow inside Isaac's place spills into the dark, and I feel a million times more alone right now than I ever do when I'm by myself.

I know where Isaac keeps his industrial-sized container of window cleaner and his mega-rolls of environmentally-friendly brown paper towels—but I refuse to ask if I can use them.

So, what if my car's windshield is smeared purple? No one except my late father could possibly miss seeing oncoming vehicles with their headlights on. All I have to do is wash my face and I'll be good for my return to the kosher food wasteland I live in and to my "pain in the ass dog" who's done zero to deserve Isaac Kahn's coldness.

The Jacaranda blossoms glommed onto my skin and hair smell like dirt and honey. I wipe my hands on my leggings, cross the lot, then step over Isaac's EMS bag and into the entry. "I'm not coming in because I'm filthy. I'm just going to use the bathroom."

Isaac stands aproned in a clean pair of clogs behind his stainless-steel work-table on which he's piled mangoes, red onions, limes and bunches of coriander. He separates a ripe mango from its pit with a serious knife, then arranges his face into a smile that is really a scowl. "Be my guest."

I duck into the cement-floored, fluorescent-lit bathroom, wash my arms and hands with Isaac Kahn's Smart & Final soap and, as I rinse, I catch myself—desolate and wet in the mirror–—my hair tangled and flecked purple, my sweatshirt spattered.

The effect is the opposite of Pre-Raphaelite innocence or disheveled sexiness. I'm a mess and afraid and absolutely sure of three things that will probably fuck up my life—especially the thing that involves Isaac—

One—L.S. Rutledge's dog didn't attack her or kill her.

Two—And though I've spent over a year looking away from and making excuses for the way he behaves around Freddie—Isaac hates dogs.

I felt that dog's gentleness when he licked my face and I saw fear and sweetness in his eyes. I think Isaac's hostility blinded him to seeing that the dog guarded the dead woman and tried to protect me from whatever had happened to her.

How long before that dog is euthanized?

Which brings me to Three. I am not sure how it can be accomplished or if I can—but I have to find a way to save that dog.

14.

When I open the bathroom door, the commercial food processor is crushing something and Isaac is excavating a bulky foil-and plastic-wrapped package from the chest freezer which gives me a chance to make a zero-conversation, no-painful-goodbye, graceful exit.

I take a step back toward the still-open door, then I topple backwards. My elbow meets metal and realize that I just fell over the EMS bag onto my ass and knocked my head for the second time today—and that the metal thing must be the hooked tool Isaac said he'd use if he had to force his way into L.S. Rutledge's apartment.

As my aunt would say, I'm lucky I didn't knock my eye out.

"Are you okay?" Isaac hastens around the worktable, still carrying the foil and plastic wrapped frozen mega-turkey or unthawed side of bison. "I shouldn't have left my bag in the entry. I'm late for a job and forgot about it. I'm sorry."

I stare at Isaac's forehead and silently command him to drop the frozen package, rush toward me arms outstretched, and recite the following—

"I'm so sorry we argued and that I used that insulting tone of voice with you. That was wrong. You didn't deserve it and I'm sorry I hurt you.

Isaac's hug will then be tight. And then he will say, "I love you, Ascher. Nothing can change that."

But Isaac says nothing.

"I'm just like new," I lie to the silent man with something icy in his arms. "And there's no need to be sorry for anything. You can put your bag wherever you want. This is your place, right?"

What a stupid thing to say. Elbow throbbing and a pain-egg swelling under my scalp, I escape to the parking lot and I'm fumbling the car door open when—though I try to stop myself—I look back and see Isaac standing under greenish light as the buttery radiance pours from the entry way.

The heavy package still in his arms is a chunk of freezing darkness.

And the man embracing it is a shadow.

15.

It is nine forty-five P.M. I'm not falling on my ass, walking Freddie to or from the "Dog Park," smoothing my aunt's sweater the way he likes it on the bed, washing my sticky, flowery hair, icing the bump on my skull or doing my anatomy reading for tomorrow's Zoom dissection of the right ventricles of a pickled human brain, or preparing for the post-dissection quiz that will determine thirty-five percent of my semester grade because I haven't been home.

I'm parking my unclean Lexus in the Home Depot lot on Victory Boulevard two spaces away from a man offering sample slices of the navel oranges and honeydew melons he's selling from his pick-up.

Home Depot closes at ten so I run along a row of fancy stainless-steel grills chained to each other to prevent what? alien abduction? —pull on my N95, pass under the ENTER sign, and, as an industrial fan heaves hot warehouse air in my direction, I find my place in the Pick-Up line. When I stick my credit card in the reader, I notice that my elbow has purpled, then I'm waving my receipt at a woman with profusely pierced eyebrows and I'm through the exit.

Now I'm driving west on Victory and listening to the weather, traffic and news station which has become the All Kill Killer Dog All The Time station. Am I the only person in L.A. County who believes the dog is innocent? The only human being who isn't worried about—what did Isaac say? —the dog that "savaged" L.S. Rutledge? Or as the guy booming on the radio put it—"the huge, enraged, homicidal creature that was roaming among us"?

16.

I tried the dry shampoo I found when I was cleaning out my late aunt's apartment and learned that it's dry but not shampoo, so I'm towel-drying my hair for the second time today—careful to avoid the back of my head—and drinking my second not-kosher or decaffeinated latte with two extra shots and inhaling the un-kosher glazed jelly doughnut I picked up with eleven just like it when I stopped for gas.

I'm definitely regressing. How many times did I lie today or violate the rules of my One Meal Per Day Low Carb/No Carb Try To Look Good For Isaac Diet?

After a stop at the dog park Freddie sleeps on my aunt's sweater pressed against my laptop on the bed. I order laser pointers and other stuff on Amazon Prime one-day, study every photo I can find of the shelter, zoom out on the Google map street view of the street it's on, replay local videos of news coverage of L.S. Rutledge's murder and keep returning to the black and white video of the dog being dragged across what I see now is some kind of enclosed patio into an outdoor kennel at the Los Angeles Mid-City No-Kill-Except-This-Dog Animal Shelter until I switch to the mayor's news conference.

The slender political up-and-comer wears his navy-blue windbreaker half-zipped, a patch with seal of the City of Los Angeles—rosary, grapes, olives and oranges floating outside the coats of arms of the United States, Mexico, Castille, León, and the old California bear flag—covering the place where his heart is supposed to be.

The mayor eyes the camera as if he's a seasick mariner searching for the storm-drowned horizon. He grips the sides of the lectern that matches his hair color and that has a plastic seal of the City of Los Angeles attached to the front. Various city council members and officials cluster behind him, their foreheads creased above their identical dark blue masks which have—you guessed it—the glorious seal of the City of Los Angeles on them. To the mayor's left are the chief of police and a man wearing khakis and a brown "EXTREME PACK ASCENT Canine Training" sweatshirt.

It takes a second before I realize that this is the dog expert with a clicker who's always on "The View" and "Today" and "Good Morning America" and who wrote "Show Your Dog Who's In Charge: How To Control Your Dog So Your Dog Doesn't Control You" —a *New York Times* bestseller.

The two uniformed Animal Services officers behind the dog guy seem antsy without noose-poles to hold.

Then the mayor speaks. The assembled alternate between seriously bummed-out and shocked expressions, then nod and lift their waxed and/or scraggly eyebrows when the mayor promises "a quick and decisive finale" to this "obscene eruption of animalistic violence." The mayor pauses, touches his patch lightly with the fingers of his left hand and intones, "the safety of human Angelenos is and will always be my greatest and number one priority."

Then I surf the local news stations and listen to the radio—AM and FM—but the only skeptics I can find are on a public access cable station's late-night interview show, "Get Real with Don." Don is former character actor who played vicious hit men and sadistic gangsters who in real life is thoughtful and soft-spoken—introduces these outliers as the founders and executive directors of YES ANIMALS ARE PEOPLE RESCUE in Menifee. The executive director is bony man with a ZZ Top beard whose over-tanned forearms appear to have become jerky. The other executive director is woman with a howling wolf neck tattoo and viscous fake eyelashes that appear to be forcing her powdered eyelids to close.

Don asks the question of the day, maybe of the year—why would a dog attack and then try to eat its owner "out of the blue?"

The woman replies that dogs are instinct-driven and that dog attacks don't just happen—they're a response to something—an aggressive dog, a jarring or disturbing canine or human behavior, a threatening or disturbing object or person. "Some precipitation factor—a threat or perceived threat—is what drives a dog to initiate a defensive biting behavior."

I was wrong—the man's arms look like petrified wood, not jerky. He tells Don that a long-time YES ANIMALS ARE PEOPLE volunteer who also volunteers at the Mid-City Shelter and whose identity he cannot divulge was so "deeply concerned" that he contacted him just few hours ago to let him know that Dog Doe is an slightly underweight, approximately four-year-old, spayed female—he saw the raised incision scar on her abdomen—maybe a shepherd-flat-coated retriever or lab mix—who is terrified and submissive and has demonstrated no aggressive behaviors at all.

The man sucks in a breath then waits a little to set it free before dropping a final, hideous truth-bomb. After the dog is euthanized, her stomach-contents will be examined for pieces of L.S. Rutledge's flesh.

17.

The salty early morning coolness flows into the open car window like zooplankton flowing into a jellyfish. I drift past auto salvage lots and pet cremation places—Furever Furwell, A Better Place for Pets, and AquAnimals Hydro-Cremations—then stop the Lexus next to a tree and across from the mint ice cream-colored Mid-Hollywood Animal Shelter.

Widely-spaced exterior lights illuminate a FIND YOUR BEST FRIEND HERE banner, glint along the sliding glass entrance doors, and brighten a rectangle of scorched, plant-free, environmentally-friendly, weedy gravel and a cement walkway.

The tree next to me is the only tree I've seen for miles—a ten-foot-wide dwarf palm that I hope will hide the Lexus from the two black-eyed security cameras installed in the building's eaves.

I remember to switch off the dome light before putting on the extra-large black sweatshirt Isaac keeps in my dresser drawer and the black latex gloves I folded inside it. Now I put on the pale pink plastic mask—the kind bank robbers wear in bad movies—and over that a costume beard.

I pull the sweatshirt hood onto my head.

I take a black plastic bag from the glove compartment and slide it into the sweatshirt pouch. The bag holds two laser pointers, six dehydrated pig ears in a baggie, a size Large black halter and matching leash, and a pocket Halogen flashlight. I open the driver's door halfway, drop to the pavement, then push the door closed. I crawl to the passenger door, open it, and reach for the Halligan tool I bought at Home Depot.

The passenger door clicks when I close it. I listen for a response to the sound—a car starting or sounds that indicate human activity—clicks, coughs, scrapes—then check under the car for headlights or the shoes of a shelter security guard doing his rounds.

The street and the shelter entrance remain desolate.

I run through what I have to do despite having rehearsed the steps in my head until one follows another with inevitability of a tipping chain of dominoes. But the mask limits my range of vision, the hoodie is dampening with my sweat, and keeping the folded Halligan thing under my arm is awkward—especially with my sore elbow.

What else did I get wrong?

I close my eyes and see Isaac holding that frozen brisket or whatever it was and watching me go—his features frozen, too.

What if Isaac is right and I'm completely mistaken about the dog?

What if I'm wrong about everything?

Will I lose him forever when he finds out what I'm about to do?

Or have I lost him forever already?

18.

Chin down, laser pointer in my right hand—which is shaking—and the Halligan tool tucked under my left armpit, I cross the empty street, then tiptoe over the gravel until I'm just outside the widening cones of light thrown from the double-bulb security fixture above me. I squeeze the Halligan tool hard in my armpit, then aim the red laser beam at the white, plastic rectangle that is the fixture's light sensor according to some guys on Reddit and YouTube.

I imagine a frizzle of electricity, a small explosion triggering a silent alarm, the scream of sirens, being dragged, maybe by my hair, then thrown into the back of a police car—but none of that happens.

What does happen is that after what feels like too many seconds the security lightbulbs dim and flicker out—temporarily, I know from the videos. But the dimming is my cue to run along the green cinderblock wall to a padlocked, chain-link gate with Dumpsters on either side of it. From behind a Dumpster that reeks of what must be a ton of saturated kitty litter, I disable the security light above the gate with a fresh laser pointer, release the Halligan tool from my aching armpit and hold it in both hands.

Even with the gloves, the metal is so cold that I wouldn't be surprised if—like dry ice—it emitted fog. But it's my own fear that's making me shiver—the padlock on the gate is more serious and the chain-link fence higher than they looked on Google Street View.

I unfold the device and replay in my head the demonstration video I memorized—then, just as the friendly firefighter in a blue parka directed, I make sure it's straight and stick the forked end through the padlock and pull it hard to the side.

The shackle breaks just as it did in the video.

I open the gate, push it quickly closed, then stand still and listen for footsteps that do not sound.

19.

I follow a gravel path past a storage shed where I disable the security light. Then I use my flashlight to navigate the network of chain-link kennels, each with a white I.D. card attached to the front.

How will I find the dog? A white-chinned pit bull whines as I pass him. My idea was that the dog would recognize me and my scent seems insane now in what must be a haze of canine and other smells.

Sweat dampening my hair and my breath fogging the plastic mask, I walk up and down the rows of kennels setting off high and low-pitched whines, cries, growls and bays.

Wouldn't they keep a vicious dog away from the others—especially if they thought she was rabid?

I reach last aisle of kennels in the back and sweep the light over the angry, frightened, pleading and blinking captives—some housed three to a kennel, some too big for their cages—until the light falls across a rusty metal sign wired to the last kennel's door—"STOP. VETERINARY ONLY. AGGRESSION. RABIES QUARANTINE."

20.

I switch off the flashlight, then wait to see things in the darkness.

Should I run back to the gate?

Or should I remove a spectacularly un-kosher pig ear from the baggie and hope that it interests the silent, murky shape in the aggression/rabies cage?

Is this a case of me thinking I know more than anyone else as Isaac said?

A fantasy I concocted?

Or am I acting on something true and real?

My face is hot and my gloved hand trembles as I push the dehydrated cartilage through an opening in the chain link gate. The shape moves from the back to sniff, gently takes the pig ear in its teeth, then returns to the back of the last kennel at the end of the last row of cages.

This must be the shelter's death row.

"Hey, you," I whisper to the being huddled at the back of the enclosure. "It's me. Ascher. Do you remember me?"

The dog chews for a few seconds, stops, and finally whines. I take another pig ear from the bag and hold it against the outside of the cage. My index finger stings with the phantom sensation of fangs ripping through the glove all the way to the bone, but I do not push this pig ear through the opening.

I realize now that eating them takes way too long.

There's a rustle as the animal advances, then a flash from black eyes as it lowers its head and waits for me to push the treat through.

I flick on the flashlight to examine the kennel gate again, then switch it off.

No padlock. Just a heavy, stainless-steel latch like the others. The Halligan tool makes my armpit hurt, but I couldn't know if I'd need it or not. I put it on the gravel, take the collar and halter out of the bag, and put them on the gravel next to it.

I kneel and peer at the dog.

This dog resembles the dog I saw in the apartment. The head and the forepaws are the same size.

But what happens if I open the door and this is the wrong dog?

I hear Isaac's disapproving voice inside my head telling me that I don't know what I'm doing, and that the worst lies I tell are the ones I tell myself.

The sharp, tiny gravel stones transmit tiny shocks into my knees and up my thighs as I scrunch down and try to discern the features of the dark dog in the dark.

Her forehead and shoulders are the right width. And I know Isaac would mock me for saying it—but this dog's vibe—patient and sad—is exactly the same.

So yeah. I'm pretty sure this has to be the dog.

My cell phone vibrates in my back pocket and the dog snuffles closer to the kennel gate.

"Good dog," I say. "Come to Ascher."

The snuffling stops.

The dog is so still and so quiet that I can't help wondering—though I don't think dogs do it—if she is holding her breath.

"Come to Ascher," I say again, —singsong this time—then pull down my mask and hold my face closer to—but not touching—the gate.

The dog's tail wag-thumps against the cement floor of the kennel just as it thumped the floor when Isaac spoke to her in the apartment.

"It is you, isn't it?"

The dog thumps her tail again.

I uncoil the leash and release the latch on the kennel door—but hold it closed.

I'm not ready. "Stay. Stay," I plead.

But the dog presses her nose against the chain link gate, and swings her tail against the sides of the enclosure.

"Wait," I command sharply, and back away from the enclosure. The dog flattens as if in fear, then whines.

What am I doing? Who the fuck do I think I am?

Clutching the leash and collar, I look at the blue-black, starless sky to calm myself.

My phone vibrates again.

"Are you the dog?" I speak into the kennel, clutching the collar and leash. "Are you the dog that tried to save me? This morning? Or was it yesterday?"

I sound insane. Out of my fucking mind.

But the dog wags its tail, then licks the chain link door.

Shaking hard, I touch the latch, then pull the door open. "Stay. Sit. Be good. Please. Please."

The dog sits just inside the open kennel.

"Stay."

The dog stays.

I reach inside, slide the chain collar with the leash already attached over its head, pull until the collar tightens, then stand and take a step back.

The sky dissolves into black Van Gogh whirls or spinning cosmic gears until the dog and the kennel are a blur.

But the leash remans slack as the dog licks the toe of my tennis shoe and the sky flattens and retreats. I pick up the Halligan tool, and stick it under my arm again.

"Come on," I say.

The dog's angular head emerges from shadows inside the kennel. Then she steps onto the gravel, tilts her head at me and waits.

"Okay," I say. "It's time to for us to go."

21.

Wearing a white N95 that Isaac gave me, I drive up La Cienega just a little above the speed limit—if I'm too slow I'll seem drunk, and if I'm too fast I'll seem high—and pull over where a perfectly overstuffed trash receptable vomits its contents onto a bus bench with a Robbie Conal "Supreme Injustices" poster stuck on it.

"Stay."

The female mutt sitting on the towel in the back seat doesn't make a move—but her eyes follow me out of the Lexus, and must be watching me push the black plastic bag containing a crumpled plastic mask, a pair black latex gloves, and the balled-up fake beard into a container of maggoty spaghetti halfway buried in the receptacle.

The flashlight is in the glove compartment under my aunt's Lexus manual and I'll toss the laser pointers somewhere later on.

I get back in the car and as I turn onto Sunset, I barely avoid running into a woman pulling a child's red wagon loaded with crushed plastic water bottles, aluminum cans and a dirty American flag. She is tan, barefoot, wears a purple sequined mini-skirt and strapless bra, and half of her head is shaved.

Did I just dream her?

Since closing the gate and leading the dog to the car, I've pulsed with adrenaline and fear, the streets have unfurled like gauze and nothing feels real—including me—except the dog.

Where did she come from?

She is all resignation, sweetness and sorrow and smells of old blood and the disinfectant and fear soaked into that death row kennel.

What do I call her?

Flecks of L.S. Rutledge's rusty dried blood stick to her eyelashes and dapple her gray toenails. But she does what I ask, and seems comfortable gazing out the car window—or, as I discover each time I check in the rear-view mirror—staring into the back of my head.

21.

I turn onto a residential street off the alley behind Hugo's Restaurant—a mix of small old houses and new apartment buildings—and drive until I reach a low, nineteen- twenties wooden house with three loaded grapefruit trees in front and no Ring device on the front door frame, and no "BEWARE OF DOG," "SMILE, YOU'RE ON CAMERA" or armed patrol signs stuck into the brown lawn.

I park and sit in the car for a few minutes, then open the passenger door. The dog waits for me to ask her to before she jumps onto the thirsted-to death grass of the parkway. She immediately squats and pees—she must have had to go for a long time—then matches my pace as I walk to Riverside, then pass through an unmarked Life Space entrance to a stairwell.

I'm not sure how she feels about elevators and I want to avoid the lobby—even at this hour.

She's tentative at the bottom of the stairs, but after I climb two steps, she follows.

Freddie's scream-barking and door-scratching reach me when I open the stairwell door, but she pads calmly down the middle of the carpeted hall to the door of my apartment and sits. Though I need to get the dog inside fast, I wait to unlock the door.

What if the dog interprets Freddie's barking as a threat just the way the dog rescue lady described the provocations for dog attacks on T.V.? And what if she—already disoriented and afraid—feels that must she defend herself against Freddie? How much does she weigh? Fifty pounds?

I don't think I can carry her in—especially if she fights me.

Fuck.

My Fitbit tells me it's 4:30 A.M. and my heart is beating one hundred and twenty times a minute—too fast. Any minute my neighbor, Mark, will hurl his apartment door open so hard the knob will crater the wall, then heave one of his very expensive, fancy bikes down the hall to the elevator in preparation for his daily pre-sunrise ride—his "spiritual practice."

I don't have a spiritual practice—unless springing a sad, strange dog that I might be wrong about from the shelter and hiding her in the studio apartment I share with an anxious, possessive, geriatric quick-to-anger canine head-case counts.

And I'm pretty sure it doesn't.

I lack the shining, lighthouse soul that my aunt and Isaac have and whose luminousness carries them forward and bleeds into everything they do.

My light burns dim and intermittent, and sometimes it hardly burns at all.

I listen to Freddie snuffling, then scratching the bottom of the door with his toenails. Then I look at the dog I brought here waiting resignedly for me to reveal the next thing that will happen to her—and her innocence is unbearable.

A person with a functioning soul would probably pray for wisdom, courage, clarity and divine guidance if he or she were here instead of me.

But I'm too afraid of the dog to close my eyes—so I squint at the tiny green light on the smoke detector and—since there's no One an atheist can pray to, and because most Jewish prayers are aren't solicitations for emergency favors but praise or thanks to the universe's Creator—I wait for truth to reveal itself.

The dog whines softly.

Well, there's it is.

With Isaac out of the picture, there is only one being in the universe who can help me—the hungry, thirsty, exhausted and starting-to-pant dog waiting for me to get my shit together.

I look into the dog's wide eyes and wonder if behind that smooth forehead some primitive part of her canine brain might be starting to see red.

Freddie yips.

I kneel. "You okay with being Linda?" I whisper into the dog's face. It's a Jewish thing to name children after someone who died or to pick a name with their first initial. "L.S." seems too formal, and "Rutledge" too attention-grabbing.

Linda tilts her head as she processes her new phonemes, then thumps her tail against the industrial carpet.

I take the thumps and the head-tilt as a yes.

"Okay. You should know that Freddie is much nicer than he seems." Linda listens, her nostrils flared as if to breathe my words. "But like you he's been through a lot—so please don't freak out when he barks at you. He just needs time to get to know you. Everything will be okay, Linda. I promise."

I knew my promise was a lie as I said it—but the lie was aspirational and sincere and was as close to a prayer as I will probably ever get.

22.

Freddie is intact.

Dissolving specks of dried blood and dog hair film the tub and shower.

Linda permitted me to shampoo and towel-dry her twice—though I couldn't defeat the cowlick in the fur on the back of her head. Then, after a hefty snack, she pretty much passed out.

I'm hungry too, and hungry for Valium, and keep thinking about the bottles I stashed for an emergency—World War III or the Big One—and argue with myself about whether getting dumped by Isaac the same day he said he loved me, dropping in on a murdered woman, and stealing an allegedly rabid, killer dog from a city facility equals a 9.3 on the Richter scale.

So far, it's a no. I don't want to go back to the way I felt—very little—when Valium was my best, most reliable friend—my parents' replacement and my aunt's stand-in.

Loving and being in love with Isaac but not admitting it for almost a year helped me forget my situation—except for collecting and hoarding memory-fragments from the old house. My situation is not solitude exactly—but the disconnect that is the erasure of first and second-degree relatives, people who know more about my aunt and my parents and my grandparents than that that they're dead, and who can confirm that a less incomplete Ascher Lieb than I am now—one who was part of a family—existed.

I can't complete my funeral science degree anesthetized. And I can't risk more possible Valium side-effects—"agitation, black tarry stools, skin-blistering, blurred vision, changes in speech patterns and rhythms, chills, confusion, cough, dark urine, discouragement, dizziness, lightheadedness when getting up from a lying or sitting position, adopting false beliefs that cannot be changed by facts, fast or irregular breathing, feeling sad or empty, feeling that others are watching or controlling my behavior, feeling that others can hear my thoughts, feeling, seeing, or hearing things that are not there, fever, headache, hyperexcitability, irritability, itching or rash, lack of memory of what takes place after a certain event, loss of interest or pleasure, lower back or side pain, nausea, nightmares, outbursts of anger, painful or difficult urination, pale skin, restlessness, seizures, sore throat, stomach pain, sweating, trouble concentrating, trouble sleeping, trouble speaking, white spots in the mouth, unpleasant breath odor, unusual behavior, unusual feeling of excitement, unusual tiredness or vomiting blood."

I developed an atrial flutter last year from too much Valium and from being sick at heart over my aunt's death.

The empty, irritable restlessness, nightmares, and the deep feeling of discouragement I suffered was probably just my temperament intensified by pandemic lockdown weirdness and panic.

"Feeling and seeing things that were not there"? I did. More than once.

Except the things that were not supposed to be there that I saw—and Freddie saw—my aunt's ghost and a shimmering, unhappy soul that camped out a few times in my old apartment––were as real as the clanking of my Life Space stainless-steel dishwasher.

But I could really use something to take the edge off—the edge being Linda damp and smelling like Freddie's "calming"—though it never calms him—Calming Organic Lavender and Oatmeal Shampoo—and the consequences of her presence here where she snores on a beach towel I smoothed and she pawed into a lumpy nest.

Freddie's furious, condensed self is tightly coiled on my aunt's sweater on my side of bed, his angry little back to Linda and his accusing eyes following my movements.

Instead of barking or nipping when Linda entered the

apartment with me—Freddie's eyes went total Margaret Keane, and he shrank into himself as if the stinking interloper I'd invited here possessed the demonic power not only to nullify my love for him, but to make him even smaller.

I sit on the bed next to him and pet his head the way he likes me to. But Freddie is stone-quiet.

"I love you Freddie," I say. "Nothing's changed. It's you and me against the universe. Linda needed help and she's nice and I think you'll really like her."

Freddie moves his head from under my hand and farts.

There is nothing to do but stretch out between Freddie and Linda, close my eyes and wait for the swirling images to slow until I do my own nosedive into the blankness of sleep.

My cell phone rattles against the quartz bathroom counter.

23.

No legit human being would text me at this hour. First, because no actual people except my parents' accountant, my paperless dentist, Amazon Fresh, Door Dash, the Beto O'Rourke campaign, scammers or Isaac ever text me. Second, because Isaac and I are incommunicado. And third because the old people home improvement scam and Medicare phishing texts I get because I was tangled up with my aunt's will and her papers never start until just before seven A.M.

I shut my eyes and try to reanimate the sensation of gliding slack-muscled into a velvet black, dreamless cocoon.

I'm halfway in when my phone buzzes again.

Linda stays asleep. Freddie throws an icy look my way as I slide off the foot of the bed.

I pick up my phone from the bathroom counter and scroll through my text messages.

There are a dozen messages from Isaac. And they all say the same thing.

24.

I hold the All-Day Max Factor Fair Pan Stick that was in my aunt's makeup bag above Linda's questioning, upturned face, and—using Freddie's as a template—I create two matching eyebrow dots.

Freddie watches me take a close-up photo of Linda's new face for reference, then flares his nostrils and opens his mouth halfway in disgust.

I consume a homemade caffeinated latte and gather the stuff I'll need on the coffee table—

The blue and gray plaid lumberjack dog jacket, gray collar and leash I bought on Amazon.

An at-home, quick COVID test.

My burial society training packets.

English translations of Hebrew psalms.

Anatomy class notes.

My aunt's pearls and the good black turtleneck sweater I wore to her Zoom funeral.

My nice black pants and black ballet flats.

I add my navy sweater just in case, connect my cell phone to the charger, then perform the COVID test at the kitchen counter.

Negative.

I take a screen shot of the results in case the mortuary requires it.

I secure my hair with the silk floral scrunchy my aunt bought me at Bloomingdale's, and rummage some more in her black satin-finish makeup bag thinking that wearing my aunt's red lipstick might make me appear confident—then remember that

I'll be wearing a mask.

I tuck the lipstick back into the bag and see that a strand of my aunt's white hair has coiled itself against the silky lining like a fern.

If my aunt were still here, what would she tell me to do?

Not what I'm contemplating doing—that's for fucking sure.

And if experienced *shomer* Isaac and I were still a thing—what pointers would he give me?

Nada.

He was hoarse and coughing in the voicemails he left while I was spiriting Linda away from the shelter. He said he had a bad sore throat and a fever of hundred and two, that he suspected he had COVID, that most of his Hatzalah colleagues had the same symptoms and were in quarantine, the problem being that he and they had signed up for five-hour shifts as *shomrim* for L.S. Rutledge, and he wondered if I could cover early morning through late-afternoon—maybe also early evening while he found healthy replacements for tonight and tomorrow.

I texted him yes—not to please him—but because this is something I know I can do.

As a chevra kadisha—a burial society—volunteer, I was repeatedly up close and extremely personal with the dead. I assisted during *tahara*, the ritual bathing and shrouding of deceased women. I also learned about the Jewish practice of keeping a deceased person and his or her disoriented soul company until burial—it's called *shemirah* in Hebrew—and about the job of being a watcher or *shomer*—or in my case—a *shomeret.*

Hanging out with the dead—reading psalms, reciting prayers, meditating on appropriate topics, and thinking good thoughts about the casketed or covered or refrigerated deceased person and her soul—isn't complicated. There are no rituals involved––nothing esoteric—or duties that must be discharged in any particular order.

Guarding the dead is unskilled labor. All that's required of a *shomer* is his alive presence and his love.

Still, I'm afraid that the job of being with L.S. Rutledge will need much more than placing my warm body near her cold one––and that a stranger's generic love will not be enough to soothe a soul so ferociously and cruelly untethered from life.

25.

I email a fraudulent excuse to my anatomy T.A. with effusive regrets about missing today's Zoom dissection and assure her that I will watch the recording as soon as possible. Then I Velcro Linda into the lumberjack jacket, connect the leash to her collar, spray her black paws, ankles, fore and back legs and the back of her head with bursts of the gray, non-toxic temporary fur dye I ordered, and take photos. It takes some coaxing to maneuver sullen and suspicious Freddie into his halter and collar, but finally I lead both dogs through the hallway, down the stairs and out for a short, no-frills, five A.M. walk in the dark.

The good news is that the dogs ignore each other, urinate and defecate promptly, and that under the street lights and bulked-up by the jacket—my grayish dog no longer resembles the AWOL, rabid female Killer Dog Doe who—according to the Internet—is waiting until daylight to commence an epic, rabies-fueled mauling and murder rampage from one end of L.A. County to the other.

The not-good news is that I completely forgot that the gray male-looking dog would squat to pee—a deficiency I can neutralize with the lie to anyone who asks about it that "Larry" suffers from a hormone problem.

Back in Life Space, I feed the dogs their breakfasts at opposite ends of the apartment—which is not far apart in a studio—fill Freddie's little bowl and a mixing bowl for Linda with water, scatter pee pads over the carpeted area, and switch on the Weather Channel because I don't want Linda watching images of her own vilified, terrified self while I am gone.

I ask both dogs to sit—only Linda lowers her butt to the

floor—it's obvious she's had training—and exhort them to be good during what will be my regrettable but necessary many hours-long absence.

Linda remains seated.

Freddie remains standing, his mouth drooping in disappointment.

I dump the rest of my latte into my battered Sea View Community College Krakens travel mug, microwave a Lean Cuisine entrée and eat it at the sink though the middle is still icy, kiss Freddie, pat Linda lightly on her made-up forehead and in my tight-in-the-heel flats and my aunt's luminous pearls, I ride the smells-like-onion-rings-this-morning elevator to the depopulated parking structure.

I drive with the window open to the blue predawn air without music or news or the podcast about human decomposition rates in aqua, green and traditional burials I'm listening to as research for my paper on green burials. The address Isaac provided doesn't take me to The Eternal Home Of Peace where my aunt is—or was—depending on what you believe about the afterlife––or to Hillside Memorial Park where the sparkly seventy-five-foot-high mosaic canopy shading Al Jolson's tomb and its eternally cascading water feature is visible from the 405 Freeway—but to a hummus-colored Art Deco building on Pico Boulevard with a faded sign—"Mount Of Olives Chapel And Mortuary Park In Rear."

In the rear I choose a space marked "Mount Of Olives Bereaved Only"— not the "Mount Of Olives Funeral Director" space or any of the four "Mount Of Olives Staff" spaces—though a *shomer* is not usually among the bereaved.

I adjust my mask and smooth my hair in the rear-view mirror in which I see a raccoon drag a dirty baguette into the alley's dark periphery.

I wish Isaac—sick as he is and sick of me—had texted me a few pointers on how to keep my thoughts centered on L.S. Rutledge and her soul's predicament and not my own problems, had told me which psalms are best to begin and end with, or had filled me in on the meditation topics that might be good for watching over a murder victim.

But it's not Isaac's fault that I won't be able to fake my way through this—it's mine.

Why was I so eager to say yes?

Perversity? To impress Isaac? To pretend I'm a better person than I really am?

Yes.

But I'm also doing this because of something Isaac will never understand—I'm doing this for the dog.

I shut down thoughts of what the dog and Freddie might be doing to or with each other and force myself to think about what has to happen.

I look in the mirror hoping the racoon reappears—but I'm alone.

No one except the God in whom I cannot believe, L.S. Rutledge's body, her anguished soul and my family of ghosts—whom I often feel are watching me critically—will know if I succeed—or how massively, cosmically and irrevocably I fuck this up.

26.

The black buzzer vibrates under my finger.

I count to seven before the inner door opens with a jangle of keys. The voice belongs to a masked face with assessing eyes and a fringe of brown hair escaping a paper surgical hat. The voice flows through the security screen the way forgiveness must flow through a confessional window.

"May I help you?"

"I'm Ascher Lieb. I'm here for L.S. Rutledge,"

"Leah Rutledge—*zichronah l'vrachah*—yes. Izzie—Mr. Kahn—said an Archer was coming. I just didn't expect it to be female."

It? Izzie? Is she kidding?

The woman who doesn't disclose her name pulls the door open. She must be a mortuary tech. People in sales don't wear P.P.E. And she said "Leah," didn't she?

"It's Ascher."

"Come with me, Ascher."

I follow her into a corridor wide enough for easy transport of a 4XL casket and truck, then past three closed, citrus green doors fitted with extra-tall stainless steel kickplates.

How well does she know Isaac?

What does it mean that she called him "Izzie"?

And wasn't it like thirty or so hours ago that "Izzie" made a huge deal of saying he loved me?

My heart flutters a warning against wondering if this woman and Isaac ever dated.

"I hope you brought *tehillim,*" Izzie's nameless buddy talks over one conceited shoulder. "We don't provide anything."

"No worries. I have everything I need." I address the back of her head, her shoulders, her small waist, her generous hips and ass, thick thighs and sensible shoes—all of which make me wonder if Isaac is attracted to a specific type—female pears like me and this one in death-business casual and P.P.E and who has Ascher-Lieb-Brown hair.

Or do I have her hair? Is she the template and am I her copy?

The woman gestures at two doors with "Biohazard" and "Keep These Doors Closed At All Times" signs screwed into them at the hallway's end as if she is about to tell me something important about them—then she elbows the wall-panel.

One of the doors gasps open to another hallway.

"I should have mentioned that the restroom is in the back where you came in. The plumbing's old, so make sure not to flush any tampons or menstrual products."

Is she joking? Or do I give off a menstrual-product-flusher vibe?

"The staff lounge slash kitchen is there. There's a charger you can use." She indicates a door. "Everything is *parve*. You can help yourself—" she looks me up and down—"within reason—to the coffee and cocoa pods, but everything else is staff-only. If you get hungry, use Grubhub and order something. The kosher pizza place two blocks from here is decent."

I follow her past the door to the lounge/kitchen and three more doors, and she speaks again. "Use of electronics is forbidden when you're with the decedent—but I'm sure you know that. Just make sure your phone is turned off before you enter, and don't leave the memorial candle burning if you step out—even for a minute. It's a fire hazard. And don't forget to sign in and sign out when you leave. Okay?"

"All the food is *parve*. Cocoa and coffee pods are permitted. No electronics. Blow out the candle before I leave to do some tampon and menstrual product-flushing. I think I'll be able to keep all this straight."

"And make sure to remember that the door on the left is yours—" Isaac's acquaintance is already walking away, her sharp elbow raised and aimed at the touchless control panel that will free her from me—"and the one on the right is the morgue."

27.

The decedent on the blond laminate table in the Room of the Leftward Door is a sheet-covered, mummy-ish form with a forehead bump at one end and an elevation at the other indicating stiffened toes.

A white and blue Star of David crocheted lap blanket delineates the curving ribcage.

An end table supports three sad, balsamic-vinegar-red "silk" zinnias trapped in resin that demonstrate the complete wrongness and futility of "cheer" in a place like this.

A memorial candle with a white-Star-of-David-on-blue design, a lighter, a box of off-brand powder blue tissues, a pump-bottle of commercial sanitizer, two Sharpies and the battered spiral notebook I'm supposed to sign have been arranged on a table next to a settee too short for even me to stretch out on. There's also a standing lamp with a knocked-in shade and a coffee table with a glass surface protector.

The walls are bare except for a framed prayer in Hebrew and in English, two floor-to ceiling cupboard doors behind the body-table, and a laminated poster of Moses raising the black and gold-engraved tablets over his tousled hair as if he's about to throw them at the viewer.

Soundproofing amplifies the fluorescent ceiling fixture's buzz and the exhalations wheezing through the air conditioning vents. The air is pungent with disinfectant, the synthetic clove, pine and anise bouquet of the jar of gel deodorizer absorbing death's mustiness, the nostril-scald of the embalming fluid some assimilated Jewish families demand, and the sick-sweetness of the emollients required for customers who request an open casket instead of a closed, kosher box.

Nothing in here reflects the decedent's violent departure from life. It's so still that a small throat-clearing could shatter the cold from the body and send the ice-needles flying around the room.

I drop my backpack on the linoleum, arrange my print-outs on the loveseat, write my name, L.S. Rutledge's—ignoring the Leah thing—and the date and time in the notebook just as my doppelgänger instructed, then light the memorial candle.

The chubby little flame that consumes the fresh white wick is the only warm thing in here except me—and I'm cooling fast.

I rub a fat, glistening glob of chilly sanitizer into my cold palms and wonder if I was supposed to recite some sort of prayer over the candle.

It's too late to worry about that—

My almost-friend waits for me like a magician's assistant waiting to be levitated.

28.

I look at my English translation of the Shema—the big deal prayer on the wall that observant Jews like Isaac recite three times a day, and that my burial society *shomer* training materials suggested be recited to the dead—then—as if I am being blinded by a celestial light—I shield my eyes with my right hand the way my grandmother did when she lit the Shabbat candles, and I read—

"Hear, Israel, the Lord is our God, the Lord is One. Blessed be the Name of his glorious kingdom for ever and ever. And you shall love the Lord our God with all your heart and all your soul and with all your might and it shall be that these words that I command you today shall be in your heart. And you shall teach them diligently to your children and you shall speak of them when you sit at home and when you walk along the way and when you lie down and when you rise up. And you shall bind them as a sign on your hand and they shall be for totafot between your eyes. And you shall write them on the doorposts of your house and on your gates"

Totafot means phylacteries. I remember watching Isaac put on his, then I look at the body on the table. The abysmal silence emanating from it builds into a roar that rumbles through me.

29.

Chilled, I take my navy-blue sweater from my back-pack, and pull it over my turtleneck.

My sweater feels like it's been stored in a refrigerator. I feel like I've been refrigerated, too—and that snow sloshes inside my head.

The silent roar was a hint perhaps that reciting the most important prayer in Judaism wasn't the friendly ice-breaker the female Death-Quasar under the sheet required—and that it didn't do a thing for her inscrutable, freaked-out soul.

I probably should have started with saying *tehillim*—reading psalms—traditional reading in this situation—but of course I had to start my hang-out session with L.S. Rutledge in my completely-doomed-to-failure, ass-backward, stubborn Ascher Lieb way.

With numb fingers, I haphazardly gather the psalms I printed out and read from the top page. "Oh Lord, do not punish me in anger, do not chastise me in fury. Have mercy on me, Oh Lord, for I languish—"

The chill pierces me from skull to feet.

Did I catch what Isaac has?

Is the dehumidifier set too high?

I can't see a thermostat anywhere. It must be next door in the morgue. And the morgue must be where the cold is be coming from.

"—heal me Oh Lord for my bones shake with terror."

A vessel adrift in a crush of icebergs, I tiptoe into the intensifying cold that surrounds L. S. Rutledge until I'm close enough to see the glitter in the yarn of the Magen David blanket

sparkle like sunlit ice crystals. I finish reading the terror-psalm–
–silently to myself this time—then read the next one—also silently—which may be the mode of delivery L.S. Rutledge prefers—

"I extol You, O Lord, for You have lifted me up, and not let my enemies rejoice over me. O Lord, my God, I cried out to You, and You healed me. O Lord, You brought me up from Sheol, preserved me from going down into the Pit…"

There's no comfort in this psalm. There's no relief in contemplating becoming a dust-blot trapped in the halfway place between the finite and the infinite.

Which—as I think about it—sounds a lot like being trapped in desolate, frigid room.

30.

I've been here what? Fifteen minutes? That's way too soon for the mental-health time-out I'm taking on the loveless loveseat—my feet in my shoes impolitely tucked under my ass for warmth.

When I close my eyes to soothe my death-boom headache, I see L.S. Rutledge bleeding into the recliner and the bloody dog giving me a pleading, heartbreaking look.

When I open my eyes I see the truth—I've failed to provide comfort to L.S. Rutledge's soul.

I have not made this place feel pure or peaceful to her body–—the sacred container of the immaterial thing that temporarily enlivened it.

I haven't acknowledged what brought her here—or what brought me.

If I were on that table, and my soul—if I had one—was terrified and lost, what would I want from an ambulatory, warm and breathing stranger? What would I need?

31.

"I apologize, Mrs. Rutledge. I should have introduced myself first thing." I address the head-end of the alabastrine shape, and rest my left hand on the spot where I guess L.S. Rutledge's hands have been folded upon her sternum.

The hand under my hand feels like a chunk of ice wrapped in a tarp. Well, not ice. I learned in a mortuary science class that the coolers in which the dead are kept are set between 37.5 and 41 degrees Fahrenheit.

Any colder and the bodies freeze.

"My name is Ascher Lieb. I'm a friend of Isaac Kahn. The day you passed away he brought me to your apartment so you and I could meet. He knew we had things in common and hoped we'd become friends. He told me about your knee surgery and a few other things. So, I'm not a complete stranger."

I wait for a beat. "He knocked on your door, then called. And when you didn't answer he forced your door open."

Do I tell her she was murdered?

Do I tell her about the dog?

Not yet.

"Then Isaac discovered that you were—no longer living."

I imagine L.S. Rutledge's frantic, amnesiac soul alighting on the lamp or on the edge of the framed picture of Moses and trying to take in what I just told her.

"Isaac—Izzie—maybe you called him that—told me you'd been a burial society volunteer. I was, too. Which is another reason he wanted us to meet and I wanted to be here with you today."

It feels colder, if that is possible. Maybe the morgue coolers are set too low. Or maybe their seals leak.

"My parents died in a car crash when I was thirteen." Wow. What hideous, awkward, hideous segue. "They'd been visiting me at summer camp. It wasn't visiting day or anything—I'd asked them to bring me something I thought I needed. Anyway, I can't help feeling that their deaths are my fault. I'm just telling you all this to let you know that I understand grief—and what it feels like to be alone."

32.

Is anyone more diminished, objectified or riven from the world than a person in a body bag?

I drag the unlovable loveseat close to the long table and sit so that my head is close to body-bag level in case some alive human closeness might make a dent in the vastness of L.S. Rutledge's separateness. And I talk.

I tell L.S. Rutledge about refusing to return to L.A. after my parents died, attending boarding school in Santa Barbara and then Sea View Community College. I mention writing for the *Mission City Lifestyle Digest,* but skip ghost-writing student papers for money, or that I regaled friends with lies about my parents and the way they died. I also tell L.S. Rutledge that my boyfriend, Hans, broke up with me and my aunt died during lockdown last year.

I don't mention the blow-up with Isaac.

Maybe all this is T.M.I., but L.S. Rutledge deserves to know what kind of person I am, doesn't she?

A full-body shame-shiver travels through me as if to remind me that L.S. Rutledge doesn't know that I'm the kind of person who lies too comfortably—especially when I'm lying to myself.

33.

What would my parents—become ash-and-grit—and my aunt all dolled-up in her casket—have wanted to know in the hours before **their vanishings into sea, earth, the pit or eternity?**

I guess that they'd have wanted to know about the people they loved and left behind—me.

And they'd have wanted to know how they died.

Which is why I pushed the settee back to its spot and now stand next to Rutledge's table pressing my backpack against my chest for warmth.

"I'm not going to lie," I warn myself as much as I warn L.S. Rutledge. "I'm going to tell you what I know—so here goes. When you didn't answer the door or your cellphone, Isaac did something to the lock and we went in. Right away, things in your apartment felt wrong. The blinds were closed. It was too quiet and too dark for late morning. And there was a weird, metallic smell."

I regret saying the last thing, so I give the icy slab-hand a pat. "Isaac told me to stay near the front door and went ahead with his EMS flashlight. He found you in the living room in your chair. Your recliner. And I'm so sorry to have to tell you this, but—you'd been attacked. And you were bleeding."

I can smell the dizzying blood smell again and see the dark shape streaking toward me. "What happened next is hazy—something came at me fast and then I blacked out."

34.

"Then a dog—covered with blood—was licking my face."

Am I making sense? Am I telling her too much?

I walk to the settee and back.

"Isaac called 911. A fire department ambulance arrived and police and Los Villas security. Then the coroner. And Animal Services took the dog away so they could put it down and examine its brain for rabies."

I know what I promised—but I just can't tell her that they planned to examine the contents of the dead dog's stomach and its feces for traces of her flesh.

"Anyway, Isaac and the police and the Animal Services believe the dog killed you—I don't."

I take a breath.

"The dog in your apartment was scared—but calm and submissive. I believe she was sitting close to your recliner not because she hurt you—but to protect you. And I think she became bloody while fighting your attacker and trying to save you from the assault. The dog must have rushed toward me—not to maul me—which she had every opportunity to do—but to rouse me after I fainted."

I notice a loose blue thread in the Star of David section of the blanket.

"The dog didn't have a collar or a tag, and on the news Animal Services said it is an unchipped female. When Isaac told me about you, he didn't mention a dog—and he would have—"I almost say "as a selling point" but stop myself—"because I'm really into dogs. Also, I didn't see a water or food bowl in your kitchen or a dog bed in your apartment. And your recent surgery would have made it close to impossible for you to have a dog around."

"So, this is the thing, Mrs. Rutledge—if the dog wasn't yours and she didn't attack you—someone took her to your apartment and made your murder look like a dog attack. And if that's what happened—then the person who killed you is still out there—free to kill again."

35.

I push the glittery, frayed blue thread through an opening between stitches, then knot it.

"That's why I feel I have to find out who killed you and convince the police to look for a human murderer—not a dog. But I can't do it without your help."

I remove my cell phone, a pair of latex gloves, an N95 mask and my burial society volunteer packet from my backpack. I locate the page with the corner I folded—"*Pikuach nefesh.* פקוח נפש, 'Watching Over A Soul.' Protecting Life" —

"I'm sure that you already knew this stuff—but when I was learning to become a chevra kadisha volunteer, two things really struck me. *Kavod ha'met*—the duty to honor and protect the dignity of the dead. And *pikuach nefesh*—the belief that preserving life takes precedence over everything else—including the dictates of Jewish law."

I fold the soft blanket into a rectangle and place it near my back-pack at the foot of the table.

"Isaac told me you were observant. I know that you honored and protected the modesty and dignity of dead when you were a burial society volunteer. So, I'm sure you would agree that, when protecting the modesty of the dead endangers life, that obligation must be put aside."

36.

"Until your killer is found, people's lives will be in danger. So, the way I see it—it's our obligation—yours and mine—to do everything we can to protect those lives."

I violate the All Electronics Are Absolutely Forbidden Near The Decedent Rule and switch on my cell phone, mute the sound, then put it on the body table.

"I did some reading—and when a fatality might be the result of a dog attack, canine behavioral and teeth and bite experts determine the dog's innocence or guilt by evaluating its behavior and examining the victim's wounds."

"It's complicated to explain how—but I've checked out the behavior of the dog we found in your apartment, and she's not aggressive. She's not reactive."

I put on the mask and pull on the latex gloves, then begin untucking the sheet at the foot-end and folding it back until L.S. Rutledge's white, envelope-style, regular size, vinyl body-bag is uncovered.

"There are only three beings on earth with knowledge of the particulars of your murder— The dog. Your killer. And you.

"The dog is mute. Your killer is out there somewhere. But—even if you don't remember what happened—your body kept a precise record of the attack. So, what I'm asking you to do, Mrs. Rutledge, is to let your body tell me what it knows."

37.

I check the pictures to see if they're sharp, then turn off my cell phone.

L.S. Rutledge's unwarm soundlessness hums like electricity as I flatten the plastic bag containing dark, blood-saturated gauze strips and flakes of dried blood and place the bag back inside the body bag. Jewish law stipulates that the body return to earth whole—which means with the blood chevra kadisha members collected after the police were finished with the crime scene.

I close the zipper sewn into the tongue-shaped flap, then cover the body bag with the sheet, smooth it and tuck it under.

I remove my mask and gloves and stuff them with my phone into my backpack.

The last thing is to unfold and arrange the blanket just so over L.S. Rutledge's sternum.

I step away from the table and check that the wrapped body looks the way it did when I entered the room.

It does.

I wave the jar of gel deodorizer to kill death's sourness, then carry my backpack to the little couch.

No thunder. No sorrow-roar or icy wave rises to rebuke me for disturbing L.S. Rutledge's peace or for violating her modesty or privacy by taking repeated, frank, close-up photographs of her wounds.

Tomorrow the female chevra kadisha volunteers will bathe L.S. Rutledge on a steel table fitted with drains, will steady her head on a wooden block and wash and smooth her blood-clotted hair, clean her nails and feet, will bathe her again and will declare her purified, will pray for her and praise her, will dry and dress her in fresh, pocketless white linen burial garments and place her and the plastic bag of gauze and blood into her casket.

I envy them their kindnesses.

There's a human murderer out there that I must find alone.

Part Two

"…we come from dust, and return to dust. We labor by our lives for bread, we are like broken shards, like dry grass, and like a withered flower; like a passing shadow and a vanishing cloud, like a breeze that passes, like dust that scatters, like a fleeting dream."

from the *Unetaneh Tokef,* a prayer recited during the Jewish High Holy Days

38.

After I stopped to dispose of the Halligan tool in a closed construction site Dumpster, I returned from the Death Space that is Mount Of Olives Chapel And Mortuary Park In Rear and entered my compact Life Space, the dogs—instead of killing each other—were dozing on opposite sides of the bed. A "Weirdest Weather" episode about blood-red rain was on the television and the British meteorologist host—wrapped head-to-chin British Royals-style in a floral scarf—was explaining that this freakish precipitation wasn't a stern message from God as the rained-on people believed—but resulted from the random convergence of heavy pollen and unusually dry, wind.

If the sky rained blood on me—I'd want to know why.

A poll I read about on X found that that a majority of Americans believe Jews control things—banks and entertainment, news, pandemics, and the weather—which must include, I guess—the Weather Channel, right?

Does this mean that when bad things happen to good people, most Americans think that certain other people are bad?

Or despite what "a majority of the American people" believe, does bad stuff happen because—although They are all-organized, all-knowing, and all-powerful—the Creator doesn't have time or head-space for every little thing?

What with eternally calculating the fates of wind-buffeted sparrows, wrangling light-eating black holes and dark energy and matter, regulating the weather and the moderating of majority perceptions of a certain minority are probably two teeny, annoying jobs too many.

Things mean nothing or everything.

Whatever instigates events is butterfly-wing-fragile and quick as a wince. I've given up trying to pin down the something—physics, divine boredom, or my own self-centeredness—that adjusted the pressure of my father's foot on the gas pedal and nudged the bird into the open window of my parents' car at just the wrong—or, depending on how indifferent or malevolent the universe seems to you—the right moment.

The Busby Berkeley symmetries of the universe—spinning galaxies, nested darknesses and big bangs that seem to collapse into chaos but then keep dancing blind me.

I squint at the reflections of the dancers' shoes splintering white against the black-mirror floor. I focus on particulars.

L.S. Rutledge's purple-black wounds and beet-red contusions.

I checked dog bite wounds and contusions online and in textbook photos of dog attacks, and yeah—a dog might have repeatedly clamped its jaws into L.S. Rutledge, drilled in its teeth, then shook its head.

But when I look closely at the photos I took—her wounds mostly look as if they were humanly devised—repeated, scraping penetrations that could have been created with a sharp-toothed object.

Linda leaps off the bed, softly licks my cold ankles, then flares her nostrils to taste the scents of disinfectant, mortuary deodorizer and death that have attached themselves to my shoes.

Freddie merely raises one toffee eyebrow dot and shoots me a disdainful Where-Have-You-Been? look.

"Don't ask where I was or what I did," I tell him.

I feed the dogs, give Freddie his meds, turn up thermostat, remove my clothes and throw away the mask I wore at the mortuary, scrub my hands with antibacterial soap, shower and wash my hair, change into leggings, a fleece, thick socks and my Uggs, and make and drink a full-caffeine latte.

I put on my puffer, leash and harness the dogs, dress Linda in her jacket, and reapply the makeup she rubbed off while I was gone.

Even with the jacket I can't get warm. I'm afraid that the chill of the decedents' room has nested inside me. Shivering, I let the two trusting, mysteriously knowing creatures lead me—the little, bossy one first—into the unsettled, bruise-dark night.

39.

I eat a microwaved, not bad, not good, not *parve*, Marie Callender's frozen dinner, sip a scalding mug of Swiss Miss cocoa made with water, then invent a flexible, extended-use lie—COVID that could bring complications or turn into long COVID—to cover missing the make-up anatomy exam tomorrow and all the classes, exams and/or papers I will miss in the near future. Then I craft an abject, touching email about my illness and send it to the teaching assistant, make another hot chocolate, wrap myself in blankets and read more about dog bites.

Dog bites are more serious than they look. A small, puncture wound that hasn't broken the skin can crush soft tissue. A dog bite can tear muscle, penetrate the chest wall and fatally damage organs.

Incidents involving more than two bites are classified as dog attacks.

It takes two tenths of a second for a dog to feel threatened, panicked or frightened enough to bite. It takes three-quarters of a second for a human being to react to an aggressive dog.

In the U.S., dogs bite forty-five million people each year, most of them children.

A dog bites someone every seventy-five seconds.

Each time you interact with a dog, you have a one-in-seventy chance of being bitten.

But the odds of R.S. Rutledge being killed by a dog in any given year were less than 1 in 18 million.

The force of a dog's bite is measured in pounds per square inch—PSI. Dogs with scary-high bite force are English Mastiffs

(556 PSI) and Rottweilers (325 PSI).

As a twice-fully-toothed-canine-adjacent adult, I can't help wondering if a few dogs are responsible for most of the biting, puncturing, organ- and tissue-crushing; what Freddie's and Linda's PSIs might be; and what I'd need to do to frighten, threaten or panic either or both of them into biting me more than twice.

40.

I'm in the Lexus on Serenity View Drive inching my way toward L.S. Rutledge's funeral where my plan is to scope-out the attendees. I did some snooping at Mount Of Olives and learned that L.S. Rutledge's funeral will happen at two P.M. at The Eternal Home Of Peace, the cemetery where my aunt chose to be buried and where she purchased an adjacent plot for me. It feels not bad, but totally weird that my aunt, L.S. Rutledge and I will decompose near each other—if not for eternity then for the duration of something that will certainly feel like it.

But Serenity View Drive is un-serene. It is that scene in every disaster movie where those fleeing The World-Ending Event are gridlocked all the way to the conflagrating horizon.

And my nightmare still fogs my head. In it L.S. Rutledge morphs into my dead aunt restrained in her hospital bed while my parents—two, slim charred smudges—writhe on either side of her.

Or maybe it's the prospect of attending L.S. Rutledge's sendoff that has me off-tilt.

But if I were being honest, I'd have to confess that last time I felt one-hundred-percent sharp was when I was with Isaac in his ambulance on the way to meet L.S. Rutledge.

Isaac.

Just thinking his name is a blow. And I think it all the time.

If he'd been with me, I might not have approached the cemetery from the end of Serenity View Drive where I'm stuck and no parking is allowed.

Cars and news vans parked at crazy angles crowd the narrow, sloping gravel shoulder, blocking the tents on poles providing shade for the people selling five-dollar bouquets from plastic buckets.

I advance until I'm parallel with Serenity View Memorial Park—The Eternal Home Of Peace's larger, ornate non-Jewish neighbor—which means I'm a little closer to L.S. Rutledge. Men shouldering heavy video cameras and large-headed, male and female local news reporters with raised eyebrows painted onto their Circus Peanut-orange makeup zigzag between cars. The only thing absent from this traffic cliché would be the spectacle of the Serenity View Memorial Park's dead rising zombified from their graves.

But the only disturbances visible at Serenity View Cemetery are two workmen creating leaf-blower dust devils, and a whirling flower spinner glitterizing the velveteen green.

I have three-quarters of a gridlocked mile to go. A man on a motorcycle threads his way past me and the flower-shaped spinner sparkles because Serenity Vista Memorial Park is not Jewish.

A fake stone sign explains that Serenity Vista welcomes people—dead ones—of all "faiths." And its website touts special "Jewish areas" in certain locations—but not this one because there happens to be a jumbo Jewish cemetery next door. Which explains why—depending on the season—Christmas trees—real and aluminum, variously-shaped helium balloons, spinners, Jack-O-Lanterns, scarecrows, solar light strings, Easter baskets, stuffed animals, five-dollar bouquets and potted plants—sweet and heartbreaking—festoon Serenity Vista Memorial Park through the seasons.

Jewish cemeteries are traditionally object- and flower-free except for the small stones of remembrance visitors leave on graves. But like many American Jewish cemeteries, The Eternal Home Of Peace made peace with its assimilated clientele and offers embalming and cremation, and provides graveside vases and water for the flowers they sell in the mortuary lobby.

I've seen deer materialize on the early morning, empty slopes and graze upon the un-kosher arrangements.

A blue and yellow News 23 van honks its way into my lane from the red gravel strip ahead of me. I turn hard onto the shoulder churning dust, park in the narrow space the van just vacated, grab my mask and my leather shoulder bag, and make my way in my nice, uncomfortable flats to what will be My Eternal Home Of Something that I'm pretty sure will not be Peace.

41.

Black and white cars with their light bars blinking and a tight line of helmeted and Plexiglas-shielded LAPD officers prevent opposing groups of noisy, jostling protesters from entering or blocking the driveway to The Eternal Home Of Peace.

Most of the protesters flourish professionally-printed placards printed in a red, dripping-blood, font—"Find It and Kill It!" "Hang The Beast!" "Put IT Down!, and "Bite Back!" Pressed against the fence an outnumbered trio of sad-eyed, look-alike endomorphs push homemade cardboard signs up and down in the air: "Dog Doe Is Innocent Until Proven Guilty!" "Dog Doe Is A ScapeDog," and "Save Dog Doe!"

Beyond the police line, a cemetery man in the night-dark suit, his gray kippah secured to his dull brown hair with a shiny clip, and his surgical mask dipping below his nostrils checks the I.D.s drivers hand him through their open windows against a paper attached to his clipboard. If the ID matches a name on his list, he waves the car in.

If it doesn't, he traces a U in the air to indicate that that driver must return to the hell that Serene Vista Drive has become.

It's clear that the angry people, camera operators and reporters are not here because of Dog Doe's alleged bite-ee, L.S. Rutledge.

They're here because they want to kill the dog that's right now sleeping on my bed—the monster they imagine pacing and salivating for sundown when she will lower her fantasy 670-Pounds -Per -Square-Inch stinking razor-teeth into her next soft and easily-punctured, human victims—them.

42.

I follow the mulched border of the ascending Eternal Home Of Peace driveway past the waterfall refreshing the Cleansing Pool where visitors on their way out are invited to rinse death's invisible residue from their hands. I adjust my leather shoulder bag—which looks heavy, but isn't—then proceed past the shuttered information kiosk toward the guy manning the clipboard.

"Excuse me," I uptalk through my mask, careful to communicate that I want something, but don't want it too much. "I'm from Mount Of Olives for the Rutledge funeral?"

The man assesses me.

I'm not wearing my good black pants or my turtleneck because, after wearing them in the decedent's room, I couldn't stand to. On the way here I ducked into my aunt's favorite Chico's and waded through cruise wear and short-waisted, exaggerated-print outfits designed for osteo-porous seniors with cataracts until I found a pair of no-wrinkle, dark navy pants with a matching V-neck, and a simple, fake gold chain on sale and which I put on in the dressing room.

I'm hoping that the fresh clothes, the serious N95 with straps that go around the back of my head instead of looping over my ears, the serious-looking leather bag, and—in case the mortuary people here know her—my freaky resemblance to Isaac's Mount Of Olives Lady Pal—will make my impersonation convincing. And all the shouting, honking, and the motorcycle growls can't hurt.

The motorcycle cop speaks into the mic on his helmet headset, rolls his bike forward, taps the cemetery man's sloping shoulder, talks, then points at the snarl of cars waiting to enter.

"Tell them this is the only public entrance," he tells the cop. "And that the mortuary entrance is for employees and transport and ambulance only." The cemetery man shakes his head. "That area is strictly private. Sensitive. And full of toxics. It's never open to the public under any circumstances." The man waves his clipboard toward the line of cars. "And tell Burbank P.D. to keep their pants on. This is memorial park, not some sort of rave. Our deceased clients are no longer in a rush."

The man's mask loosens until it lands along his upper lip. "Have overflow enter through Embalming? Can you believe that? I'll bet the genius who thought of that doesn't know the difference between a casket and a coffin or between a mortuary and a cemetery."

"Dealing with the living is hardest part of the job," I shrug. "But today is nuts."

"Tell me about it," the man says. "You're from Mount of Olives you said?"

"Yep. I'm here for the L.S. Rutledge graveside service and interment at 2 o'clock? Management wants somebody from M.O.F. there and to sign the visitor book."

"Sure. Horrible, horrible thing. They'd better find that killer dog soon."

"I know," I say. "I won't be able to sleep until they do."

He doesn't ask for my I.D. Good.

"Follow the main road past the mausoleum and turn left at Queen Esther. And be glad you're strictly mortuary and don't deal with celebrity or victim interments."

"I am," I say. "Every single day." I step beyond the open, tall wrought-iron gates and the dark, silent markers unfurl in perfect, austere rows before me.

43.

These thin ballet flats are worse than heels—maybe because everything connected to ballet is designed for maximum suffering and pain. But I keep to the pavement and avoid the lawns when I'm here except when necessary to reach my aunt's grave.

I'd planned to leave her the smooth, mottled stone in my pocket that I found walking the dogs yesterday, but it's too late.

I move past knolls and dells engineered for gentleness. They ripple through Ruth, Isaiah, and Moses, past the butterscotch Mausoleum and the King David section where my aunt reposes and where I will someday be deposited. When the road lifts to meet a section of freshly constructed and precisely-mown hills––I've reached Queen Esther.

Cars pull over to park with their front wheels turned into the curb and unload figures in suits and shiny shoes and somber dresses. The only sounds issue from two hawks surfing a rising thermal, car doors thumping shut, and the chirping of remote locking devices.

I pause near a polished black SUV with an LAPD officer in the driver's seat. I'm pretty sure the passenger in a white linen kippah and a mask printed with the official seal of City of Los Angeles emerging from the back leather seat—his thin scapulae showing under his suit—must be the mayor.

The trees of Queen Esther are new and thin on shade. Slender from crown to base, fat rubber ties connect them to sturdy supports. Folding chairs have been unfolded between the trees' fresh, breakable trunks and arranged in rows facing an excavated grave lined with fabric turf. A pair of shovels recline against the pewter-colored bier—*mitah* in Hebrew—that seems to float the plain pine casket under the thin blue slice of Hollywood-Glendale sky.

A traditional Jewish funeral at The Eternal Home Of Peace would have begun with a gathering in the chapel next to the flower shop. Then would have come the pall-bearers' removal of the casket and the casket's transfer to the mortuary hearse parked in the special Hearse-Parking-Only spot indicated by a blue-painted curb. A slow vehicular procession to the grave site would follow. And after that, the pall-bearers would haltingly transfer the casket to the *mitah*.

The crush of protesters and media must have made the chapel gathering impossible. Or maybe like my aunt, L.S. Rutledge made her pre-need wishes known to The Eternal Home Of Peace counselors and told them she wanted to go out clean and lean.

I move behind a big-assed, mahogany Escalade with a casket profile parked a few cars down from the lustrous Mayoral Ride and watch the arriving attendees choose their seats. I also have a view of stragglers making the turn into the Queen Esther section.

No one does anything weird. No one stands out. People are somber—but no one is distraught. And I recognize some people—

The harassed-looking gaggle of aides that collect behind the mayor when he makes a statement or gives a speech.

That dog expert with the clicker, an "EXTREME PACK ASCENT Canine Training" t-shirt visible under his sport coat.

Three city council members under investigation for taking bribes from developers, each of them speaking urgently into their cell phones.

The guy with the dog in a stroller from Los Villas del Fairfax Village with a moon-faced man. His husband? His friend? A neighbor?

The man who whittled that hedge into a heart nods at the man who had the bow-tied dog, but he sits in the back row with a group of Villas del Fairfax Villagers. I recognize a few of them as people who gathered behind the police tape on the night of the murder.

Taking a hint from the council persons, I pretend to listen to someone on my phone, and move to a white Suburban with an official parking decal on the back bumper. I have a clear view of the seats reserved for the decedent's family and I want to see who claims them.

Two mustached men wearing shades and a woman with deep frown lines in a dark green blazer with shoulder pads stride onto the grass and choose aisle seats in the middle row. The woman's overbearing perfume defeats my mask and hangs in the air after she passes me.

I know the men are talking because their moustaches move up and down. And I know they must be plain clothes police because I could see the outlines of their ankle holsters as they stepped over the curb.

I transition from the road to grass, careful not to step on grave markers and decide to occupy the empty seat behind the woman in green and wonder where she stows her weapon. In her purse? In an armpit holster?

From here I can see what they see. But what or who are they looking for?

Suspicious or incriminating behavior—whatever that might be.

Or maybe one of L.S. Rutledge's neighbors saw something. Or had a security camera.

Either way, they must be looking for the person who brought the killer dog to L.S. Rutledge's apartment.

And for the person who stole the killer dog from the shelter.

44.

I shift my weight from one aggrieved foot to the other in the line of living people waiting to perform the *mitzvah* of twice-depositing fresh shovelfuls of soil into L.S. Rutledge's grave. The Los Villas del What the Fuck contingent is ahead of me, some with their arms around each other's shoulders, some touching their eyes with crumpled tissues.

The dust that is L.S. Rutledge has been lowered into the earth.

I'm not sure where the undercover police officers went. Maybe they slipped back to their station in a nondescript vehicle. Or maybe they've positioned themselves on the mausoleum roof where they can scan the license plates of departing vehicles.

L.S. Rutledge's rabbi wasn't the rabbi The Eternal Home Of Peace provided for my aunt's Zoom funeral last year. This rabbi was an un-jolly Jewish Santa who intoned the service exactly as it was printed in the right-to-left booklet placed in the center of every hard, cold metal seat:

"*Adonai* is my Shepherd; I shall not want…"

"Oh God, full of compassion, who dwells on high, grant perfect rest beneath the

sheltering wings of Your divine presence, among the holy and the pure who shine as the brightness of the firmament unto Linda, who has gone to her eternal home. Author of mercy, bring her under the shelter of Your wings, and let her soul be bound up in the bonds of eternal life. May you be her inheritance and may her repose be in peace. Amen."

Then Kaddish.

The rabbi did not cut the black ribbons traditionally pinned to the clothing of the deceased family as a symbolic rending of garments. Though three people—two women and one man in dark business wear—claimed the family row a few moments after the service started—they were ribbon-less and were probably what they looked like—lawyers, not relatives.

The rabbi introduced a white-haired woman as the president of the Los Villas del Fairfax Villages residents' association. As she delivered a choked eulogy for her friend, her flowy palazzo pants became progressively electrified until they'd plastered themselves to calves and thighs. Between sobs, she shared the same information Isaac gave me—that L.S. Rutledge was smart, generous and kind, had earned a couple advanced college degrees, had "worked with troubled children." But I learned one new mini-fact: Unless it rained, L.S. Rutledge read the newspaper in the jacuzzi in her sun hat every day between nine and ten A.M. I also learned that Mrs. Rutledge moved from D.C. into her Los Villas apartment a year after she became a widow.

And she didn't say anything about L.S. Rutledge having a dog.

My heart raced when a group of Hatzalah volunteers arrived very late—but their jacket insignias identified them as from North Hollywood—not Isaac's Mid-City group.

45.

Sunset burns the world into blankness—which feels right after a funeral—until the gray-blue Subaru Cross-Trek with wraparound black tinting started tailgating me as I turned from Serenity View Drive onto Victory Boulevard. I saw it again on Riverside and Cahuenga. And here it is making everything feel wrong as I drive west on Ventura Boulevard.

Am I paranoid? Maybe.

But I can't lead whoever is driving that Subaru to Life Space and Linda.

I cut through a gas station, then backtrack east until the light at Barham stops me.

From here I can detour to Burbank, return to Serenity View Drive, enter Universal Studios, or I can drive to Hollywood.

The sun in my rear-view mirror blinds me. I choose Hollywood.

I squeak through the light at Cahuenga, then run a fresh red light at the Hollywood Bowl parking lot. The heavy traffic crawls toward the Valley, so there are few southbound trucks or buses to hide between.

When I pass the Egyptian Revival American Legion Post, the Subaru's roof is visible—more gray than blue in the intensifying twilight— three cars back.

I turn onto Franklin at the last second, consider entering the Magic Castle driveway, but turn onto a dead-end street instead, back into a driveway and wait to see if the Subaru followed me.

I wait for a count of five and wish I had a nice fat Valium, take Franklin to Highland and turn onto Hollywood Boulevard to activate my new plan to take Laurel Canyon back to the valley without seeing a Subaru.

Chill out, Ascher, I tell myself, attempt a slow yoga breath and have a coughing fit instead.

My eyes watering, I pass Temple Israel as the street lights ignite and the black insect-eye that is the Subaru's windshield fills my side-mirror with its reflection.

46.

Objects in the mirror are closer than they appear and the Subaru appears way too close.

Fuck the Subaru. Fuck yoga. I make a hairy left-turn on red, then change lanes abruptly.

Should I pull over in a driveway or find a bright, public place and call the police?

Should I open the windows and put on my emergency lights and yell for help?

There's a CVS ahead that has a big parking lot in the back. And apartment buildings after that. I know there's a supermarket at Santa Monica and a big gas station at Melrose. Then the Farmer's Market and The Grove.

A red light traps me in the right lane at Melrose. A woman stands on the bus bench in front of a dry cleaners and gestures at the traffic like a Rose Queen on a combusting float, her tattered white granny dress absorbing the cool light of the indifferent headlights flowing north. A sign repurposed from the side of a cardboard box with "NEED HELP! GOD BLESS!" written in pencil sprouts from the stuff in her shopping cart.

Will anyone pull over and help her? Has anyone asked Alexa to call 911?

Why would they? What could the police do to fix her catastrophe except arrest her on a seventy-two-hour psychiatric hold or dump her in the women's jail miles from here? The last time they did a count, seventy-five thousand, five-hundred and eighteen people were living in cars or RVs, or on L.A. County sidewalks, underpasses, parks, freeway overpasses and flood channel embankments because there is nowhere else for most of them to go.

If I park the Lexus somewhere and start yelling about a gray-blue Subaru following me like a shark—what can I expect?

Two dogs who don't really know each other—one of whom is an emotional mess and another that has been recently traumatized—have been locked together in my studio apartment for hours.

The more I drive, the farther I am from them. I have to find a way back.

47.

It's dark. The traffic tightens the farther south on Fairfax I go, so I can't make a U-turn or execute a sudden lane-switch. I'm stuck in the right lane no matter what the Subaru five cars back in the left lane decides to do.

I auto-dial a number on my phone, listen to the ring, the away message, then after the beep record my own—"Hey, it's me. I'm on my way to your place. Someone's following me and I'm really scared. Please meet me outside. I'm almost there."

Why was I so sure Isaac would be home?

Because he has COVID and he's isolating, that's why.

Then why was I so sure that if he was home, he'd answer his phone?

Because I need him to.

I make it through the intersection at Third ahead of the Subaru and just as I'm about to pass it, I swerve into the parking lot at Partridge Place.

Isaac's security light—no, lights—he's added some—sour the Jacaranda tree's purple and make some white stuff on the ground and the hood of the ambulance glow green.

Isaac is not outside waiting for me.

Headlights bounce behind me and my rearview mirror goes white.

48.

The Subaru accelerates and jolts my car forward, then a man-sized shadow pounds on my window".

"Put it in park, Ascher! Open the door!"

"It's in park!"

The Subaru rams me again.

"Unlock the car!"

I unlock the car. The door opens and Isaac's unmasked face is close to my unmasked face. "Undo your seat belt, Ascher, then run inside and lock the door. And be careful not to twist your neck."

I release the seat belt and slide out of the seat on wobbly legs. "He followed me here from the Valley and I have no idea why."

The Subaru flashes its brights, then backs up a few feet as if readying to ram my car again. Isaac jogs toward it carrying something black that he slams against the Subaru's windshield and driver's-side window.

I stay where I am, but I don't twist my neck. And though I can't see what it is right now—something is wrong with Isaac's face.

The Subaru's door swings open and a thick man in a red t-shirt angles his round rare-beef-patty head toward me and opens his mouth. "That fat bitch cut me off twice, bro, and I was just giving her a little driving lesson is all. Isn't that right, bitch? Learn to fucking drive, bitch."

49.

Did that asshole just call me fat?

Isaac says something. The man shrugs, and Isaac raises the black object above his head.

The man nods, then holds up his hands.

Isaac turns and I see that his weapon is a leaf-blower. He lowers it and pushes the blower-nozzle into the Subaru driver's ribs.

The man flinches, gives me the finger, mouths the word, "bitch," grins, then gets into the Subaru, and—with the car door still open—lurches backwards onto Fairfax.

I do not hear tires screaming and metal crushing metal—just some honking.

Isaac puts the blower on the ground, steps to my car, opens the door, scoops my key fob off the seat, then slams the door and locks it.

He hands me the fob, then he crosses his arms like a pissed-off Mr. Clean. "I told you to go inside, Ascher. You should have. Road rage is no joke. What if he'd had a gun?"

"Did I say anything was a joke? And I have no idea why that lunatic was enraged at me."

"Where did you first see him?"

"On Serenity View Drive at the Eternal Home Of Peace. Right after I left the funeral."

"Well, maybe he's one of those guys who doesn't like Jewish cemeteries or the Jewish people who visit them."

"That's a stretch, isn't it? All kinds of people attended that funeral."

Isaac frowns the way my CPA parents did whenever I brought

home a math test—with a frown that signified their disappointment in me once again.

"He rear-ended you pretty hard. Do you have any soreness in your neck?" Isaac touches his neck with his index finger as if to illustrate what "neck" means.

"My neck is perfect," I say. But my neck is stiffening as I utter the lie. "And thank you for saving me from that asshole. But I didn't cut him off. And I don't need to be more freaked out than I already am."

A motorcycle backfires, then a bus gasps as it passes Partridge Place. But Isaac is silent. I decide to lose the game of chicken and speak first. "I know you have COVID. How are you feeling?"

"It's complicated." Isaac takes a step back, and the light from one of his new security fixtures falls across his face. A shiny black gash slices through his left eyebrow. The bridge of his nose is bruised and swollen, and there are black marks under his eyes.

"Oh my God, Isaac. What happened?"

Isaac steps back into the shadows. "Like I said, Ascher. It's complicated."

"Well, it doesn't look complicated. It looks like you fell, or you were in an accident, or you were attacked. Am I warm?"

Isaac picks up one of the white papers from the asphalt and hands it to me. "Okay. Since you insist on knowing, this happened."

50.

It's a flyer with "The Order of Christian Manhood" in an awful font with Iron Crosses along the top and a disclaimer that the flyer was distributed "randomly and without malicious intent" at the bottom.

I read the flyer twice. I count the sixteen Stars of David bracketing each slur—and I recognize the hunchback, rat-like, leering, hook-nosed caricature of a Jew from a *Der Stürmer* cartoon I saw at the Holocaust Museum during a fifth-grade field trip.

Hundreds of the same flyers rustle like snakes beneath the Jacaranda tree and ride the breeze onto the ambulance's hood, then to Isaac's doorstep and the sidewalk beyond.

I look again at Isaac's beautiful, damaged face. "Did the—um, people—who left these here have something to do with what happened?"

"Yeah. The same ones who hung up that banner. They've been driving their van around, shouting slurs at Jews walking home from *shul* or eating outside at kosher restaurants. They harassed some Haredi boys skateboarding near the Nazi lampposts on Wilshire yesterday."

"The Nazi lampposts?"

"There swastika lampposts in the group of antique street lights in front of the museum. You know—where people take selfies?"

"I knew about the lights and selfies, but not the swastikas. And the museum people are okay with swastikas now?"

"There were a few complaints, but they insist they're Hindu good luck symbols. The community that installed five hundred of them in the twenties had a lot of open Hitler-sympathizers—

they even named a park for Heinrich Himmler and held Bund gatherings and Nazi Youth picnics. I checked and the neighboring community ordered lampposts from the same manufacturer—but without the swastikas."

"Where was this?"

"Glendale. And the lampposts are still there. There was a lot of pro-Nazi activity there, in L.A., and around the country then."

And now, I think. "So, you had a run-in with the Order of Christian Manhood?"

"Yes." Isaac's pupils catch the light. "I heard male voices, and found three of them dumping garbage bags full of those flyers all over the lot. When I told them to leave, one guy ran away, but the other two started talking shit about my kippah and the mezuzah and the Hebrew on the ambulance. They called me a Christ killer, a kike, a groomer and a child rapist. After the child rapist thing, I lost it."

Don't react, I tell myself. Just float above everything you feel. "So, I guess this means you don't have COVID?"

"I have a cold. But I couldn't show up at Mount of Olives or the funeral with my face like this. And I knew how upset you'd be if told you what happened, so I didn't. I'm not proud of lying to you, Ascher. But I felt I had to."

51.

Isaac—who absolutely did not have to lie to me—corrals the flyers into piles with the leaf blower and I stuff them into garbage bags.

After throwing the garbage bags in the Dumpster, Isaac approaches me until he's a generous six feet away. Is this virus-distancing or something else?

"Thanks for helping me," he says from the other side of the Ascher-Free-Zone.

"Thank you for saving me from that creep." I don't say what I want to say.

"You should file a police report. I remember his license plate number. I'll text it to you."

"No report. I want to forget him. And I want him to forget me," I say. "But I'm worried about you, Isaac. Your safety."

"Don't be. The Order of Christian Manhood say horrible things, hang banners and distribute disgusting flyers—but they stay within First Amendment limits. Did you notice the disclaimer at the bottom of the leaflet that says 'no malice intended'? They're always covering their cowardly asses."

"I read a little about them after they hung that banner—they also post videos and have followers who might not care about first amendment limits. They punched you in the face, didn't they?"

"One of them. But I hit him first."

"Okay. But what if they decide to come back?"

"They won't. And I won't be surprised again—I'm installing cameras and an alarm system tomorrow. And Shomrim and Magen Am have set up patrols for the next few weeks. I'll be fine."

"You don't look fine."

"Stop making this into a huge deal, Ascher. This isn't the first-time people like them have behaved badly around someone like me. And it's not the last. You know very well that that this is just the way things are."

I get what Isaac is saying. Last year a woman we knew—a Holocaust survivor who was bullied by some antisemitic neighbors—jumped from her balcony and died of her injuries.

But the Order of Christian Manhood is dangerous. They have a national reach online. What's to stop them or one of their fanboys from engaging in violence?

Isaac should stay in the Valley with me—but I can't ask him to. I might be able to come up with a good lie to explain Linda—but he's sure to recognize her, and the moment he does, he'll call the police or take her to animal control himself.

"Cameras and patrols are good," I say carefully. "But you shouldn't have to live like this. And Holocaust survivors shouldn't have to jump off their fucking balconies to find peace. Could you make yourself less of a target—just until they move on?"

"Do racists and Islamophobes attack Black people and women wearing hijabs because they make themselves targets? I'm being who I am—living my life with a kippah on my head and a mezuzah on the doorpost and an ambulance with Hebrew on it parked out front. You've got this ass-backward, Ascher. Scum like the Order of Christian Manhood need to stop what they're doing. Not me."

I duck into the car, start the engine, start to back out, then stop to open my window just enough for Isaac to hear me. "I apologize for saying a wrong, stupid thing, Isaac. All I want is for you to be safe."

"Ascher? Wait." Isaac lopes to the window, then lowers his flushed face close to mine. "If your neck begins to hurt, take two ibuprofens with milk or food every four to six hours, then call your doctor first thing in the morning. You'll need to be checked out."

52.

The elevator that levitates my fat bitch neck, the other parts of me that ache, the demonic ballet flats incarcerated in the leather bag, and the bruised heart caged inside my ribs to the hushed Life Space hallway smells like macaroni and cheese.

I do not hear Freddie barking when the elevator door opens. The hallway is too quiet. And now that I've reached the door to my cozy, single-occupancy residence—I do not hear his welcome-home snuffling, door-scratching, or recriminating whining.

Why isn't Freddie making noise? Did I forget to give him his anticonvulsant? Or—and I don't want to even consider this—have I been wrong about everything and did Linda bite Freddie more than once?

Could Linda be lying in wait so she can bite me more than once, too?

I unlock the door, and open it a hair. The only sound is the Weather Channel guy droning about cells and hail and atmospheric rivers.

53.

I push the door until there's space for me to limp across the threshold into the fuzzy T.V. glow—I forgot to leave a lamp on. I drop the leather bag on the floor, ignore the mail someone slid under the door—it must have been delivered to the wrong box downstairs—and switch on the overhead light.

Freddie blinks and wags his tail from his spot on my aunt's sweater on the bed. Linda sits near the sweater's edge, her haunch touching Freddie, her fake eyebrow dots raised.

Freddie leaps off the bed to dance around my feet, then Linda follows him, her tail swinging.

I kneel and kiss them. They kiss me back. There are no punctures or lacerations on the dogs' faces. No blood on their fur.

And when I lift my eyes to check, the white sheets on my unmade bed are clean.

54.

I meander with the dogs among lovely, anonymous surfaces under the sky that canopies Isaac and L.S. Rutledge on her first night beneath Queen Esther's starlit grass.

I hope Isaac is safe.

And that L.S. Rutledge is at rest—whatever "at rest" means for the murdered. And, I hope that her memory will point me toward what is right and true.

Kumquats flicker like embers in the branches of the parkway tree Freddie has chosen to pee against. Linda—in her Larry coat—lifts her nose to receive the firmament's soundless sounds, then lifts her leg and pees, too.

I laugh out loud despite the pain in my neck—for which I refuse to take ibuprofen with or without food to spite Isaac and probably to punish myself.

I feel too emptied out to decide where to go next, so I follow Linda as she follows her new friend through a darkness that carries a premonition of summer and jasmine.

The moment feels like a precipice.

Will I be here this summer with the dogs and the thinning ghosts of my parents and my aunt? Or would the smart thing be to pack up the dogs and my stuff and drive as far from L.A. as I can stand to and start over?

I'd have no problem fashioning the lies necessary for a transition. My mortuary school tuition is paid, the first year and a half is all online, and I could take a leave of absence if I needed to. My lease is month-to-month. Linda would be much safer if she weren't in L.A. And I can't see the few friends I still have here until the Linda is out of danger and L.S. Rutledge's murderer is caught.

I don't owe any living person anything.

The evaporation of Ascher Lieb from the greater Los Angeles area would be the swift erasure of the almost-invisible. The removal of a faint smudge. The silencing of an almost inaudible sound. The fading of a shadow into a darker shadow. Single women constantly migrate seeking affordable rent, jobs in hot real estate markets, in Bitcoin, the wellness industry or A.I.

Or to chase the lies that people call dreams—well-paying, meaningful careers in solar or sustainability or podcasting or Substack blogging. Lives shared with significant others or solitary lives filtered and doctored into white-toothed, toned-body, live-laugh-love, living-my-best-fucking-life Instagram photos taken in a wellness spa in Mexico.

Women are probably heading out right this minute despite the traffic—fighting their way to novel communal living arrangements in revitalized urban centers that offer invigorating activities like spelunking or plunging earthward after jumping out of small aircraft.

Women pissed off at their loneliness. Women who decide to fuck it. To fuck everything.

But will a new start in a new place produce a fresh, invigorated me?

Or will I always be hung up on my aunt- and my parent-ghosts? And will I always be a liar shocked and outraged when someone I've lied to lies to me?

The ironies of my situation are not lost on me.

But Isaac—who lied to me, who is angry at me, who loved me until he didn't—and who is in danger—isn't just someone. He's the one living person I was sure would save me if I began to drown.

Well, I'm drowning now.

And—though he won't admit it—so is he.

55.

The dogs doze on the couch. I open my laptop, find the Order of Christian Manhood online and watch their most recent video. It has three thousand likes.

I press play—

The two women resemble each other enough to be mother and daughter. Both have large limbs, long, thin auburn hair, cream-white, wide foreheads, and matching weird, frayed patchwork jeans. Their gazes are fixed Diane-Arbus-blankly on the camera's eye. When the camera pulls back, we see that the women stand in front of a stone wall supporting a carved wooden sign that says, "Temple Beth Jerusalem" under a carved Star of David. The older woman holds a professionally-printed image of a black cartoon rat wearing a large Star of David around its neck and coughing a mist of black droplets with the caption, "THE JEWS CONTROL CHINESE COVID LABS. WHAT ARE THE JEWS CONTROLLING NOW? WHAT WILL THE JEWS CONTROL NEXT?"

The young woman operates a small portable sound system that blasts a looping message delivered by a deep male voice: "Everything about the COVID pandemic is Jewish. COVID is a Nazi-Soros-Talmudist plot to genocide Patriotic White American Christians. So was AIDS. Stop the globalist Jew conspiracy or you will die! You must act now!" Four thousand likes.

The second video is a montage of grainy, black and white security footage shot from various locations. A city street—maybe New York. A modestly dressed Jewish woman—her head covered with a scarf and her ankle-length skirt swaying—briskly pushes two toddlers in a double stroller across the frame. A young man wearing a dark hoodie and surgical mask flashes toward her, then delivers a full-force kick that upends the stroller and pitches the children onto the sidewalk. Six thousand likes.

The third video unfolds on an urban street. Three young men, one of them carrying a baseball bat, assault a tall, Hasidic man wearing a large fur *shtreimel*—it must be Shabbat—from behind. The blow to the side of the man's head sends his hat spinning into the gutter and—as a gash widens in his scalp—collapses him onto the ground. Twenty thousand likes.

A sunny place with palm trees—A white man in a White Lives Matter shirt runs onto a jogging path and throws a large cardboard cup of coffee at the face of a Black female jogger, then mouths, "Sorry, not sorry," at the camera and laughs. Fifteen thousand likes.

"Just look at this disgusting kike, will you?" In the third video, the camera follows a man in his forties with black swastikas and blue iron crosses tattooed on his cheekbones and forehead as he tails a gray-bearded man wearing a black suit and a kippah and carrying a lumpy mesh bag filled with groceries across a strip mall parking lot "You fucking human filth" the tattooed man laughs, then begins to run behind the old man. "Run faster, bedbug! Faster! Or I'm going to kick your ass!" The camera lingers on the frightened, hastening man, then moves to his tormentor as he knocks the old man forward and down. "The only place a kike belongs is in a nice hot oven!" Isn't that right, you filthy Shylock?" Fifty-four thousand likes.

56.

I knew already that Jews are blamed for every calamity—including Hitler. I've seen the photographs of Kristallnacht, of rusty canisters of Zyklon B, the mountains of human hair, pyramids of wedding bands, the trophy-photographs the Nazis took of the colorless, horizontal, stacked emaciated dead, and the women they watched strip before they shot them and pushed them into murder pits.

And I've seen cruelty. Lynching photos. The cavernous scars whipped into the backs of slaves. George Floyd's slow-motion, asphyxiation murder.

And I knew without thinking about it that people must still call Jews kikes. But not that they still did it to their faces. Or that swastika lampposts were a thing. Or that L.A. was once swarming with Nazi wannabes.

Why didn't I know?

Perhaps the people who could have told me didn't want me to know. Maybe they hoped that an antidote for this poison would be discovered before it sickened me.

Or maybe they didn't want to feel what I felt after I saw the flyer, or looked at Isaac's face, or watched those videos.

Because seeing *Der Sturmer* cartoons, knowing there were festive, openly Nazi picnics in Heinrich Himmler Park in Glendale, and that the Order of Christian Manhood has targeted the man I can't stop loving changes things.

And changes me.

57.

Images from the videos jostle each other in my head like sharks in a too-small tank. I decide to exorcize them with some heavy-duty, overdue Life-Space cleaning, but Freddie hates the hiss and smell of glass cleaner, the vacuum is too loud, and when I take out the broom to sweep the tiny kitchen floor, Linda cowers.

I pick up the mail from the entry floor—two supermarket coupon throwaways, an envelope from the dean of my mortuary science program, and a café au lait envelope from The Eternal Home Of Peace. I attach them—unopened—to the refrigerator with magnets, sort my green burial notes on the coffee table, line up Linda's fur color products on the bathroom counter, unfold the Order of Christian Manhood flyer I took from the parking lot outside Isaac's and slide it into the bed table drawer, wash my face, start a latte, kill the impulse to call Isaac, then sign into the account I opened on EveryoneSearch.com, and check the results for L.S. Rutledge.

Linda Smith was born in Rochester, New York in 1952. Her father worked at Xerox. Her mother was a teacher. She went to college at SUNY Stonybrook, where she earned a Bachelor's of Science degree with a major in social work. She then moved to Albany and got a Masters in Social Work and a degree in family therapy, became a licensed family counselor and then became Linda S. Rutledge in 1980 when she married her husband, a geography professor at SUNY Albany.

Linda worked for the County of Los Angeles Division of Children's Services, then at Isla de la Familia, a nonprofit serving families with children and teens with emotional problems, had a private practice, and then, after retirement, volunteered at a homeless service center called Beit Chai.

L.S. Rutledge had never been arrested, had not been sued, had not sued anyone, had not filed for bankruptcy, did not have a social media presence, had co-authored a number of papers about art therapy—"Fluency in the Language of Color" — and addiction—"When a Child Is Addicted, the Family is Addicted" —and published articles in various social work journals.

I checked Open Secrets which showed that she'd donated small amounts of money to Democratic candidates. An image search produced a group photo of a book club gathering in 2016 that showed her holding her hardcover copy of Barack Obama's *Dreams from My Father*; and a headshot of her on the Beit Chai "Meet Our Volunteers" website page.

While Isaac's friend conducted a private staff meeting over private kosher pizza, I located L.S. Rutledge's social security number during a brief break-in to the Mount Of Olives computer which confirmed my suspicion that all Jewish mortuaries have passwords containing the number eighteen or multiples of eighteen, and "shalom," "Zion," or "Sinai." The social security number coughed up no aliases that would indicate that L.S. Rutledge had a secret life or lives.

All I have learned about L.S. Rutledge is that she was generous, smart, lovely, dedicated and thoroughly vanilla.

So why would anyone go to the trouble of murdering her?

Maybe I will begin to find out at her Memorial brunch tomorrow.

58.

I was late leaving for L.S. Rutledge's memorial potluck brunch at the Los Villas del Fairfax Village because I stopped at the contactless Whole Foods in Sherman Oaks for a coffee cake, and before that I had to freshen Linda's makeup and touch-up her dye with a new organic spray color for dogs I got online. I also took the dogs to the "Dog Park" and back, then emailed my anatomy T.A. requesting extensions for the make-up exam and the already-extended green burial paper because the fictional case of COVID afflicting me seems to be lengthening into long COVID.

And it took a while to decide on an outfit.

I finally made it out of the house, and right after I drove past Casa Vega, I saw it—a new billboard with a giant blurry black and white photo of blood-spattered Linda advertising a twenty-five-thousand-dollar reward from Anonymous for information leading to the Apprehension of Dog Doe Dead or Alive.

Now I'm stuck in traffic near one of the places where the road rage guy scared the shit out of me, and—as if engineered by an active curse—the sullen clouds congeal into a cold and freakish storm.

Hail rat-a-tat-tats the windshield and smacks the nasturtiums into the chocolate-dark hillside, and I wonder if the boulders balanced on the softening ridge above me are loosening and wait for the nightmare Mount Olympus traffic light to change.

Imagine the hubris required to name a merely upscale housing development "Mount Olympus," then to advertise your creation with a-fake-Greek-pillared lighted, rectangular sign. Or the chutzpah of arriving late with a crappy, gluten-free coffee cake––the last cake at Whole Foods, so it must be stale—at a gathering honoring a murdered woman while her alleged murderer—who slept and dreamed curled up against you last night—is busy killing the jumbo Busy Bone you bought her.

59.

The Los Villas del Fairfax Villas guard who smiled warmly at Isaac does not smile at me as she hands me a Day-Glo orange Los Villas del Fairfax Blah, Blah, Blah parking pass.

I should be figuring out which “Calle” is Calle Del Comunidad in the maze of little one-way streets that makes Los Villas del Fairfax Village so village-like. But L.S. Rutledge’s apartment pulls me toward it like something dim and deep that you can’t help standing at the edge of and staring into.

The closed vertical blinds in L.S. Rutledge’s living room window are smudged. LVFV-stenciled sawhorses strung with crime scene tape block the sidewalk and fingerprint powder blackens the red door with the number forty-nine. A pile of hail-battered bouquets wrapped in cellophane wilt on the curb next to the black Dodge Charger in the space right in front of the apartment—a Dodge with a CA Exempt license plate and a radar gun hanging from its rear-view mirror and no orange parking pass displayed on its dashboard. A car that must be just what it looks like—an unmarked LAPD vehicle.

If Isaac were with me—because he’s an EMT, and because he’s so genuinely charming—he might have found out what is happening inside L.S. Rutledge’s apartment.

But Isaac is the opposite of here. And—though I’m a good liar—I’m not good enough to lie to a bunch of cops.

60.

Having located the Community Room, I search the *calles* for a parking space and wonder how Linda and her human companion got inside L.S. Rutledge's apartment without neighbors or passing drivers seeing them enter. Because if someone had seen them—the police would be circulating a description.

I circle the block again, then slow as I pass the Charger. If a car had been parked where this police car is parked now, only a person standing on the sidewalk would see L.S. Rutledge's door. A car parked in that spot after dark—especially something big like an SUV—would have blocked the view of L.S. Rutledge opening her door or her lock being bumped to admit a medium-sized black dog jumping from the SUV, or being dragged inside.

The rain falters into mist. I find a parking spot across from the empty, gated pool whose surface rockets steam at the shattering clouds.

I'm in the navy funeral pants with a cream cardigan over a white V-neck I found in my aunt's Chico's stash, hoping the storm is a good-enough excuse for wearing clunky low-heeled boots with interior space for my tube socks, gauze-wrapped toes, and bandaged heels.

I bobby-pinned and tortured my hair with spray into what my aunt called a "chignon" —another thing that made me late and that my aunt always urged me to do that I regret not doing just once to humor her. And I forgot my umbrella. Well, it was my aunt's umbrella. So, with only the cake box to protect my chignon from the hair-unraveling moisture, I clomp and slosh until I reach the wide, cold puddle that moats Los Villas del Fairfax Villages' "Room de Communidad."

I hope L.S. Rutledge's neighbors won't remember seeing me outside or inside the ambulance or recall the man I was with. And that the lies I cooked-up for this occasion will work if I need to use them.

I balance the cake box on the edge of a wet planter, force some rebellious strands of hair back into my chignon, and pull on my N95.

61.

The Communidad air penetrating my mask is the same warm, chickeny, fat-loaded air that circulated in my aunt's kitchen when she'd celebrate my presence by heating a Marie Callender's frozen chicken pot pie for our dinner.

Two long, folding tables with red plastic tablecloths in the center of the room display the spoils of a manic Costco run—dozens of bottles of water and soft drink cans buried in a tub of ice. Tall coffee and hot water carafes. A half-gallon of half and half, a tower of inverted Styrofoam cups. Mini-mountains of sugar and Splenda packets. Tea bags and plastic stir sticks in big baskets and a massive platter of cubed cheeses. The other table displays a cookie tray, two glistening chocolate-chip babkas that must be from Diamond Bakery, pre-sliced bagels arranged like petals around a tub of cream cheese with a plastic knife stuck in it, and a steaming foil-covered casserole on a hot plate that must be the source of the very good smell.

I linger near a laundry basket full of rolled-up yoga mats, folded chairs, and a microphone and speaker set-up, and read the notices on the corkboard locked inside a glass case on the wall–– A Los Villas del Fairfax Villages Food Truck schedule, an Updated Laundry Room Etiquette explainer, a Residents' Association Do's and Don'ts, Los Villas Holiday Décor Tips—"Extension Cords Prohibited In Walkways!"—an invitation to "All Artists and Crafters" to participate in an upcoming Los Villas Residents "Fairfax Villas Arte and Crafte Faire," an invitation to join the Amigos Brigade, a weekly movie night film schedule, a call for volunteers for this year's "La Fiesta de la Communidad," and a warning to "ALWAYS Keep Windows

Closed During Windy Days and Nights."

I step over the heavy-duty orange extension cord extruding from the hot plate onto the floor to which it is duct-taped, arrive at the cookie and bagel table and remove my offering from its box.

"Just loving the boots." The voice comes from the shimmery sapphire Disneyland-level hologram that has manifested at my elbow. "So whimsical. And thank you for the cake." It's the silver-tongued, silver-haired eulogist from L.S. Rutledge's funeral whom the rabbi introduced as the president of the Los Villas del Blue Eye-Shadow Association.

"I hope it's good," I say. "My Whole Foods was low on coffee cake this morning."

"That pecan streusel topping looks delish. And please, help yourself to anything and everything." Her voice is just like the upbeat female voice that narrates those T.V. commercials for drugs with sci-fi names that promise to slow your fatal disease. As she straightens the cookies on the platter, her Blue Cherry blue long skirt undulates like kelp, and her turquoise teardrop earrings sway above her vibrational mauve, bell-sleeved blouse. If she begins to hum like a Tibetan singing bowl, I will not be surprised.

"I'm April. President of the Los Villas residents' association," April says as she expertly amputates a babka slice with the flimsy knife. "Were you a friend of poor Mrs. Rutledge? Or a new resident who's somehow eluded our Association outreach?"

I leave the beckoning slice on the paper plate where April put it. "I'm Evelyn Mandel," I say, poaching my dead aunt's name––about to add that I'm "a friend of a friend of L.S. Rutledge" before I realize that it's safer to be vague.

"Just an acquaintance," I say. "I feel so terrible about what happened and I wanted to pay my respects."

April smiles a sparkly smile, then fastens her Anderson-Cooper-super-blue-eyes on my face and curls a purple-veined, baby-blue-nail-polished hand around my right arm.

62.

The sky-radiance that is April that powered me to the wall of windows, now assaults me with a round of rapid, first-name introductions to Jennifer. Tim. Wendy, Mitch, Bob and Lauren. Sylvia. William. Then Karen, Fritz, Naomi, Terri and Joseph.

The owners of the bow-tied dog with the stroller are Chris and George. The man who shaved the unruly hedge into a heart is Gary.

Chris does not to recognize me as the dull brown, loose-haired woman in sunglasses he spoke to as Isaac forced open L.S. Rutledge's door. A few other people I saw the night of the murder or at the funeral don't seem to remember me, either. There's nothing like dressy, stiff, synthetic elder wear, an outdated twisty bun, mega-hold hair spray, close-toed footwear and a mask to create the opposite of my regular careless vibe.

April shoos the people gathered at the window back toward the food and drink tables, then nudges a local reporter I recognize and a camera operator toward the mic.

I stay where I am and examine the three framed photos on the windowsill—

> L.S. Rutledge, half-rims perched on the edge of her nose, the brim of her sunhat shadowing most of her face as sunlight fractures the surface of the Los Villas swimming pool hot tub.

L.S. Rutledge with 49 visible on the red door behind her. She looks at something or someone beyond the camera's lens. Her gray curls are soft and short—not blood-dark and stiff as they were at Mount of Olives.

L.S. Rutledge in a creased black and white photo. She wears a white short-sleeved dress. Her hair is dark and parted on the side. She holds a child in footed pajamas in her arms. Mother and child—I think this because the baby looks so comfortable in the woman's arms and the woman's arms are so comfortable around the baby—stare into the light. Standing close to her is a wide-faced man in a suit—his eyes slits because of the brightness.

The guest book has been opened to two fresh pages. I cannot examine the signatures on the previous pages, so I write, "With deepest sympathy" with one of the Los Villas del Fairfax Village Rental Office pens provided, and try think of something else to say when ear-splitting feedback entwined with April's liquid, amplified voice attacks the room.

"Everyone! Everyooone! The triiiiiiiibutes to dear Lindaaaa are about to beginnnnnn. Please join meeee here at the front of the roooom. You toooo in the back, Ellennn Naaaadelllllll."

April got the fake name I gave her wrong. Good. In exaggeratedly legible script, I write, "Sincerely, Ellen Nadel," and close the book.

63.

I haven't asked people for their first and last names or interrogated them about how well they knew L.S. Rutledge, or where they were, or what they saw on the day Isaac and I discovered her body. But April—even though she's got my false name wrong—has directed attention to me. The longer I hang around, the more likely it is that someone will connect the woman named Ellen Nadel with the woman they remember or think they might have seen after L.S. Rutledge's body was discovered and whose real name they might have overheard me or Isaac say.

I should leave now. But how? Surely April—and probably other people, too—would remember the woman who arrived late, then ducked out just when the person the event was about honor was being memorialized. I find a place in the back behind a tall, long-necked man I hope will shield me.

"Linda Rutledge was a sweet lady," Chris breathes into the mic. "My husband and I recently moved here from Palm Springs, and every time we'd walk past Linda watering her plants, she'd compliment whichever bow tie Dr. Phil—he's our purebred Pembroke corgi—was wearing that day. She loved dogs."

Tepid applause. April pats Chris's hand and waves a woman in head-to-ankle pomegranate Lululemon forward and hands off the microphone.

"Go ahead, Jan," April urges.

"Linda was a good person," Jan begins. "She kept to herself and was really shy, but she was always nice. We'd chat at the pool most days after I finished doing my laps. She always read the newspaper in the hot tub, so she knew lot about politics and current events." Jan falters and April pats her shoulder. "I didn't know Linda well, except that she cared about people and didn't deserve what happened to her." Jan's voice rises. "My God, no one does. And until they find that horrific dog and put it down, no one in the village will be safe."

Distress ripples through the room. The camera operator trains his dazzling light on Jan, glitterizing her tears. "I mean, if that creature could find its way in here once, what's to stop it from coming back again?"

"Everyone knows it came from the encampment," a lean, sharp-jawed, man in khakis and a brown denim jacket breaks in. "I'm not the only Villager who's complained about what goes on over there. And I'm not ashamed to admit that I complained more than once about the person we all know supported those goings on. If it weren't for people like Linda Rutledge, that encampment might have been gone by now—not a cancer metastasizing from the museum all the way down Wilshire Boulevard."

"Please, Dean," April says.

"Not now, Dean." A man in an L.A. Dodgers windbreaker holds up his large-palmed hand.

"Bob is right." April's earrings swing and her voice fills the room like incense. "This isn't the time or place to discuss the encampment. And, if you can't let this go, Dean, I will have security escort you from our gathering."

"No one listened, April," Dean thrusts his face forward. "Or if they did, they were too cowardly to do anything. And now we have a tragedy and a deadly threat to our safety. So, when would be a good time to chat about all this, April? After another Villager is mauled to death?"

64.

The slamming shut of the Room de Communidad door after the uniformed Los Villas del Fairfax Village Isn't Fucking Around security officer led Dean outside ruptures the shocked silence.

Gary, the topiary man, steps to the mic, and takes one of April's hands in his. "We all know that Linda meant well when she'd take toiletries and whatnot to the homeless over there. And Dean knows that, too, I'm sure. But he's upset. Can we blame him? This may sound petty after Linda's been murdered and all—but since the encampment really got going, I've had things stolen—a bird feeder, some Christmas decorations, nice wind chimes and my new garden tools from Williams Sonoma––right off my front step. A few times after I went inside for a few seconds—poof. Gone. And I've heard that other Villagers have had things stolen, too. Those vagrants have to be the ones doing it. I mean it's not hard to slip into the Villas in the middle of the day."

"Dean and Gary are right." A short woman with rhubarb pink braids strides to the front. "The elephant in the room is the Wilshire encampment. Why do the authorities say they have no idea where the killer dog came from or where it is now? We know where it came from. And where's it's probably being hidden. Something has to be done! We shouldn't have to live in fear!"

65.

I tiptoe—not easy in these boots—toward the door as the group presses close to the camera operator recording the reporter's interview with a woman in an abstract Marimekko poncho who started a petition for the encampment's removal, the euthanizing of animals there, and an F.B.I. investigation into the encampment's connection to L.S. Rutledge's murder.

I ease the door open and close it slowly, then run the way I'd run from a fire. Once inside the Lexus, I pull off my mask and gulp the chicken-free air flowing from the open window, then start the car.

As I pass the guard at the Sixth Street exit, I notice how many people enter and leave Los Villas del Coffee Cake with leashed dogs.

Isaac said he'd first met L.S. Rutledge last year at a Los Villas community services event where he represented Hatzalah. Was L.S. Rutledge attending as a Los Villas resident or as a member some group where she was a volunteer?

I wish I could ask Isaac about that meeting. And about other things. But I dread saying anything to Isaac now. Every time we talk, we argue. And arguing hurts too much.

66.

I go to the 99 Cents Only store at 6th and Fairfax and buy bottled water, a few dozen bottles of hand sanitizer and some protein bars, then stop at the Whole Foods on Third for a triple-shot, caffeinated latte, a ginormous apricot scone, and two boxes of natural turkey—what is an unnatural turkey? —dog treats with a cartoon turkey wearing sailor hat on the front of the box.

I enter the underground LACMA parking lot as most of the cars are leaving and park facing the wall on the lowest level.

I stay in the car and inhale the scone and savor the hot, bitter coffee, unpin and shake my hair free, then swap the long, dressy sweater for the emergency sweatshirt I keep in the trunk.

It's a unisex, extra-large, blue and goldenrod UCSB sweatshirt I bought in the campus bookstore the day Isaac and I drove to Goleta for a picnic on the beach near campus, and I spilled kosher wine all over my new, supposed-to-be-pretty-and-flattering, white, a little low-cut, Anthroplogie blouse.

The front of the sweatshirt has a big, fancy, goldenrod seal with an open book in the middle and a ribbon wafting across the book that says, "Let There Be Light." It was overpriced, it's ugly, and it reminds me of my gracelessness—which is why I keep it in the trunk.

I pack the boxes of dog biscuits, protein bars, and hand sanitizers in one of the reusable Trader Joe's shopping bags I also keep in the trunk, and ride the odorless glass elevator up through the underworldly shadows while I soundlessly repeat like a mantra the motto of the university that rejected me—

Let There Be Light.

67.

I follow the slick walkway past the LACMA ticket office toward Wilshire Boulevard and artist Chris Burden's "Urban Light" installation—two-hundred single and double-globed antique street-lamps painted a glossy, pearl gray and planted in a raised, concrete platform.

I locate the swastika lampposts right away—there's a whole row of them. And—except for rotating counter-clockwise—the symmetrical symbols ringing their bases are mirror-images of the swastikas that do not signify good health or good fortune or good anything.

Did the Orthodox kids on skateboards notice them? Does the wedding photographer or the shivery bride corseted into a sparkly mermaid gown and posing for Golden Hour photos with her groom know there are swastikas here or what they are supposed to mean?

The newlyweds and the beefy photographer dressed in a black suit have the symmetrical forest of streetlamps to themselves. No museum-goers take selfies. No skateboards rasp against the cold concrete. No Order of Christian Manhood creeps shout hateful things into bullhorns. No hate-flyers butterfly among the lampposts' white, unlit globes.

Alone on this raw, anemic afternoon, I watch the groom and bride kiss, hold hands, lean on opposite sides of a lamppost, gaze at their wedding rings, look into each other's eyes, then—after the photographer counts from five to one—leap into the cold, failing, honeyed light.

68.

I walk eastward—away from unlit Urban Light and along the encampment—a procession of tents and tarp-covered boxes lined shoulder-to-shoulder that swallows the sidewalk.

These rain-stained tents are not unlike other L.A. tents that look as though a tsunami landed them where they are—always a place where it is illegal or dangerous to camp.

Stuff swamps everything—bike parts, collapsed boxes, wheelless shopping carts, cracked plastic bins, wet blankets, towels, sofa cushions, crumpled plastic sheeting, gallon water bottles, gallon bottles of urine, hibachis, bent beach chairs, crushed plastic bottles, toys, tilting tables, cracked mirrors and trash.

I scan each tent as I place a protein bar and a bottle of water and a hand sanitizer on the curb in front, not sure what I'm looking for except dogs.

I stop as a man crawls out of his tent, then pulls out a battered, green backpack with a frayed, patched strap and a sleeping bag–—both wet. He leaves the sleeping bag on the ground, and shakes out the backpack near the gutter where I stand.

"Could you use some water, hand sanitizer or a protein bar?" I ask. "I've got dog treats, too, if you have a dog."

The man hangs the backpack across the handlebars of the bicycle propped against his gray tent. "I could use some dry smokes." The big hands that produce a cigarette butt and a lighter from his back-back are scratched raw. "Everything got soaked. Especially my backpack. And I need it. You don't happen to have a spare back-back, do you?"

"I'm sorry, no. All I've got are dog treats, protein bars, water, and hand sanitizer. And this shopping bag. I can leave it here for you later when it's empty."

The man works the lighter until it flames, then holds his cigarette butt to the fire that sallows his stubbled face.

"Why are you still here?"

"I'm looking for the owner of a dog that lived here until recently. A medium-sized, black mutt. Female. Do you know that dog?"

He inhales, and in the failing light, the smoke swirling through his scarce, brown teeth looks violet. "My policy is to stay the fuck away from dogs. A policy I recommend for you unless you're LAPD or a bastard sheriff or from Animal Services. In which case you can go to hell."

"I'm not," I say. "A friend of mine—Linda—comes down here a lot—told me she's interested in adopting that dog. I'm asking for her."

"Linda?"

"Yes. She injured her leg, so I came here for her."

"You mean the old counselor or something?"

"Yes. She's the one."

"Well, you can tell her that Anthony doesn't know anything about a black dog."

69.

I give Anthony two protein bars, two bottles of sanitizer and two twenties, then move on—emptying the Trader Joe's bag as I check out the tents. Most are zipped shut and tarps enclose the makeshift shelters. But the eyes I sometimes see inside the murky interiors of the few open tents I pass look through me.

I'm almost to the Page Museum when I see a dog—a Husky stretched out on the wet cement in front of a blue tent close to the Tar Pit Pond. The dog produces a long, deep growl as I pass, but doesn't lift its head.

A scruffy miniature poodle with rust-stained eyes sits wrapped in a blanket in its tarp-covered kennel a little past Curson Avenue.

An obese woman in a purple polyester track suit under a black chenille robe brushes a white-muzzled dachshund who sits on her lap. And an old beagle is leashed inside a newspaper-lined shopping cart in front of her tent.

"Excuse me."

The woman ignores me.

"I wonder if I could ask you about a dog."

The rhythm of the brushing slows. "I'm busy."

"I have treats. Can I give some to your dogs?"

"No—I don't let them eat junk."

"Do you to know an older woman named Linda? She arranged with someone around here to adopt a black dog, and then she got sick. A medium-sized, female, mutt? Do you know that dog?"

The splat-shaped, blown blood vessel above the woman's left pupil vibrates as she pauses the wire brush mid-air. "I don't know any dog like that here. But you're sure about her wanting to adopt a dog? That can't be right. Linda always keeps her distance from Charlie Brown and Lucy because of their dander. She told me was allergic."

70.

I sit on the edge of my casket-sized Life Space tub immersing my cold feet in hot water in which I've poured Epsom Salts from the box I inherited from my aunt although I'm not sure what Epson Salts are. To banish the faces of the people at the memorial and at the encampment, the swastikas, the road rage guy and Isaac's bruises, I watch Freddie and Linda cozy up on the fuzzy bathmat.

Since I got back, the dogs have stayed close each other and to me. Maybe they can read my feelings, or maybe they share a premonition.

I drain the tub, dry my feet, apply fresh Neosporin and new band aids to my heels and toes, put on fresh tube socks, sweatpants and a sweatshirt, and go into the kitchen, the dogs right behind me. I make a fresh latte, and when I shut the microwave door on the last two kosher, blue corn, cheese and Hatch chile enchiladas that Isaac made for me and left in the freezer—the sneering face of the man April called Dean appears on the dark glass.

What is his problem? So what if L.S. Rutledge handed out toiletries? The people living at the encampment need everything. And how would L.S. Rutledge's little aid missions incite the people camping on garden-less sidewalk to steal wind chimes or a bird feeder except to sell them on the street? Sell them to whom, though? Why would a homeless person from that encampment murder her? Or go to the trouble of sneaking a dog into Los Villas, then into L.S. Rutledge's apartment before doing it?

The stuff Dean said doesn't make sense unless L.S. Rutledge's murder was a warning from someone to the Los Villas residents to stop trying to get the encampment moved.

I have to check somehow if L.S. Rutledge's dog allergy was real—but what reason could that woman have to lie about something like that? And why plant a dog in the apartment of someone who stayed as far as possible from dogs? Maybe the murderer didn't know about her allergy.

Dean just might be afraid to show that he is scared shitless like all the others. Or maybe the murder is an opportunity for him to pressure the city to clear the encampment with bulldozers and trash trucks the way they've cleared others after the neighbors complained loudly enough.

Or maybe Dean's outrage over the homeless encampment is a cover for his anger at L.S. Rutledge—for what I don't know—and a way to deflect attention from what he did about it.

I burn my fingers removing the last two Blue Matzo enchiladas from the microwave and watch them cool.

I have to find out more about Dean and the others.

And about L.S. Rutledge who, while cordial, seems to have kept space between herself and her neighbors.

71.

Paws trembling and farting on and off, Freddie dream-chases something big. Linda—as she does often now that she's settled in—looks at me as if she's trying to communicate something I should know.

"What is it?" I ask her and study the sweet, sad mystery that is her face, then pat the place between her fake eyebrow dots.

I sip latte number three—decaf. And—so much for de-carbing—I give Linda half of my graham cracker from the box I stole from my earthquake kit as I check out the Los Villas Villagers I saw at the memorial.

April is easy. The Los Villas del Cheese Cube Platter Residents' Association has a Facebook page on which April has listed her full name—April Felice May. And she has her own page with a bio. She's seventy-three, a realtor, and the widow of January A.K.A. Janus—the two-faced Roman god of doorways and beginnings—V. May. Janus owned a successful maternity-clothing business in the San Gabriel Valley called "Expectational Fashions." Until Janus's death from a stroke-while-golfing, the Mays entertained friends who looked like them—dressy, dressed up, color-coordinated, fit and tan— on their flagstone Pasadena patio under a giant, twisting oak, golfed, visited wineries, and cruised to sunny places that resemble Pasadena. Despite the maternity business, they seem to have had no children. A photo captioned, "My new job!" and dated October, 2016 shows April in front of Los Villas del Fairfax Villages rental office. Another shows her moving into one of the Villas' apartments, and a third shows her holding a gavel signifying her ascent to the power-apex of the residents' association.

I go back to the Los Villas Residents' Association page and check the tagged photos for faces I saw today and find almost most of the last names I need—

The guy I thought of as Chris is Kristof Bleekerson, Palm Springs resident until early this year when he and his husband moved into Los Villas del Bowties for Purebred corgis. A USC communications graduate and creative director, Kristof Bleekerson's website explains that he "…conceives and implements concepts and strategies in creative projects and oversees them to completion and collaborates with creatives to produce strategic visions."

Kris's resume is dense and his list of LinkedIn connections is stuffed with fellow creative directors and people who call themselves "creatives." And I find him on Instagram—@BowtieCorgiBoyBoy—an account devoted to his dog, Dr. Phil, Dr. Phil's neckwear, selfies with the dog, and to his retiring husband, George, in that order.

Husband George is an interior designer. His website gallery features photos of the interiors of mid-century modern Palm Springs houses inhabited by sharp-cornered furniture and Jonathan Adler ceramics.

Gary—whose voice didn't ring a bell—is a voice actor whose website lists his work in commercials, independent animated films, a few big movies and provides links to audio samples that demonstrate his range. Jan is a tax lawyer at a big Century City firm. Jennifer is an Ob-Gyn resident at the nearby Masada General Hospital. One of the Bobs tends bar at a West Hollywood fusion restaurant I've read about. Tim, Wendy, the other Bob, Lauren, Mitch and Sylvia are a CPA, a teacher at a private girls' school, a researcher for an environmental non-profit, a graphic designer, and lawyers.

Quick searches of William, Joseph, Terri, Fritz or Karen turned up nothing weird.

The only problem person is Dean—Dean Stockhauser—widower, retired aerospace engineer, cyclist, mountain biker, and hunter. He hid his Facebook friends list, but forgot to hide his "about" information or photos of himself cycling in Joshua Tree, mountain biking through a steep, arid canyon, camping, smiling from the deck of boat while two-handedly holding the huge fish he hooked. Dean outfitted in camouflage clothing with a long gun and a big, dead deer with a bullet-piercing leaking blood from its side, and a German Shepherd panting at Dean's booted feet.

Does it mean something that Dean had or has a dog and enjoys killing things?

Dean is also an active Nextdoor poster about litter, noise, weed smoke, cigarette butts, bus exhaust, bus sounds, homeless people living at bus stops, the proliferation of weed shops in Mid-City, shoplifting, bicycle thefts, "vagrants," Los Villas residents who leave dry laundry in the dryer, extension cords outside, and celebrating the wisdom of imposing strict limits on the duration of outdoor holiday displays.

Linda's eyes droop, then close. She relaxes into sleep, her head pressed against Freddie's back. I close my laptop, eat the last half-graham cracker which—if you believe the nutritional information printed on the side of the box—counts as two crackers, which, with the enchiladas must count as a year's worth of carbs. I brush the crumbs off the sheet, listen to the dogs' soft breathing, then stretch out and do my nightly survey of the ceiling.

The ghost of my dead aunt that I saw the night she died is a no show again. She has not ventured from wherever she is to cross the pockmarked expanse of ceiling above me the way she did that night like a doomed explorer afraid and alone in the freezing universe.

Though I'm alone and Isaac is absent from my bed—I'm not frozen out like that. Sure, my dead parents are aloof. And they've halted all transmission of the colorized memory fragments I moved here to receive. A joke's on me, I guess. But they're still always with me in their way—invisible two-ton weights squeezing the chambers of my heart open and closed.

I check the ceiling again just in case. No aunt. Just a new, delicate fissure that extends from the overhead light toward the corner where—if I turn my head just so—I can see the Daddy

Longlegs.

One of the papers I wrote for money required research into these stiff-limbed members of the genus Opiliones that are also called Harvestmen. But they're not man-like at all, and they're not spiders, either. They don't make venom and they aren't a threat to people. For some nonsensical reason, after I finished the paper, I decided that Daddy Longlegs weren't just benign—but that they bring good luck to benevolent human non-victims who leave them alone.

I was taking a lot of Valium when I came up with the idea. I was still living in Goleta with Hans—before Isaac—a time when running into something alive and nonvenomous was as rare as seeing a double rainbow.

Is the venomous someone who killed L.S. Rutledge dreading the arrival of her anguished, maybe angry, ghost during the dusk between wakefulness and sleep?

What turns a grievance into a murder? What made the killer see red? How does a crank become a member of the Order of Christian Manhood? How does a neighbor hate a neighbor enough to kill her the way L.S. Rutledge was killed?

Is there one precipitating event? Or a smoldering that requires time to ignite?

It took time. L.S. Rutledge's murder wasn't spontaneous. To make her killing look like a dog attack required knowing something about dogs and their bites, finding the right dog, and planning.

72.

This morning's trip to the Dog Park was quick. I smooth a fresh towel across on the back seat of the car, lift Freddie inside, signal Linda to join him, give them each a liver treat, then drive north past the very little Little Brown Church where—my aunt always reminded me—Ronald and Nancy Reagan were married.

A fresh row of zipped-up tents has popped up overnight like a broken fairy ring under the 101 Freeway overpass I drive through. I return to sunlight, then turn onto the eucalyptus-littered cul-de-sac.

I park at the dead bottom of the dead end where I parked last year—the first time I visited the house since the accident. My parking spot is a few houses away from what was the one-story ranch that—after the accident—I couldn't stand returning to—and which I insisted to my aunt and the accountant must be sold. Since then, the owners have transformed the place into a two-story French-doored, balconied Mediterranean/chateau mash-up with a square of turf in the front and two Teslas in the widened driveway. A thick black cable umbilicals one of the Teslas—the white one—to a clean power source thrumming somewhere beyond the porch mail slot that swallows it.

I take off my shades, get out of the car, open the back door for Linda, and slip on her Larry coat although the morning is warm. Note to myself—get Linda a summer jacket. I leash her, place Freddie on the ground, secure his leash to his halter, and lead the dogs forward.

In the year since I've been here, gravel and agaves have replaced more big, old trees and mottled lawns. The yolk yellow, white-trimmed one-story my mother called the "bird house" because of the roof's ornamental dovecote has been demolished, and the emptied lot flattened and fenced. And two other houses have been updated into mega-Craftsmen.

The dogs trot happily in the street—there are no sidewalks or street-lamps here—past a trio of hulking "modern farmhouses" —McMansions with wood shutters signifying the pastoral and with Range Rovers, Jeep Rubicons and nannies' Camrys in the driveways.

I wonder what these farmers keep in their garages.

A woman wearing Air Pods and a linen dress pushes a blanket-covered pram down the driveway of a huge white two-story you-know-what, then advances toward Freddie. I'm relieved when he growls, but doesn't bark. Linda briefly assesses the woman, then resumes sniffing a pot-hole filled with an interesting soup of old sprinkler runoff and rotting eucalyptus leaves.

The next house has been boldly designed to look like a white box with another white box on top with both attached to boxy garage with a smoky glass door. A poinsettia the color of the dogs' favorite desiccated liver treats dehydrates on the porch. When I lived next door, this door was dusty blue and Dutch, and Shirley—the lady who lived inside—had a dachshund named Heidi and a rose garden where cacti now push their pin cushion heads through gravel mounds.

Last year it was just Freddie and me when we glimpsed the defeated-looking dog someone let out to pee on the square of artificial turf fronting the former Lieb Homestead. This time I still have Freddie, I have Linda, I saw the woman with the pram which must have had a baby inside, and the snaking charging cable—all of which should count as proof of life.

But what I'm here for is proof of death.

No, not death. Not life after death, either. But life-in-death. Proof that some sort of dead-parental-post-life vestige exists which would prove I didn't dream them and that my parents really existed.

I imagine a faint but detectable repelling or attracting force like the force a weakened magnet exerts—with just enough juice to excite a few of my brain waves or retinal cells and accomplish the transfer of one brief, final something from them to me.

A portent. A foreshadowing. A sign that despite having been eaten by the ugly ocean, the parental scintillae still have enough oomph to give me a nonverbal pull or push.

So I guess my little field trip is really a séance on the cheap. A disorganized summoning of wrecked souls from wherever the fuck they've been since I refused to hug or kiss them goodbye at Camp Whispering Stones because I knew that if I did, the Whispering Pebbles who were watching would never stop mocking me for it.

A silver pick-up with two skimmer poles hanging out the back glides in front of the face-lifted, former Lieb Family Manse. A sunburned driver removes one of the poles and a jug of chlorine, sidles past the Teslas to the fake-wood gate, enters a code, then fades into the rear of the property.

I wonder if the pool is still shaped like a kidney. I do not hear the sad dog bark. Did it die or is it stashed too deeply inside for its bark to reach me?

Absence stays with you. I have to hand it to the vacuums that are my parents for never disappearing even for a second. I can always rely on their time-stopping, blurred and melted Dali faces to remind me that no matter what my Apple Watch says, it's always They're Not Here O'clock in Ascherland.

As if I needed to be reminded of their departure when the cycle which augured it calibrated itself from my very first period to mark the anniversary of their bird-and-conflagration deaths on the dot every twenty-eight days.

As if menstruation wasn't already a form of weeping.

73.

Linda, Freddie and I stand at the edge of the flattened square of turf that replaced the generous persimmon tree and a shade tree and the house's grassy yard. The dogs sniff several spots, then pee. The solar panels, the white rain gutters and the Roman-shades defeating my view through windows with security system decals look new. The security camera installed on the porch eave makes me think we should move along—but I don't. If the new owners throw open the front door and demand to know why I am loitering here—for once I'd have no reason not to tell the truth.

Or at least some of it.

What am I looking for so hard? What am trying to see? To hear? My mother's wavy black hair, its gray strands flashing silver? My father's wide, round face? His voice when he called her from another room? Her voice when she'd answer? The endearments they used when addressing me?

I want to hear those failing voices. I want to feel their touch––not just remember how touching them felt.

They are the two removes through which I experience my life. They are the foggy veils I can't wash from my eyes.

The dogs seem perplexed that I stand here willing some nothing inside or underneath this house to just this once make itself known to me and by doing so, help me make personal adjustments and clear a few things up.

But the house is an ugly tomb millions of lightless light years away from me.

Inert. Blank.

A container for the two zeroes inside it.

74.

Sirens swell in the distance as the dogs finish their liver treats in the back seat and I contemplate the two envelopes I freed from their refrigerator magnets and brought with me here thinking that some quality time with Mom and Pop Lieb might give me the courage I need to open them.

It didn't.

The house that was once my house shrinks to nothing in the rear-view mirror, and I'm the same needy coward I was when I arrived. As I defer to the red STOP hexagon at the top of the cul de sac, then turn onto Coldwater Canyon Boulevard, it feels as though I have somehow relinquished the heavinesses that were my parents to nothingness forever.

Will my lungs work without the descending pressure of their absences? Will the world I gaze at without their blurs be too sharp? Too bright?

The sirens become insistent. I can't tell if they're coming from the fire station on Burbank Boulevard or from the police station in North Hollywood, or if there's a crash on the 101 Freeway. I open the window, but I don't hear the choppers that always hover above the freeway when something there goes wrong. I sniff the air—no smoke—then turn on the radio.

"Live traffic with Crime on the Nine has an update on events unfolding in Mid City from our Crime Chopper pilot, Jed Bushwick. What can you tell us, J.B.?"

"We've had no official word from Mid-City P.D. or F.D. on what is a very fluid situation," J.B. shouts over the engine-whine and the rotor's chuffing. "Police and fire have surrounded the two-story building housing a number of offices and the first-floor Beit Chai Jewish center which, I understand, provides walk-in services to homeless in the area."

Bushwick pronounces "Chai" "kai."

"Building occupants have been evacuated and gathered with police at a dry cleaner across the street. Some of them wear skull hats, if that's the correct term. A bomb squad vehicle is right in front of Beit Chai and also LAFD paramedics and a pumper truck. Social media posts reported smoke coming from the building—but no smoke is visible right now as I circle the roof. Unsubstantiated rumors have been flying on TikTok and X that the first anonymous 911 call referenced a bomb."

75.

"Chai" means life. I have no idea about "Beit," but Beit Chai is where L.S. Rutledge volunteered, and where, I remember now, Isaac once mentioned being called to treat one of their clients—a homeless man who'd been hit on the head with a bottle.

Why didn't I remember this before? Or that he said they offered used clothing, sandwiches, cold and hot drinks, showers, toiletries and access to representatives from Health and Housing Services, and referrals to addiction rehab programs?

Even if Isaac had been there when the 911 call was placed—he's fine, right? He's safe with the others at the dry cleaner with the police.

I drive to Life Space—AKA Chai Space—listening to news radio all the way. Once I get inside my apartment, I turn on the local T.V. news station. Nothing has changed except the police and bomb squad in the Beit Chai building's parking lot seem to be waiting for something. No one on the news mentions hostages. But why else would the authorities be so tentative about going inside?

Why doesn't the LAPD bomb squad send in their robot? Isn't going inside a place where there might be a bomb what these machines are for? I give in and do a search on X for #BeitChai, then scroll—Deranged, homeless meth addicts planted a bomb. #George$oros paid for the bomb. The Jews faked a bomb just as they faked the 9/11 and the Holocaust—except it's spelled KikeOcaust. There's a #RothschildBank down the street and they planted the bomb. The homeless are making bombs. The people who run Beit Chai aren't "real" Jews—they're #Khazars––they're imposters—they're Nazis. Beit Chai is a Mossad operation designed to bring more homeless people and immigrants into L.A. The homeless are animals—do not feed them, put them to sleep. The Jews planted the bomb and are now extorting the city for money because money is all Jews care about. Oven jokes inspired by the real or mythical 911 call reporting smoke. Memes about other purported Jewish hoaxes and Jewish crimes. And humpbacked, Jewish rat guy memes.

For fuck's sake. Each new calamity is an opening into the light for these subterranean, venomous freaks.

76.

I order a lightweight, navy blue windbreaker for Linda on Amazon Prime. I found a really cute sailor jacket, but don't want anything that attracts attention. I feed the dogs, give Freddie his meds and Linda a new Busy Bone, reattach the still-unopened envelopes to the refrigerator door with magnets, swap nice jeans for my leggings, a white shirt for my aunt's yellow Sunny Morning Elder Care t-shirt, find my Converse sneakers, grab the long sweater, change the T.V. station to Animal Planet, refill the water bowls, remember to turn on the lamp, and kiss and hug the dogs goodbye.

And drive toward Beit Chai, I remember that Jews are point one-percent of the world's population. That's around fifteen million—fewer than there were before the Holocaust—bobbing in a choppy sea of eight billion Normies.

I didn't stash this fact away because I discovered it while writing a paper for money for some C-minus slacker. I found it for myself because I'd begun to realize that all my life I'd been buoyed—not by progress—but by moving along in the lukewarm current of steady improvement that seemed headed—maybe not to the Promised Land of Justice—but to a place that was Promised Land-adjacent. I never almost-drowned because the gold Star of David I don't wear around my neck got too heavy. I didn't get pulled under or out into treacherous, open water because I didn't regularly enter and exit a synagogue even during the High Holidays except with my parents and my grandmother when she was alive.

After the accident when I was hiding out in boarding school and later in community college—and then when I lived with

Hans in Goleta—though I attended the Sunny Morning Elder Care seders with my aunt—I didn't visit the Chabad of Goleta to decorate the sukkah, or attend shabbat dinners at the UCSB Hillel, or light candles at sundown on Fridays. And I laughed when—after decorating our Christmas tree, I brought out my grandmother's—formerly my great-grandmother's—Hanukkiah, and Hans called it a "Jew candelabra."

I flowed with the flow and when it became turbulent, I smoothed out my attitude. I didn't mention that the correct word would have been the singular "candelabrum", or that "Jew" is always either a religious descriptor or a pejorative that means to haggle or to steal. I kept floating—if being half-submerged qualifies as buoyancy—on my lies and the Valium that deadened me.

77.

I see the police cars and barricades when I get close to Beit Chai. I make an illegal U-turn via a strip mall entrance, backtrack the three blocks to Partridge Place and park in the lot at Isaac's. The ambulance is in its parking place. The Jacaranda tree's purple is fading to mauve. A Ring camera has been installed above Isaac's door and the mezuzah—people keep stealing them—is still attached to the door frame.

All is leaflet-free and calm. I've been checking the Blue Matzo website so I know Isaac doesn't have a pop-up today or a catering event, but even if he's not on call, Hatzalah can request his help. Is he home?

Or is he out somewhere or out somewhere with someone?

I text Isaac.

`saw news re Beit Chai r u ok?`

But he doesn't text back.

I'm wearing my Converse low-tops, so I can run. Not like a machine or like the wind—but efficiently enough to get to the news vans, then past them. I thread my way into the group of onlookers gathered behind the barricade closest to Beit Chai—about a long half-block away. Then I stand on my toes and scan the huddle of people under the dry cleaner's awning for Isaac.

78.

A high-pitched siren sounds, then two police officers move us back, then wave through a small, white van with tinted windows and "Bomb Detection K-9" inscribed on the side.

`where r u?`

I text Isaac again.

`pls let me know`

Where is he?

"They're going to detonate whatever it is," a man in an ankle-length, stained red apron and wearing a hair-net says. "It's a bomb for sure."

"If it was a bomb, why was there smoke earlier?" I ask. "Bombs don't smolder, do they?"

A man on a low bicycle turns to me. "Because the smoke call was just to get the authorities here. It's on TikTok. Whoever called 911 wanted to get the authorities here so they could blow them all up. Fuck up the police, you know."

"It's a bag," the woman behind me says. She has her mask around her neck. "I work at the nail salon over there. My friend works in the dry cleaners. She texted me that somebody left a bag in that Jewish place."

The air thickens with an intuition that flows like a seismic shudder through the crowd pressing itself against the barricades––something is happening or is about to happen.

I ready myself for the detonation inside the bomb squad containment vessel I've seen a few times on T. V.

Then two strong hands seize my shoulders from behind.

Part Three

> "Step back/From the graveside where nothing flowers…"
>
> —Freida Hughes, "For the Living Left Behind"

79.

I'm not fortifying myself with caffeinated coffee and my favorite side—a little dish of Canter's perfect potato salad—because Canter's isn't kosher. I'm sipping good black coffee at a wobbly table outside a kosher bakery and café on Pico and attacking a tender, sesame-seed-studded, goat cheese boureka. Isaac settles into the chair across from mine now that he's failed to stabilize the table's base with a carefully engineered paper napkin. He sips his Israeli coffee and takes a bite of his toasted everything bagel plastered with unsalted butter.

"Maybe it's the sidewalk that's uneven."

"If I had tools," Isaac says. "And some plywood, I could fix this in a few seconds." Isaac stirs his coffee again.

I take another bite of the boureka and chew slowly before I swallow. "You do know you scared the shit out of me, right?"

"I'm sorry. When I saw you there at the barricade, all I thought about was getting you as far away from the bomb as I could."

"Thank you for swooping in and saving me from a bomb—"

"—that didn't turn out to be bomb, thank God."

"Not a bomb, just a backpack full of filth. I would have preferred an empty backpack or one full of these bourekas."

"Shush. You're not supposed to know that a backpack was left at Beit Chai, or that it was stuffed with Order of Christian Manhood flyers until the LAPD has their press conference."

"Well, I know because you told me and because one of your LAFD buddies told you. And now I can't help thinking about it."

"It's bad. But it wasn't a bomb. Sticks and stones, right?"

Isaac's bruises have faded from purple to beet, but the bridge of his nose is still swollen—and words are what made those people do that to his face. "I thought they moved around. At least their videos make it seem that way. Why would the Order of the Christian Manhood hang around here?"

"You watched their videos?"

"Three—but one was a montage. Three was enough."

A bearded Jewish man strides past our table, the *tzitzit* swaying from beneath his shirt.

"They're probably hanging around because this is a very Jewish neighborhood." Isaac spreads more butter on what's left of his bagel.

"Who comes to neighborhood like this and—instead of eating—litters it with shitty flyers?" I'm trying to keep things light.

"Um, let me think who that could be. Neo-Nazis, maybe?" Isaac covers my hand with his. "I missed you."

"Ditto," I say, surprised and grateful for the pleasure-jolt that is his touch. "You know how you said that when you saw me, all you wanted was to get me as far away from what everyone thought was bomb as you could?"

"Yes?"

"That's how I felt when I saw what those Order of Christian Manhood assholes did to you—I just wanted you to be safe. I've never wanted you to hide, Isaac. I'm always proud of you."

80.

Isaac powers on the big flat screen with the remote, then settles against the pillows with me as the news conference comes on with the chyron repeating, "Jewish Center Bomb Scare. News Conference to Begin Soon."

I haven't had a chance to ask Isaac why he was near Beit Chai today, if he knew that L.S. Rutledge volunteered there, or any of the other questions I packed away with the questions for my parents that will never be answered.

I listen to the huh, huh of Isaac's breathing and the companionable, perfumed silence between us. Isaac has a batch of kosher—no lard—sweet corn, cheese and apple tamales going in the pressure cooker.

A commercial comes on for that amazing weight-loss drug I keep reading about whose side effects include suicidal ideation.

I didn't lose the weight I planned to on my no breakfast, no lunch, no carb diet. I didn't lose weight when I lapsed into my current three-meals-a-day-plus-snacks carb-fest after I was sure I'd lost Isaac.

Do I have him now?

Why did I order that boureka when I could have had a dressing-less salad? Why did I forget that cheese is probably much worse than carbs and then snarf a cheese-carb thing down?

I pull the sheet up to my neck.

The mayor hurries to his special podium. The uniformed LAPD, LAFD and HIS officers, and men and women in suits standing behind him straighten. The mayor wears his black windbreaker with the seal of the city of Los Angles embroidered on it. He taps the microphone and frowns.

"There is no place for antisemitism, racism, anti-Asian hate, homophobia, Islamophobia, anti-Latino or anti-Hispanic prejudice, sexism or ableism in the great city of Los Angeles."

"Not this again," Isaac pulls the sheet back, kisses my breasts, my bare shoulders, my neck—then pushes my hair back and kisses my forehead.

"I, the chiefs of the Los Angeles police and fire departments, and representatives from Homeland Security and the religious leaders who have joined me today are here to put the person or persons who left a backpack filled with vile anti-Jewish hate literature on the premises of a vital Jewish service organization on notice. We know who you are, but we will not amplify your message of hatred by speaking your name. You are not welcome in the vibrant, diverse city of Los Angeles. Let me repeat—you are not welcome in our great, loving, diverse City of Angels."

"Not the mayor's best day," I say. "But his new windbreaker is cool, don't you think?"

"You should wear your bangs pulled back sometimes." Isaac strokes my dull brown hair as if it were spun gold. "The world deserves to see your beautiful face."

81.

"The world doesn't deserve anything," I blush.

"Today I'm proud to announce that I've established an inter-faith, inter-agency task force that will be single-mindedly focused on stopping hate wherever and whenever it chooses to rear its ugly head in this great city."

"This is just B.S.," Isaac scowls at the screen. "The mayor knows those flyers are protected speech. He knows that leaving a bunch of them in a backpack in a bathroom is not a crime. There's nothing he or his task force can do."

"But the hoax 911 call about a nonexistent bomb or fire? Isn't that swatting?"

"Yes, that's a crime. But the call could have been an honest mistake. What I heard from a Shomrim friend is that that a volunteer found the backpack in the Beit Chai restroom and—because they get death and bomb threats all the time—they were afraid to open it or move it, so they called the police. That was the right thing for them to do."

"They get death and bomb threats all the time?"

"Often. That's the way things are. Every Jewish business, school or organization has to be on guard."

"LAPD, LAFD. and HSI are analyzing security footage and examining the backpack as I speak." The mayor grasps the podium's sharp edges with both hands. "Until I receive their determinations, I will refrain from comment. But we have a photo of the offending backpack, and we've set up a dedicated, toll-free hot line to receive anonymous calls from anyone who recognizes this backpack or knows the person who owns it. That toll-free number is S-T-O-P-H-A-T-E-N-L-A."

A close-up of a battered backpack with a frayed strap replaces the mayor's face on Isaac's television screen with "DO YOU RECOGNIZE THIS BACK-PACK?" and the toll-free number superimposed across it.

The backpack is green.

82.

"There must be thousands of backpacks just like that in L.A. So, good luck finding the owner." Isaac sniffs the air above the pressure cooker. "I pronounce these tamales done."

Isaac releases the pressure valve and the cooker hisses and spits. Seeing that backpack has freaked me out, but I can't show it. "That smells so good. Can I eat my tamale now, or do I have to get dressed first?"

"Undressed, please," Isaac says. "This is like the dog that killed Mrs. Rutledge. It hasn't gone public, but a Shomrim friend told me that people have been turning in random black dogs to claim the reward, and Animal Services and the police have no way to identify the killer dog even if someone turns in the right one. And if the dog is roaming out there, there's no way they will find it. But they can't admit it, and I'm sure the mayor insists that they keep pretending that they're close."

The only time I was punched in the face when was I was a lowly Pebble at Whispering Stones—so I'm no expert.

But that was some punch in the face just now.

I roll out of bed, slip Isaac's extra-large Blue Matzo sweatshirt over my head, take a long, humid, breath of the Isaac-scent inside it, then pull my head through the neck-hole.

Does this mean Linda is free?

Almost.

She's not free if Isaac recognizes her. And she's not free until I find L.S. Rutledge's real killer.

And is Anthony a neo-Nazi? A member of the Order of Christian Manhood? That backpack is definitely his. He held it maybe two feet away from me at the encampment.

I have to find out.

And Isaac has to know.

But how do I tell him? I could lie that I met Anthony somewhere. Where?

I could lie about why I was at the museum. And about why I attended the Los Villas memorial potluck under a false name. And I could lie about a lot stuff I did and saw before that.

The mouth in my unbeautiful, dishonest face opens and though—for the first time in a long time I'm not hungry, more lying words come out—"I'm starving."

Isaac removes the steaming, aromatic tamales from the cooker with heavy-duty, silicon-tipped tongs and arranges them on a stainless-steel tray. "We can round out our tamale lunch with cilantro rice and the pepita, lime and jicama slaw I'm experimenting with for a catering thing. How does that sound? And why is my old sweatshirt covering your nakedness?"

"That sounds delicious. And, Isaac and—it's complicated—but, I'm wearing your sweatshirt because I know who owns that backpack."

83.

The soles of Isaac's chef's clogs slapping the cement LACMA walkway and the thwap-thwap of the emergency flip-flops I keep in Isaac's dresser with my extra underwear and tampons punctuate the quiet.

Isaac wanted to walk from his place to the encampment—but he agreed to my request to take the Lexus and park in the underground LACMA lot. I didn't tell him that I wanted to drive because the foggy, bad feeling I have about coming here is hard to describe.

And my feet still hurt. And with every step, my body—buoyant with my renewed closeness to Isaac—sinks.

Isaac's clogs clack past Urban Light, then stop. "I didn't mean to leave you behind. I was just thinking again about what you told me."

I told him about going to the memorial potluck for L.S. Rutledge—but not that I used my aunt's name. I explained that most of the Los Villas residents there believed a person with a dog from the encampment is responsible for her murder. And that the residents are angry and afraid.

I told him I went to the encampment because I wanted to see it for myself and wanted to ask about a black dog. And I told him that no one remembered one—or at least no one said they did.

I told Isaac that L.S. Rutledge was known to a few people there—including Anthony—and that one person said that L.S. Rutledge was allergic to dogs. I told him that the backpack we saw on T.V. was the one I saw Anthony carry out of his tent.

I didn't tell Isaac that I had liberated Linda from the shelter, or that she's living at my apartment with Freddie and me.

I didn't tell him that I photographed L.S. Rutledge's wounds.

I didn't mention that I suspect that Dean might be L.S. Rutledge's killer.

I plan to tell him all of it—just not yet.

"It's my feet," I say. "The shoes I wore to the funeral did a number on them."

"I'm sorry," Isaac says. "I love your feet."

But how does Isaac feel about the rest of me? What does what happened today mean?

"You should speak to Anthony if we find him. You're the one with experience with people living on the street," I say.

"But he knows you, Ascher. And you're so good at thinking on your feet. And people sometimes react badly to my kippah. I think you should take the lead."

84.

Isaac follows me along the red curb. Tarps and tents sit open to the strong, generous sunlight. People are outside eating, shaving, bathing, listening to music, smoking cigarettes, smoking weed and sorting through piles of stuff.

Things look and feel different, and I don't know why. And I fear that I won't find Anthony's gray tent again. But I remember that it wasn't too far from where Urban Light ends and the encampment begins.

Isaac takes my hand—the one that isn't holding the handles of the Trader Joe's bag—and we walk in the gutter side by side.

"Did I mention that his tent is gray? And that he smokes?"

"Yep."

We pass a shirtless woman sleeping on a collapsed, orange sofa. Then a young man braiding a young woman's white-blond hair.

"About three tents down," Isaac shades his eyes. "Gray. Could that be his?

85.

Anthony sits on an overturned blue plastic milk crate and trims his toenails with a silver clipper. The sun has burned the June mist away and the hot light makes the clipper and the limpid sweat on his neck shimmer.

Isaac releases my hand and we wait for Anthony to see us or to feel our presences.

Still hunched over his bare feet, Anthony turns his head. "If you're here to convert me, fuck off."

"Jews don't proselytize," Isaac says.

"I wanted to talk to you again and I brought a friend with me."

Anthony waits.

I pull a carton of Marlboros from the Trader Joe's bag. Anthony puts the clipper in the pocket of his jeans and straightens.

I give the carton to Isaac who steps up on the curb and passes the carton to Anthony. His huge, raw, red hands are spattered with blisters.

"How long have your hands been inflamed like that?"

"Do I barge into your living room and ask you personal questions? I don't know you. I didn't ask you to come here. And I don't give a shit if you're some doctor who likes to go slumming."

Isaac backs up into the street. "I'm not a doctor. I'm an EMT––an emergency medical technician. I think you have eczema—dyshidrotic eczema. It comes from stress and can be treated with topical corticosteroids."

Anthony opens the carton, removes a pack of cigarettes, tosses the carton into his tent, opens the pack, removes a cigarette, sniffs it, then lights it with his lighter.

"Goody. I'll just drive over to the pharmacy and get some of that cream."

"I have some. I'll bring it by later," Isaac says. "Just try to lay off hand sanitizer."

Anthony looks at me. "Well, this has been fun. But I have a Zoom meeting with Elon Musk in a few minutes and have to pull my notes together." Anthony places the plastic crate on the seat of the bike still propped against his tent.

"Anthony, wait," I say. "We're here because you're in trouble. LAPD and the mayor and the sheriffs are looking for you and blasting a photo of the backpack you left at Beit Chai. It's on TV right now. And it won't be long before they're circulating your photo."

86.

"I left the backpack at that Jewish place by accident. I went there for something to eat and to pick up some drinks before walking to where they wanted me to drop those papers."

I want to ask how Anthony could leave the backpack there "by accident" if the next thing he was going to do was distribute the papers inside it—but the waiter shows up.

The red-vested man unloads two stoneware mugs from his tray—Anthony's coffee and my latte—and two little white bowls——one holding individual creamers and another with packets of sugar. "The full order of hotcakes with bacon, sausage and a side of three eggs over easy will be out in a minute." He looks at Isaac sipping the can of Coke he bought at the ice cream stall nearby. "Are you sure I can't bring you anything, sir? Water? A cheese burger? A slice of our famous chicken pie? Welsh Rabbit? A salad?"

"No, thank you," Isaac smiles. "This is fine for me."

I eat the latte foam with a teaspoon. Isaac sips his Coke. Anthony empties four packets of sugar into his coffee mug, adds the contents of four mini-creamer containers, then stirs the mixture vigorously.

"What else was in your backpack besides the leaflets? I.D.? Anything"

"I lost my I.D. a while ago. Just the sandwiches and the bottles of water and some personal items."

I look at Isaac Kahn.

"What place?" Isaac asks. "Where were you taking the leaflets?"

Anthony lifts his cigarette from the edge of the cement planter he's using as an ashtray and gives us a demonstration of slow-motion exhaling of smoke through one's nose and teeth.

"Are you a member of their group? The Order of Christian Manhood?" I ask.

"Why should I tell you?" Anthony flicks ashes under the metal table near a sparrow waiting for crumbs.

"Because we know it's your backpack and because the police are looking for you, and because Beit Chai has security cameras inside and outside their offices. So, even if you don't tell us anything, if you work for them, they will think that in a few hours you'll be telling the police all about them. And they'll look for you." Isaac runs his fingertips along the water beads on the side of the diet Coke can.

Anthony flushes. "I not a member of anything. I just did shit for them a few times because they paid me. I got laid off from my brain surgeon job at that big hospital down the street and I need to make my Beemer payments."

87.

Anthony pours melted butter and maple syrup from the little stoneware jugs onto his full stack and my stomach—which was not hungry enough to do more than pick at Isaac's tamales, rice and slaw—grumbles.

I consider ordering a short stack—but I don't. First, DuPar's isn't kosher, which is why all Isaac is having is a Diet Coke in a can. The second reason is the carb thing. And the third is gravitas—Isaac has tons of it—but I don't have much or—or maybe I have none. And what happens next depends on whether or not Anthony believes that not just Isaac, but that I, too, am a serious person. Snarfing up eight dinner-plate-sized perfect buttermilk pancakes loaded with butter and syrup that Isaac will never taste right front of him would be pure selfishness.

And eating with gusto is always a bad look for a woman.

Isaac removes his cellphone from his pocket, looks at it, then blandly watches people enter and leave The Farmers' Market parking lot through the opening in the white vinyl picket fence that encloses the patio.

I'm silent until all the hotcakes have exited Anthony's plate. "When they hired you to distribute leaflets, how many of them were there?"

Anthony dips his bacon in the syrup pool that has formed in the middle of his empty-except-for-a-yolk-smudge plate, then chews it.

"Three white guys. Same ones each time. In their thirties or early forties. Once they picked me up at four in the morning and dropped me on a street corner in Beverly Hills, and then picked me up at a bus stop they told me to go to when I was done. Another time they left me in Beverly Wood. Lots of Jews there they said." Anthony glances at Isaac's head. "And lots of Jews in Beverly Hills."

"What about this time? Where were you supposed to take the flyers?"

Anthony backs his chair away the table. "I need to use the restroom."

Isaac rises from his chair. "I think I need to use the restroom, too."

88.

I leave the table and enter the restaurant through the door the waiters use, tell the man behind the cash register where we were sitting and what we ordered, give him two twenties and a ten, then run through the cozy dining room and out onto the patio.

I make my way among colorful metal tables where diners eat pizza and gumbo under a broad Ficus full of noisy birds, scan the people waiting for their orders in the shade of awnings, then find an empty table near Charlie's Coffee Shop where I can watch the open, dead-end hallway leading to the restrooms.

The men's room is the first door, so I will see Isaac and Anthony as soon as they come out. But I know that while I sit here, Anthony and Isaac could be crossing the parking lot, or on Fairfax or Third Street, or moving through the maze of shaded food and produce stalls, or entering The Grove. Or in the huge Grove parking structure.

And if they are in any of these places—they are lost to me.

89.

I stay where I am and notice that most of the people entering and leaving the hallway are women shouldering heavy diaper bags while holding the hands of toddlers, or pushing strollers with babies in them.

How long have I been here? My cell phone tells me I've been here for eight minutes— which means that Anthony and Isaac have been in the men's room for ten or eleven minutes.

Which could mean that they were never in there.

I'm not an expert on how long it takes men—on average—to pee, wash and dry their hands and glance at themselves in a restroom mirror—but I know from experience that a man who takes eleven minutes to accomplish these things is not typical. And two men using up eleven minutes doing the same thing is probably impossible.

If I were Anthony, where would I run?

The members of the Order of Christian Manhood follow the news. Their channel is full of replays of T.V. news stories about them harassing people. They must have enjoyed the bomb scare Anthony accidentally created at Beit Chai. And they must have watched the press conference and know that the L.A.P.D is circulating a photo of Anthony's backpack and will soon be circulating his description.

Anthony would run away from them, from Isaac and me, from the police—from everybody.

`where r u????`

I text Isaac, though I know I am stupid to do it.

Nothing.

90.

I put on my shades and—holding the Trader Joe's bag in front of my Blue Matzo sweatshirt—I wait until the hallway is empty, then slip into the men's room.

A plastic sawhorse that says PISO MOJADO stands under the hand dryer near the door.

A man in an orange and black San Francisco Giants t-shirt stands behind a boy using the low urinal in a row of them on my left. On my right is a cement counter with five sinks. Beyond the urinals are five stalls. The doors to the first four are open—but the door to the last one—a large one wide enough for a wheelchair—is closed.

My head down, I move past the man and boy, enter the fourth stall, lock the door, sit on the toilet and pull up my feet so that the dad and the boy already in here and anyone entering do not see them. The urinal flushes, then the man asks the boy if he wants to "go number two." The boy declines. Water ripples into the sink, the hand dryer roars, then the door creaks open and shut.

I get on the floor and look into big, last stall. Two pairs of legs—one in black jeans, the other in blue—are visible on the cement floor. The black clogs under the black jeans face me. Tattered brown leather shoes show under the blue jean cuffs behind the clogs.

I put my flip-flops in the Trader Joe's bag, hang the bag on the coat hook, then nudge the stall door open, move the sawhorse in front of the last stall's door, grab the metal footstool under the sink, and take it with me back into the stall.

I lock the door and stretch out on the floor, my feet sticking into the stall behind me and the top of my head almost touching the partition.

The just-mopped, gray-green cement floor smells of urine and the industrial cleaner I've smelled in mortuaries.

The gap between floor and partition is about a foot. What if I'm too thick to slide all the way through?

I flatten my breasts against the floor and tense my buttocks—then decide that my ass will be flatter if relax it—which is not an easy thing to do right now.

I hold my breath, push the side of my face into the floor's repellent moistness and wriggle into the last stall.

91.

The two-headed, four-legged creature writhes against the wall of the big, handicapped stall. One of the heads has Isaac's face except that it wears a contorted frown. And though it's dim in here—I can see that the pupils Isaac aims at me are pinholes. Anthony's head is behind Isaac's. His wide forearm pressed against his mouth and nose pushes Isaac's head back and his big red hand presses a short knife blade against Isaac's Adam's apple.

One of Isaac's arms hangs at his side. A gash runs from his elbow to his palm, and blood drips from his fingertips onto his black jeans.

I lift the stool above my head and smash it against the top of Anthony's skull as hard as I can. I do this twice.

And then I scream.

92.

The scream I hoped would reverberate through the closed door, into the women's restroom, down the hallway, past Charlie's Coffee Shop and through the populated patio did not summon a panicked crowd into the men's restroom.

But it inspires Anthony to raise one of his heavy-brown-shoed feet and use it to kick my kneecaps.

I pivot and Anthony misses and rocks forward. Isaac snaps the back of his head into Anthony's face. The move connects with a squishy thud and loosens Isaac's black kippah.

Anthony says "Uh." His nostrils fill with blood that quickens into a gush that he tries to staunch with the hand he was using to lock Isaac's head.

Then Isaac twists Anthony's knife-hand with his good hand until the knife drops into the red mess on the freshly-mopped floor.

93.

"Ten minutes on. Ten minutes off." Isaac gives Anthony a bag of frozen peas wrapped in a soft dishcloth.

Anthony lifts the bag to his purpled, swollen nose. "I don't have a watch," Anthony says—the icy bag on his nose and lips thickening the words.

"I have a timer," Isaac removes the digital timer he keeps on a shelf above his commercial stove, sets it, and puts it on the table where Anthony—in one of Isaac's Blue Matzo sweatshirts–-perches on a stool. Also on the table is Anthony's rolled-up t-shirt stained with Isaac's blood that has turned the color of uncooked liver.

"The ice will reduce the inflammation and the swelling. Can you tolerate ibuprofen?"

"I think so."

Isaac opens a stainless-steel cupboard with the hand at the end of his unbandaged arm. While I drove, Isaac applied pressure to the cut, and when we got here and had hustled Anthony inside, he explained how to clean the wound—which wasn't as deep as I thought–with hydrogen peroxide, to apply antibiotic ointment, wrap it firmly with gauze and then cover the gauze with a snug, plastic bandage.

Isaac must be in pain from the cut and the back of his skull must ache, but his movements are light and graceful. He taps three white bullet-shaped pills from a bottle onto his bandaged palm. He puts the pills on the table next to Anthony's shirt, steps to his oversized refrigerator, removes a gallon jug of milk, takes a glass from a row of glasses from an open shelf, fills it almost to the top with milk, and puts it in front of Anthony.

"Take the ibuprofen with the milk. That way your stomach won't get upset."

"Now?"

"Yeah. Now."

Anthony carefully lowers the bag of frozen peas to the surface of the steel table as if it contains snowflakes—not pebble-hard, frozen, vegetables. His red hands are shiny from the steroid salve Isaac gave him. He slides the caplets into his mouth and drinks half the milk in one swallow. "I guess I should thank you or something."

"Or something," Isaac's pupils have returned to being normal apertures. He's in the same bloodied clothes, but he wears a fresh kippah. A stinging bruise must be growing on the back of his head. Why doesn't he take some ibuprofen and pour himself a glass of milk?

Anthony—who's either chastened, exhausted, or plotting his next assault—returns the bag of peas to his battered, sad-sack face. I look at my watch and once again count the six going on seven hours Freddie and Linda have been confined inside my tiny apartment and try to numb my worry.

We were so in sync a little while ago, but now I am not sure what Isaac is thinking or doing—or thinks he's doing.

After I put the PISO MOJADO sawhorse sign outside the men's room door and locked it, and Isaac pinched Anthony's nostrils to stop the nosebleed, I picked up the kippah, put it in the Trader Joe's bag I'd left in the other stall, wiped the floor, walls, toilet seat, partition and door with damp paper towels, pushed them to the bottom of the full trash receptable, then scrubbed my hands and rinsed them.

As the afternoon darkened and we walked from the Farmers' Market to the underground LACMA parking lot, Anthony pressed a wad of paper towels to his nose. Isaac hid is bloodied arm inside the Trader Joe's bag, and kept his working hand clamped to Anthony's elbow. I had my arm around Anthony's shoulder.

If anyone looked at us, they see a guy with a bloody nose being helped by his friends.

That walk and the drive to Isaac's place did not include conversation—though Isaac and I made a telepathic pact to never leave Anthony by himself. Which explains why—though I'd like to pee—my unrelaxed buttocks are planted right here on the futon.

"Anyone want coffee?" Isaac says. "Food?"

The timer dings. Though Anthony just had a full stack and bacon, he says "Yes," before lifting the bag of peas to his nose and forehead.

"I'm fine," I lie as Isaac turns this mini-abduction into an impromptu supper.

Anthony watches Isaac grab rubber containers from the big refrigerator—this afternoon's slaw, rice and tamales. He pops them open one-handed on the table, shoves the tamales in the microwave and starts it. With his unbandaged arm, Isaac slides three white plates from an open shelf, pulls flatware from a drawer, then sets everything down with a clatter on the long, steel table.

Is Anthony wondering if the containers are heavy enough to brain Isaac and clobber me with?

Isaac's precious, scary-sharp chef's knives glitter against a strip of magnetized maple above the commercial stove. Why bother with clobbering when he can knife us?

The timer hasn't sounded, but Anthony removes the bag from his nose. "How long am supposed to do this?"

"Until the swelling goes down." Isaac pulls a chubby, braided challah from a cupboard and sits it on the thick walnut cutting board at end of the table. He takes a long, serrated knife from the magnetic rack and places it on the cutting board.

Is that a good idea?

Isaac opens another cabinet and produces a short, silver kiddush cup, a pair of weathered brass candlesticks, a box of wooden matches and two short, white candles.

The bag of frozen peas sweats on the table. Anthony aims his swollen, discolored face at me. "You know how you said they have video cameras at that Jewish place where I left the backpack? And that the police would find my picture from their videos?"

"Yes."

"Well, they can't. I was wearing a mask—like for COVID. And a hoodie. There's no way the police can know it was me."

94.

I stand close to Isaac because he asked me to. The pair of brass candlesticks, the white candles, the challah on the board, the wine bottle and silver cup and the table come between Anthony and us.

"Ascher, will you please light the candles."

I am not ready. I am not feeling this.

A little while ago I was whacking the head of Isaac's surprise–okay, I knew it was Friday—Shabbat dinner guest. The guy involved with the Nazis who beat him up. The guy who cut his arm and held a knife to his throat.

I look away from the candlesticks etcetera and question Isaac with a look. He replies by lightly touching the small of my back–– *the best spot in my geography* is what he named that place—and nods.

I hardly ever do this. I never do this. I do not light the Shabbat candles in my Life Space. I do not celebrate Shabbat or observe the Sabbath except when I'm with Isaac—and he does everything. I do not say Shabbat prayers with or for the dogs. For sure I did not do Shabbat with Hans.

Sometimes my aunt would take my grandmother's silver candlesticks out of her cabinet and light the candles the way my grandmother did—covering her eyes as if she was looking at something invisible and sad—and then she'd say the prayers and I'd say them along with her and think about my mother and father.

But I strike the side of the box with the wooden match, watch it spark, then lower its full flame over the wicks until they catch.

I drop the match on the steel table and watch it burn out.

Then I lightly cover my eyes with my hands and say the words: *"Baruch atah Adonai Eloheinu melekh ha'olam asher kid'shanu b'mitzvotav v'tzivanu l'hadlik ner shel shabbat."*

I don't understand Hebrew, but I know that the words mean, "Blessed are You, Lord our God, Ruler of the Universe, who has sanctified us with commandments, and commanded us to light Shabbat candles."

I uncover my eyes. The candlelight is honey and gold. The flames repeat themselves as soft, round dots on the surfaces of Anthony's choppy-ocean-blue eyes, and the dots combust like tiny fires.

"Shabbat shalom, Ascher." Isaac hugs me and kisses my cheek. "Shabbat shalom, Anthony." Isaac extends his good hand toward Anthony. "Shalom means peace. You up for that?"

Anthony leans across the table and instead of shaking Isaac's hand, gives it a soft fist bump and nods at me.

Isaac washes his hands, pours wine into the kiddush cup, blesses the wine and bread, then blesses the bread and slices the sweet loaf.

"Now we eat," he says. "And talk."

95.

I eat some of my tamale, but I cannot taste it. As Isaac pushes the tray of tamales closer to Anthony so he can take more, I feel that I am dreaming. Or high. Except I stopped getting high in eighth grade because it depressed me so much.

"Rice? Slaw?"

"I'm full," Anthony says. "But I wouldn't mind some of that wine."

"With all the ibuprofen you took, wine could cause a gastrointestinal bleed."

"Oh." Anthony looks at the challah. "That bread's good. What kind is it?"

"Egg bread," Isaac says. "The yolk gives it that rich flavor and the buttery color. On Jewish new year the loaf is round. On special occasions and Shabbat—the sabbath—it's braided."

"It's good," Anthony says. "Soft but not too soft."

This is crazy. Isaac's Cheerful Jewish Explainer schtick is about what? Keeping me hostage, too? He knows the dogs—-I mean he knows Freddie—who is old and sick and needs anti-seizure medications at certain times and is emotionally fragile—has been locked in my apartment since late morning.

Anthony finishes his tamales. I hope this means that he will want to visit the bathroom, and that I'll have a private moment with Isaac.

But Anthony remains seated. "What was all that about with the chants and the candles? Do you and your wife do this for dinner every night or what?"

"Just Friday nights—on the Jewish sabbath—Shabbat," Isaac

says. "Friday sundown until Saturday sundown. Jewish people refrain from work during that time, stay close to home with family, and say special prayers."

"So, you don't go to church on Sunday?"

"Observant Jews go to services on Friday, Saturday morning and Saturday evening. Others go to services on Friday evening and Saturday morning. Not in a church—in a synagogue. They usually walk because they're not supposed to drive."

Anthony scratches a blister on his left hand. "But what if you have to drive somewhere or have to work? Or there's an emergency? Then what?"

"It depends," Isaac stacks the plates and gathers flatware and opens the dishwasher. "If it's a life-or-death situation—if someone's in terrible trouble, or in danger or very sick, it's okay to drive to or do whatever's necessary to help them."

96.

Anthony has finally absented himself from the Shabbat Fest to visit the bathroom. Isaac and I stand close to the churning dishwasher and whisper—but Isaac keeps eyes on the bathroom door.

"What are you planning to do about him?" I uncurl the little twist-tie on the plastic bag holding what's left of the challah on the counter, reach inside, and yank off a chunk of bread. "I don't know what's happening, Isaac. I'm worried."

Isaac watches the bread disappear into my mouth. "I'm feeling him out. Trying to figure out when he's lying and when he's telling the truth. Are you hungry?"

I twist the metal thing back onto the end of the bread bag. "No. I'm stress-eating because I'm scared because he held a knife to your throat and slashed your arm. Why haven't we called the police?"

"Because he did those things because he was scared. He panicked. Before we do anything or call anyone, we need to find out who he's afraid of."

97.

Anthony drifts toward us like a fog rising from a derailed poison train. "Why are you doing all this stuff?"

"What stuff?" Isaac takes a few steps toward him.

"Dinner. Stopping my nosebleed. Giving me that cream. The peas. Taking me here. You're both perverts, right? You have to be." Anthony's pupils are granite. "I've heard about Hebrews doing things to people. Kids, even."

"We're not perverts," I say and sound very stupid as I say it.

"What my wife says is the truth," Isaac sounds wise and rabbinical. "We don't do bad things to anyone—though I really wanted to smash your face in that men's room."

"Why didn't you? What do you want?" For some reason Anthony addresses the Wife. "You know I don't have anything."

"You do have something," I say.

Isaac steps close to agitated man. "The Shabbat dinner was just a Shabbat dinner. It had nothing to do with you. And I'm an EMT, so when someone is injured, I help them. It doesn't matter who it is. But I should tell you something we didn't mention. My wife and I have a personal interest in the men who paid you to distribute those leaflets."

98.

Anthony has returned to what has become his seat. Isaac sits across from him, and I'm in the wife-spot on Isaac's left.

"How many men hired you for the leaflet drops? Were they the same ones each time?

"Three. Just those three."

"Did they approach you at the encampment or somewhere else?" I ask.

"They started talking to me one day when I was leaving that Jewish place. They were standing down the street. Watching people go in and out, I guess."

"What are their names?"

"They never said." Anthony jiggles his foot under the table.

"Did you ever hear them address each other by name?" Me again.

Anthony crosses his arms across his chest. "I don't know. Maybe. I can't remember."

"Think. It's important," Isaac urges. "They won't ever know that you told us. I promise."

Anthony pulls off a piece of challah from the loaf in the bag that has been moved back to the table and lifts it almost to his mouth. "James."

"James what?"

"Just James. I think he's the head of everything."

"What's 'everything'?"

"The papers. And I heard them talking about some videos." Anthony puts the chunk of bread on the table and embraces his own chest. "I need air. I don't feel so good. I need to get the fuck out of here."

Anthony's bends forward. His face pales to skimmed-milk bluish white and his forehead shines with sweat. "Oh fuck. Oh Jesus. I'm having a heart attack."

99.

The brown paper crinkles as Anthony inhales and it deflates. Then Anthony exhales into the swelling lunch bag Isaac took out of his EMT duffle.

"Nice and slow," Isaac says. "That's good. Long, slow breaths. That will restore the CO_2 in your blood. When you're anxious, you breathe too fast and your CO_2 level drops too low."

Isaac monitors Anthony's breathing. I try to ignore the fluttering of my own anxious heart.

When Anthony's color and his breathing return to normal, Isaac tells him he doesn't need the bag. Anthony puts the bag on the table.

"I'm very sorry that we upset you," Isaac says.

I deliver a wifely nod.

Anthony is really afraid of something. And if it's scary enough to frighten him like this—why would he tell us what it is?

"You're not sorry," Anthony's contracts his inflamed hands into fists. "You're both bullshitting me and I know it. You're dicking me around. You're both Jewish fucking perverts. That's what you are."

Anthony shakes his fat red index finger at me. "And your wife is big fat liar. If you were so interested in James then why did ask about some dumb dog? And that old lady?"

Anthony looks at Isaac "If you're not perverts, you're cops. Lying, pervert fucking cop bastards."

"No, we're not." The liar and woman who is not Isaac's wife by a long shot says. "That lady I asked you about? She was our friend and she was murdered, and the police think a dog killed her. She came to the encampment often, and I was trying to find out where the dog came from."

"That's true. Isaac says. "I promise you, Anthony, my wife is not a liar."

Ouch. Every time Isaac says "wife," an angel somewhere drops like a lump of lead to earth.

Anthony replies by jiggling his foot so hard against the leg of the table that it shakes.

"Whenever somebody's promised me something, they were lying. Maybe she's lying and you just don't know it. Did you ever think about that? Maybe she's fucking around on you."

But Isaac doesn't answer—maybe because he's completing his one-handed excavation of a deep hole and Anthony is helping him. And every time Anthony kicks the table leg, the hole widens beneath us.

A few more words from Isaac or kicks from Anthony and the floor will give way.

100.

The three-quarters-eaten braided loaf of challah sits on the crumpled plastic bag. A scattering of crumbs dehydrates on the table. Isaac's laptop is open. Anthony sits next to Isaac and looks at the screen while chewing a piece of challah crust.

"Run faster, bedbug! Faster! Or I'm going to kick your ass!"

"The only place a kike belongs is in a nice hot oven!" Isn't that right, you filthy Shylock?"

"I don't want to watch any more of this shit."

Isaac closes the laptop. "The people connected to James don't just dump flyers and hang banners over freeways," Isaac says. "They harass people, record themselves doing it, then post the videos online and get other people excited about doing the same thing. Last year a guy who believed their flyers and watched their videos shot at Jewish people walking home from religious services."

"Did he kill them?"

"No," Isaac says." But a man who thinks like James entered a synagogue in Philadelphia and shot eleven people with an AR-15. It's inevitable that more people James and his friends have hyped up will try to do the same things."

Anthony's stool scrapes the cement floor as he backs it away from the table. "I already told your wife I don't know anything about a dog. And I don't know about James or that online shit. I'm getting the fuck out of here and don't you try to stop me."

101.

The drive from the Isaac's place to Wilshire takes a few minutes, but I stretch it a little give Anthony time to think while he's still locked in a car with the husband-and-wife Jewish perverts who spent their afternoon and their sabbath evening feeding, caring for and interrogating him.

Isaac is silent. I am silent.

And Anthony is a Dr. Who statue sitting on the yellow towel I put across the back seat for Freddie and Linda's morning pilgrimage to the Lieb family homestead. Next to Anthony is a shopping bag Isaac filled with food in plastic containers, a loaf of challah that Isaac had in the freezer, some apples and bananas, Ibuprofen caplets in a baggie, paper bags, and another Blue Matzo sweatshirt.

The bag reminds me of the one Isaac prepared for L.S. Rutledge and that at any moment, Anthony could come to life, lean forward, stretch his arms and punch Isaac.

And then punch me.

Inside Anthony's pocket are ten twenties and Isaac's Blue Matzo business card with his phone number that Anthony folded in half longways and placed between two bills. And he has a burner phone we bought him at a dollar store during a little detour.

I turn left on 6th Street and drive east behind the Academy Museum of Motion Pictures, the crown of its illuminated dome glowing magenta and blue high above a new collection of tents along the sidewalk. We pass the entrance to the LACMA parking structure, and then the Page Museum.

"I go over to the Tar Pits sometimes." The Anthony statue

sounds weary. "And listen to the tours. The animal they found the most of is dire wolves."

"I didn't know that." Isaac says. "I guess the wolves thought they were just getting a drink of water and fell in."

I turn on Hauser and then right on Wilshire.

"They didn't fall in. There was water and leaves and shit on top of the tar so they never knew it was there. They walked right into it."

"Sad," I say.

"Yeah," Anthony says. "They didn't have a fucking chance."

The lumpy haystack shapes that are the tents and shelters of the Wilshire encampment melt into each other in the dark. At the end of that darkness is Urban Light.

"There, before that light thing," Anthony says. "There's my tent."

I pull as close to the cluttered gutter along the curb as I can. A bus driver honks as he swerves to pass.

"You're sure about the motel? We'll help pack up your stuff."

The shopping bag rustles. Then Anthony opens the passenger door. "When you said that you could drive and shit on the Shabbat if it was an emergency, did you mean it? Or did you lie about that, too?"

"I didn't lie," Isaac speaks to the Anthony in the rear-view mirror. "If it's a life-or-death thing, I can drive or do whatever I need to do. Protecting life comes before everything else."

"Jesus," Anthony says as the scent of garbage decomposing in the gutter fills the car. car. "Fuck."

"You don't have to stay here," Isaac says.

"No fucking motel." Anthony speaks to the Anthony in the mirror. "But if something really bad was going to happen, and you didn't say anything, it would be your fault, right? Like when those people got shot?"

In the mirror I watch the cold light from approaching headlights sweep across Anthony's anguished face.

"There's going to be an emergency. A life-or-death thing that has to do with James. Tomorrow."

102.

As I drive through Laurel Canyon toward the Valley, I keep looking for Isaac's ambulance behind me.

I don't see it—which is okay because I have to get to Life Space before Isaac arrives.

The light at Mulholland cycles to red, so I'm stuck staring at the NEPOBABY license plate on the white Range Rover ahead of me, and at the cornsilk grasses quaking under an invisible breeze.

What personalized license plate best describes me?

PANTSONFIRE

NOTHISWIFE

The light cools to green and I begin the always free-feeling descent down the hill. The light-haze that is valley floor shimmers under a moonless, starless, vertical, lapis lazuli sky.

Every vista that doesn't have people or animals in it is beautiful—the opposite of dire wolves struggling against that thing that pulls them under the trick water-mirror and into the suffocating pit.

Sheol.

The opposite of the Order of Christian Manhood and what Anthony told us.

And what about the wolves in my apartment? Will I find what I'm always afraid I'll find when I've been away too long?

Traffic is light and I sync my speed to the traffic lights—green, green, green, green. But it still feels as though the car is pushing through something thick.

I park the Lexus in my assigned space, then take the fire stairs three at a time. As I push open the heavy fire door into the hallway, I hear the sound I've waited so long to hear—

Linda and Freddie are barking their big and little heads off.

103.

The dogs are crazy happy to see me. I sit on the floor and receive their sloppy, adoring welcome, kiss them back, praise them, hug them, refill their water bowls, feed them, and give Freddie his meds.

They pee as soon as we're outside the building, then trot ahead of me toward the Dog Park. I left my apartment door locked, but Isaac has his key.

There was no time to straighten up. To put out the kosher cups and plates and plastic silverware for coffee. To refresh Linda's eye dots or to even out her fur color with that spray I bought. Or to hide the spray in the back of the bathroom cupboard.

And I haven't come up with any lies good enough to cover what is about to happen.

Linda is my neighbor's dog. I am just taking care of her while he? she? they? are away on a cruise— to Alaska? The Caribbean? Cabo? Which neighbor does the dog belong to? Isaac always chats with my neighbors, so knows them better than I do. That won't work.

I found Linda wandering in the hellscape that is the Valley while I was walking Freddie one evening. I posted her photo on Nextdoor and Facebook, but no one claimed her. I took her to the vet to be scanned, but she wasn't chipped—so I decided to keep her. When was this? Right after Isaac and I had our big argument? Which big argument?

Linda and Freddie do their thing inside the exclusive, members-only Dog Space Life Park, then execute a collaborative, olfactory forensic examination of the plasticized green surface. I try to put on "my thinking cap" as my sociopathic second grade teacher would urge us—"or else."

But my thinking cap is defective. And "or else" is about to happen. Nothing can fix it if Isaac recognizes that Linda is Dog Doe. No clever, audacious lie from me will prevent her from being shoved back into that death row kennel at the shelter.

104.

We enter the elevator, dogs first. It smells like nutmeg and liquid soap, and I feel the way the thirsty dire wolves must have felt right before they went out for a night of guzzling H_20 at the La Brea Tar Pits.

When the elevator doors open, the sound of a male voice speaking Hebrew travels through the hallway from the not–quite-closed door to my Life Space. Linda's ears go up. Freddie growls. The dogs scramble forward, straining their leashes.

Anthony said that something horrible is supposed to happen tomorrow. That's why Isaac was in the Life Space elevator. That's why he's in my apartment talking on this phone.

And that's why I can't pull the dogs back into the elevator and run.

105.

The coffee machine gurgles. Isaac is in the kitchen, his cellphone to his ear. His laptop sits on the counter next to a stack of cardboard cups, plates, plastic flatware, a notebook and some pens.

"Hey."

Isaac turns and smiles. Then he sees Freddie and Linda in her jacket.

"The dire wolves have arrived," I say, then watch my stupid joke fail to land and die.

Isaac says something in Hebrew into his phone, then ends the call. Now that it's quiet, it's impossible not to hear Freddie's low growls.

"What's this?" Isaac gestures at Linda with the back of his bandaged hand.

"What's what?" What's wrong with me? So far, every word I've said has been perfectly designed to piss off Isaac. "'This' is dogs who were locked in all day and are still hyper. They'll calm down in a few minutes."

"I can't believe you got another dog." Isaac scowls at Freddie, then adjusts his head slightly so he can scowl at Linda.

"Believe," I say as I unleash Freddie, then Linda—then hold my breath as I remove her jacket with shaky hands.

Freddie takes a few steps toward Isaac, appears to sniff his aura, then trots to the couch, jumps up, settles in and farts. Linda sits at my feet.

"At least it's well-trained," Isaac sniffs. "But why get another one when you live in such a small apartment? And why didn't you tell me?"

"She found me. Also, I was lonely. And I didn't tell you because you broke up with me and refused to speak to me."

"You're going there, Ascher?" Isaac reddens and puts his good and bad hands on his hips. "I can't believe you're rehashing this now."

So far Linda is just Linda to Isaac—not the billboard dog. Not the monster in L.S. Rutledge's apartment.

"I'm not going anywhere. I'm not rehashing. And nothing's really changed." I kneel to stroke the alleged canine murderess's silky head. "Let start over, okay? Linda, meet Isaac. Isaac is being not very nice right now, but he can be really nice when he feels like it."

Isaac's jaw muscles begin to work.

"Isaac, this is Linda. You'll discover that she's a total sweetheart and not moody like me." I look at Isaac. "And I'm not joking about this—Freddie and I love her."

Does Linda remember Isaac from L.S. Rutledge's apartment? Does she recognize his scent? She gets up and I permit her to advance—still leashed—as far as the toes of Isaac's clogs.

Isaac tenses. I hold my breath.

Linda sits again, raises her pretty-good-if-I-say-so-myself eyebrow dots and eyes to gaze at Isaac—then lifts her paw for a shake.

106.

We see what we expect to see.

We saw what we've been told we saw.

Or maybe we don't see anything at all—we dream.

Freddie dozes. Linda lounges next to Freddie on the couch and chews the new Busy Bone I gave her.

Isaac did not shake Linda's paw—but he didn't connect her to Dog Doe.

Why was I so sure he would? Nothing about this black-dark gray, social, deferential mutt with cute eyebrows screams murderer because Dog Doe is a fantasy and Linda is a real dog--sweet and smart.

And Isaac is too busy calling Shomrim, Hatzalah, Magen Am and other people—and jotting things down to notice her.

I'm busy, too—watching more sick-making Order of Christian Manhood's videos and taking screenshots of faces that match Anthony's description of James. I find six that are James-like and show them to Isaac.

"Him. He's the schmuck who punched me." Isaac points to the picture of a slender man with short, tea-colored hair who is ordinary except for his self-satisfied smirk. He shows up three times in my captures—

> In one, he's giving a thumbs-down and holding a poster of that famous picture of Anne Frank sitting at her desk captioned, "Fuckable? Ja oder Nein?"

In another he's yelling slurs through a megaphone aimed at a cowering elderly Asian woman who covers her ears with her hands.

In the last one he waves a coffee can with Zyklon-B written on it above the kippah-ed head of a man wearing a huge, fake hooked nose.

I crop the best screenshot, increase the resolution, and do an image search which gives me a LinkedIn photo of the same face with a name—James Adolf Aguilar, a solar panel technician employed by Green Flare Solar Panels in Whittier.

Because it's Shabbat and most of Isaac's earlier calls went to voicemail, people are just now calling him back. I wait for a lull, then show Isaac what I found.

"Adolf is a nice touch," Isaac says, then lightly touches that spot he likes so much on my lower back. "This is very valuable information, Ascher. Excellent job." Isaac removes his hand. "But, remember, we're not going after him. At least not now. If Anthony told us the truth and we figure things out, James will be coming to us."

Of course. Isaac is right. I see that now and I feel sick. "I can't believe how badly I blew this and how much time I wasted. After watching the videos, I just focused on James."

"And you found out who he is, so if we see him, we'll know it. That's gold, Ascher."

"Not when Anthony said the attack will happen this morning. I should have made a list of the most likely targets first. I'm so sorry."

Isaac coaxes me into hug. "Don't ever feel sorry about anything. You are my beautiful Ascher always."

107.

The apartment does not smell like a Life Space. It smells spicy the way the elevator did with good, strong coffee added. We occupy our sides of the bed with our laptops open, and sip fresh caffeinated and decaffeinated kosher lattes from kosher cups on the bedside tables. The dreaming dogs share my aunt's sweater at the foot.

It's a little past midnight which means the attack Anthony warned us about will happen today if it's really going to happen. I narrow the target list while Isaac communicates with his Hatzalah and Shomrim contacts.

Isaac has shown zero interest in Linda or Freddie—but ignoring Freddie is normal for him.

Isaac has shown tons of interest in me.

I'm interested in him too—but I still don't understand his coldness and silence after our argument. Or what "always" means to him—or how he really feels. It feels right and good to be close again—but I can't help wondering if I'm the right person for Isaac to love.

I touch Isaac's knee. He removes his Air Pods and covers my hand with his—and the familiar, delicious, full-body Isaac-disturbance travels through me.

"There are fifty-four synagogues in the Valley. I'm trimming the list down to the medium and small ones. And I included the Home for the Elderly. Agree?"

"That's good. What about that west Valley Jewish community center where there was that shooting at the preschool?"

"I thought about it. But that was the nineties and their security must be extremely tight now." I notice that one of Linda's eyebrow dots has faded.

"This is hard. I'm scared I'll eliminate the right target."

"A lot of people are on this—not just us. Shomrim has activated the city-wide phone tree and is in contact with LAPD and every Jewish organization and shul has received a warning and James Adolf's picture."

"Okay."

"But what Anthony told us isn't specific enough for the police to act on. It's just too vague. It's not a suspicious package delivered to a building. Or even a phone threat. And shuls and Jewish schools and centers get threats all the time."

"Where are you saying, Isaac?"

"Don't expect a huge LAPD response. What they're doing now is looking for Anthony."

"They won't find him. They should be picking up James Adolf Aguilar in Whittier. And his asshole friends."

"I'm sure the police here and HSI were already aware of him. And the groups that monitor people like him. But James and his friends haven't done enough to get arrested."

"Wait. You mean everyone already knew who he is?"

"It makes sense that he'd be someone they're watching. Which is part of the problem. But we didn't know his name, right? And now we can share it."

"How is knowing who he is a problem? I don't get it."

"Because the police already know the Order of Christian Manhood harass people and say ugly things, and also that so far, they've never been violent. Talking about bad things happening to Jews is their brand. So, James saying something vague about targeting a synagogue isn't a credible threat."

"But Anthony told us when, Isaac. Isn't that credible?"

"To you and me it is. But Anthony could have been lying. And we don't really know who Anthony is. What we have is second-hand."

108.

It's seven-thirty Saturday morning. The car windows are open to the sputter of sprinklers and petrichor as I drive east on Camarillo in North Hollywood. I make a left on Vineland, drive a few blocks, then turn at the NoHo Pooch Emporium corner onto La Naranja Way. I see open spaces in the parking lot Noho Pooch Emporium shares with a vegan doughnut shop, a fish-and-chips place and a pool supply store—but I need to park on La Naranja.

After I eliminated large, well-secured synagogues, day schools and high schools from my list, I did Google Street View searches on the rest to see how vulnerable they looked. I also checked to see if any had been targeted with Order of Christian Manhood flyers or had been vandalized recently. Two stood out—

A Russian congregation in a strip mall storefront in Tarzana, and a North Hollywood house that is home to a dwindling Orthodox congregation. The storefront was spray-painted with slurs and swastikas three times in the last six weeks. And someone threw a brick through their front window two weeks ago.

A message on the Russian congregation's website thanks donors to a GoFundMe that raised enough to cover a Ring system and to pay for a night security guard.

Isaac and I agreed that James's most convenient target would be the NoHo house.

It looks the way it did in the street view image. It's a small, nineteen thirties, beige Spanish bungalow with curtained, arched windows trimmed in green. A huge, old magnolia tree canopies the front. A sign near the front step says "Adath Tzedek" —

which Isaac said means "Community of Justice." A brass mezuzah hangs on the doorframe.

The magnolia's roots have broken through the sidewalk. The short street is quiet. I can see the side of the NoHo Pooch Emporium on the corner in my rear-view mirror. A Google map showed that the Emporium's parking lot opens to an alley that runs behind La Naranja Way. It would be easy to park in the lot and use the alley to reach the chain link fence at the back of the synagogue house.

I turn into the stubby driveway of a four-unit dingbat apartment building with "Holly North" in raised, cutout letters angled against its peeling coral front. The leaves of the orange tree in its tiny square of plastic turf are waxy green. I turn the car around, then drift back toward Noho Pooch Emporium looking for a parking space and checking the parked cars for occupants. The cars look uninhabited except for one that someone must be living in. It's stuffed almost to the roof with clothing, boxes and Beanie Babies.

And there's a burgundy Toyota Corolla with blackout window tinting, and a white pick-up with a wraparound silver sunshade long enough block the passenger and driver's windows.

At the corner I turn right on Vineland, then circle around and enter La Naranja from the west end. I don't know where Isaac is parked.

His ambulance with the Hebrew lettering in red would catch the attention of Order of Christian Manhood assholes—but especially this Shabbat morning. And if James were around, he'd recognize it.

109.

I keep circling until a woman in a Weird Barbie sweatshirt, leggings, running shoes and carrying a kettle bell exits the dingbat and prances to a Prius, puts the kettle bell in the trunk, and drives toward the Noho Pooch Emporium.

I take her spot. It's not perfect—farther away than I want—but I can see Adath Tzedek and I can watch the pick-up and the Corolla.

I compose a text to Isaac, but don't click "send".

Do I add a heart emoji at the end?

What if I Isaac thinks I'm too gushy?

But what if something terrible happens and I didn't? So I add one—

> parked near adath tzedek burgundy corolla w/ blackout tint pickup with sunshade all quiet where r u? ❤

110.

My cellphone vibrates.

> parked behind tire shop on camarillo service to start early ❤ ❤

I reply—

I touch the two heart emojis in Isaac's text with my index finger. They're as flat and smooth and cool as my cellphone screen. But in my eyes, they throb like hearts in old cartoons—Ba-Boom. Ba-Boom. Ba-Boom. Ba-Boom.

Why "early"?

I check the Adath Tzedek website on my phone—

"Saturday Shabbat Morning Services: Psukei D'Zimrah 9:00 A.M., Shabbat Morning services at 9:30 A.M."

Isaac said that Psukei D'Zimrah is a recitation of prayers and psalms that precedes the Shabbat service. The service requires a *minyan*—ten men in Orthodox synagogues or a mix of men and women that adds up to ten in other congregations. But they don't need a minyan for *Psukei D'Zimrah.*

Does James know this? If he does, he'll wait until after nine to do whatever he's going to do so he can maximize the damage.

It's eight-forty-four now.

Here we go.

Two middle-aged men step around NoHo Pooch Emporium corner onto La Naranja Way. Both wear black slacks, white button-down shirts and black jackets. As they approach the synagogue house, I can see the edges of the black kippahs on their heads and the square, zipper pouches that hold their prayer shawls in their hands.

Two pairs of similarly dressed men proceed toward Adath Tzedek from the other end of the street. Then another pair that includes a stooped, gray-bearded man wearing a black, brimmed hat. Now, five men turn the corner opposite the Pooch Emporium onto La Naranja. Then five more. All wear kippahs, black jackets with white shirts and have *tzitzit* showing under their jackets. All carry pouches.

That's eighteen men. In Jewish tradition, the number eighteen is considered fortunate because it's associated with the letters in Hebrew word, "chai" —"life."

The men come together on the uneven sidewalk in front of Adath Tzedek, then walk single file up the curved, stone pathway to the arched wooden door and enter without knocking.

Isaac isn't with them.

Where is James? In the alley in the back? In the pick-up?

Or did we get this completely wrong?

The driver's side door of the white pick-up opens.

111.

The tall white man in orange mirrored sunglasses who gets out of the pick-up is about James's age, but he isn't James. A red scar severs one eyebrow and runs to his jaw. His jeans are ripped and his belly strains against his white T-shirt emblazoned with a fake Voltaire quotation popular among white supremacists—"To learn who rules over you, find out who you are not allowed to criticize."

The guy crosses Naranja, passes Adath Tzekek, and disappears around the Noho Pooch Emporium corner. Is he going to cut through the lot to the alley behind Adath Tzedek? Or is he picking up fish-and-chips or doughnuts?

He doesn't look like the vegan doughnut type. Do people eat fish and chips for breakfast? And if his t-shirt is a coincidence, it's a big one.

I watch the Corolla to see to if there is movement inside—but the tinted windows seem to become more opaque as the morning brightens.

Eight-fifty.

I take my aunt's blue and green floral scarf from my purse, wrap it around my head, then knot it at the nape of my neck below my painfully-tight chignon.

I look in the visor mirror and assess my allegedly beautiful, worried, un-made-up face, then check my clothes. My headscarf and my outfit—my aunt's ankle-length, dark green skirt with my black leggings underneath—I couldn't find my tights—a long-sleeved, high-necked white top, and my boots—have replaced Ascher Lieb with a melancholy Orthodox Jewish woman I do not know.

I grab my purse and the shopping bag I put on the passenger seat, get out of the car, cross the street and follow the sidewalk opposite Adath Tzedek.

I slow near the Corolla—and though an Orthodox Jewish woman wouldn't use her cellphone on Shabbat—I take mine out of my purse and, while pretending to read a message, I sneak a photo of its license plate.

The Corolla is quiet—no music or voices leak from the interior.

I cross the street and walk where the men did up the path to the Adath Tzedek front door—but I don't climb the front step. I continue to a dirt and gravel walkway along the side of the house, step around the air conditioning unit and past a row of hollyhocks as the buzz and ring and the rise and fall of male voices singing in Hebrew reaches me through the screened, open windows.

The gravel path that layers my boots with dust stops at a small back yard—paved-over except for raised flower beds thick with nasturtiums, and roses—red, pale pink, and hot yellow—climbing trellises, and overtaking the rusty clothesline.

A birdbath holding a pink and red geranium stands next to a black garbage bin by the screened back door.

My leggings feel like heating pads as I walk between the cedar planter beds to the chain link fence at the back of the property and peer into the alley. No cars. No vans. No guy in the white t-shirt. Just a daylight coyote with a limp dove in its mouth.

All there is to see in the yard are three city-issued, wheeled, lidded trash bins lined up against the fence—blue for recycling, black for trash, and green for leaves and garden trimmings.

A mix of grass clippings and brown magnolia leaves rests at the bottom of the green bin. The blue bin contains two empty plastic Mountain Dew bottles. A black plastic bottle of engine oil and a crushed, pink, cardboard doughnut box with grease stains are all that I see the black bin. The soda bottles, engine oil, clippings and leaves, and the doughnut box must signify a gardener's presence.

So why is there a second black bin near the kitchen? Why

would a house that no one lives in require two black cans for trash? Especially when the city charges sixty dollars a month for each of them?

It wouldn't.

I text Isaac—

`trash bin near back door` 

112.

As the voices in the synagogue house rise in prayer and my cellphone vibrates inside my purse, I clomp along the nasturtium beds past the solo black bin to the gravel path on side of the house. I pull off the skirt, the scarf and the long-sleeved shirt, push them into the shopping bag and put on the sunglasses I had in my purse. I unpin my chignon, straighten my maybe-too-snug spaghetti-strap top, and step to the front of the house.

I move along the tall hedge separating the Adath Tzedek property from the house next door, trip on a thick, sidewalk-colored Magnolia root, catch myself before I fall, then hurry along the sidewalk to the Lexus. A Smart Car has replaced the white pick-up. But the Corolla is still there—a shiny wine-dark beetle in the sun.

After I've passed it, I glance at the back window and see the "Ask Me About Green Flare Solar Panels!" sunburst-shaped decal in bottom-left corner.

I slide into the drivers' seat of the Lexus and lock the door, shivering as it hits me— nothing James does is worth anything unless he records it and posts it online.

And James can't record what's about to happen unless he's already here and sitting in the stifling car preparing for his big moment.

`J must be in corolla idk if alone or not`

113.

"It's Saturday for us goys but shabbat for the lazy-ass kikes who can't be bothered to lift a finger from Friday to Saturday night while all they do is drink and eat and fuck like the pigs they are." James laughs. The dark red upholstery of the car seat is visible behind his head. The camera pushes so close to his face that the tiny mole with a curving, black hair growing from it under his right ear glistens under the harsh white light. "But today is trash day and the trash going to be taken out. Kike, pedophile, dancing Israeli, Rothschild trash."

hes livestreaming now ❤ ❤

I mute the livestream and—though Isaac texted me with two more heart emojis and told me to lie down on the floor of the back seat and stay there—I get out of the car, jog to the dingbat and stand under the orange tree with my cell phone to my ear and wait.

The traffic is a soft, white-noise hiss. A screen door slams somewhere, and "Layla" with amped-up bass ripples from a car on Vineland and snakes up La Naranja Way.

My cell phone says nine-ten.

Isaac's ambulance—no lights or sirens—turns onto La Naranja from the Noho Pooch Emporium corner just as the white pick-up appears at the other end, and turns sharply until it blocks the street.

The ambulance advances until there's a car-length between it and the Corolla. Isaac—wearing an N95, a Dodgers' baseball cap and his Day-Glo EMT vest—jumps down, walks around to the passenger door and helps the stooped old man in the black hat I saw enter Adath Tzedek descend to the pavement. I hear the doors in the back of the ambulance open. Men in kippahs, black pants and white shirts with tzitzit showing appear on both sides of the ambulance. Some trot to the white pick-up. Others run toward the Corolla's rear passenger door just as it opens and James Adolf Aguilar leans out.

"Please stay inside your car, Mr. Aguilar." The stooped man stands before the open door.

"Get out of my fucking way, kike!" James shoves the door into the old man and knocks him to the ground.

Isaac steps around the old man and with his good hand knocks James back into the car, then forces the car door shut. The other men surround the car and start to rock it.

James pounds the rear window with his fists as the car flips on its side.

Isaac returns to the ambulance and drives it forward until it's parallel with the overturned Corolla. He looks through the windshield at the white truck and the men in kippahs gathered around it —and that's when his eyes find mine.

My scalp prickles. The ground ripples under my boots and I hear a thump.

Behind the ambulance's windshield, Isaac opens his mouth and says something—but I can't hear him because Adath Tzedek's tile roof rises and shatters, and the big magnolia's leaves have become white flames.

114.

Firefighters train hoses on Adath Tzedek—a smoking, reeking, roofless, black half-bungalow with a maimed magnolia, a blown-out back wall, and a sink-hole for a kitchen. One LAPD black and white blocks the Vineland side of La Naranja and two more are parked at the other end. The Bomb Squad SUV is halfway in someone's driveway and halfway on the grass. A uniformed man leads a skinny shepherd in a black vest to the white Bomb Squad Canine Unit truck parked behind the SUV. Inhabitants of the little houses that seemed so sleepy before the blast observe the action from behind the yellow tape strung between the dingbat orange tree and a lamppost.

The stooped old man sits inside Isaac's ambulance sipping a Diet Coke from a straw. A gauze bandage with a fresh blood stain on it is taped to his cheek. Isaac told me that he is the rabbi at Adath Tzedek and that he's okay.

The LAPD bomb squad officer with black hair pinned up in a chignon and wearing ballet flats that don't appear to hurt her feet writes something on a lined yellow pad.

"You said the house was empty, Mr. Cohen. But neighbors reported hearing chanting around nine A.M."

"Yes," Isaac says. "It was empty. And my last name is Kahn. We thought Aguilar might attack today and we wanted to make sure nobody was inside."

The officer pauses her note-taking and looks at Isaac. "Who was praying in there then?"

"No one," I say.

"They heard a recording," Isaac explains. "One of the congregation members set it up so he could remotely signal a recorded service to play when the Shabbat services usually begin."

"When was this arranged?"

"I don't know for sure," Isaac says. "I think around five a.m. The rabbi gave him the key. He set up the computer inside, and opened the side windows so anyone outside would be sure to hear the voices."

"But people reported seeing men enter the building at nine this morning."

"They did," I say.

Isaac nods. "We wanted to make it seem like a normal Shabbat. The men entered, walked through the house and out the back door, then climbed the fence in the back to the alley where I was waiting with the ambulance to pick them up."

The three of us watch four uniformed police officers right the Corolla, then lift a squirming, arms-swinging James out of the car, spin him around and cuff him with zip ties.

Isaac squeezes my hand.

"Do you know what kind of bomb it was?" Isaac asks.

"Not yet. But the squad suspects that an improvised explosive device made of fireworks was placed inside a trash receptacle at the rear of the structure."

The woman writes something with her scratchy pen. "How do you spell your last name, sir?"

"K-A-H-N."

"And you, Miss?"

"L-I-E-B. My first name is Ascher. A-S-C-H-E-R."

"Unusual name," she says. "Pretty. And you two are colleagues or?"

"She's my fiancée," Isaac says and squeezes my hand again.

115.

Isaac drives the ambulance toward Life Space since I won't be able to retrieve the Lexus until Naranja Way opens up again—which the police said might not happen until after eight tonight. We have things to say and questions to ask each other. But since the bomb people and the police moved their vehicles and a policeman stopped traffic so Isaac could back the ambulance with me in it onto Vineland, we've been sipping diet Cokes to quench our thirst and speechless.

And we still vibrate with the boom and thud of the explosives.

I stare out the big, high, open ambulance window. Gone is the morning sprinkler mist and its perfume. This world is arid and bright—all glaring surfaces and heat.

At the red light at Whitsett, I notice the sign someone put up on the far bank of the flood channel—a painterly red heart against a black background. And the question that's been ricocheting inside me rises to my tongue and flies out of my mouth. "Isaac, what did you mean when you told the bomb squad person that I was your fiancée?"

"What do you mean?"

"I'm asking what you meant, okay?"

Isaac's jaw muscles do not contract. He does not wrinkle his brows or scowl—he smiles. "It means I love you and I'm in love with you and you're beautiful and smart and interesting and funny. And a badass. And I want to spend my life with you." Isaac kisses the side of my head.

I feel myself falling into the smoking sinkhole behind Adath Tzedek—but in a good way.

And then I cry.

"What do you mean when you say 'spend your life with me'?"

"You're kidding, right?"

"No."

"I mean go to bed together every night, and wake up together. I mean live together until death. I mean travel. Have kids. The whole schmear."

"How many kids are you referring to?" In my mind's eye, the frazzled Orthodox woman I saw in my rear-view mirror pushes a heavy double stroller and herds six, eight—maybe ten cranky kids through The Grove.

"As many as you want. Or none—if you want that."

"But what about the dogs?"

"What about the dogs?"

"You totally hate them."

"No, I don't. I just don't love them. When I was a kid, I got a very bad bite, and since then I've been nervous around dogs."

"Why didn't you tell me?"

"I don't know. I guess I thought I could change the way I feel. But so far, I can't."

"But I'm not Jewish enough for you. I'm an atheist."

"Am I too Jewish for you?"

"Not at all," I say. "I love your Jewishness. It enriches my life."

"Okay. And your whatever you call it—your questioning and your worldliness—enrich my life, too. We don't have to be the same, Ascher. We just have to respect and support each other."

116.

Isaac stops the ambulance outside Life Space and leans over to kiss me before he looks for a place to park the ambulance. The apparition of Ascher Lieb kisses him back, steps to the sidewalk, watches the ambulance turn the corner, floats above the walkway and drifts through the lobby and into the empty elevator like mist.

I don't feel real. The THREE button isn't solid when I push it. And the fried chicken smell clinging to elevator walls seems almost floral.

Each breath, each heartbeat and each weirdly light footfall in the hallway asks, "Do I say yes? Do I say yes?"

Well, do I?

Can I?

I open the door to my Life Space and the dogs gallop out to greet me. Linda runs halfway to the elevator and back for joy and Freddie performs his usual choreography. "Isaac doesn't hate you," I want to tell them as they follow me in and I the unlock the door before I close it.

We see what we want to see.

Fear blinds us.

I roll Freddie's meds in into little cream cheese balls, make an empty one for Linda, then get the dogs' dinners ready.

Isaac enters the apartment carrying the two empty Diet Coke cans and a skinny, cellophane-wrapped and rubber-banded bouquet of dark red roses.

"Oh, come on."

"They don't count because they're a couple days old and from the liquor store around the corner. They're the floral equivalent of an airport tuna sandwich."

"You've never eaten an airport tuna sandwich," I say.

"True. But I've seen one close up. And I've smelled it."

Isaac puts the cans on the kitchen counter, then presents flowers to me. "You were amazing today, Ascher. So brave."

I put my face close to the flowers—they're cold from the liquor store and have no scent. "I wasn't brave, I was just being nosy. You were the brave one, Isaac. And a regular mastermind."

Linda trots from her water bowl to Isaac's feet—and I notice again with a pang that one eyebrow dot is lighter than the other.

"What does she want?"

"Maybe a handshake. Or a pat on the head."

"How about I give her a treat?"

I dig a dog biscuit out of the jar on the counter and give it to Isaac.

"Hey, Linda," he says. "Shalom."

Isaac stretches the arm that ends with the hand holding the biscuit toward Linda. She takes it lightly in her mouth, then carries it to the couch.

I free the roses from the cellophane, pull off the rubber bands, cut off the woody parts of the stems and put them in the vase that was my aunt's, then fill it three-quarters full the way she always told me to.

"These are really pretty. Thank you."

Isaac looks at me strangely.

"Are you okay?"

"Tired, but fine. I'm going to walk the dogs and then I think we should eat something. What do you feel like? I'm hungry. And after that it might be late enough to pick up my car."

"Are you sure?" Isaac moustaches his nose with his index finger right below his nostrils. "Touch your nose."

I touch my nose. It's wet. Then I look at my finger and it's the same color as the roses.

"You're having a nosebleed. Sit down, lean your head forward, then pinch your nose—the soft part, right above your nostrils. I'll get some tissue."

I know the drill from watching Anthony, but I don't mind

hearing Isaac repeat it all to me.

I sit on a stool at the kitchen counter, pinch my nose and lean forward. "You didn't head butt me when I wasn't looking, did you?"

"Not that I remember." Isaac has returned from the bathroom with a box of tissues and stands behind me gently brushing the hair back from my forehead. "Breathe through your mouth and try to relax."

"I can't relax because my nose is bleeding and I'm breathing though my mouth. Why is this happening?"

"Dry air, probably. You need a humidifier in here. Or it could be anxiety or stress."

"Oh."

"Are you stressed about something besides the Adath Tzedek thing, Ascher?"

I look at Linda's face, release my grip on my nose so I can talk to Isaac, but blood drips onto the counter. I pinch my nose again, and Isaac wets a paper towel and cleans my face.

"Keep pinching. It can take fifteen minutes, but it will work."

"This is so embarrassing I can't believe it." I begin to cry and–-because I'm pinching my bleeding nose—it sounds as though I'm crying underwater.

"Please don't cry," Isaac touches my lower back with his fingertips. "There's nothing to be sad about. Today was a very good day, my love."

Part Four

"…Now the fire rises and offers a dozen, singing, deep-red
roses of flame. Then it settles
to quietude, or maybe gratitude, as it feeds
as we all do, as we must, upon the invisible gift:
our purest, sweet necessity: the air."

—Mary Oliver, "Oxygen"

116.

I have been working on my green burials paper and studying for a make-up exam all week and most of today—so I decided to take a break and drive the dogs to an informal dog park in Encino my dental hygienist told me about. I went to the Starbucks drive-through first, and now I sip my iced Grande decaf latte in the warm, purple shade of a big California oak. Freddie devotes his whole small being to surveilling a ground squirrel hole. Linda runs in circles with two beagles—the woman who owns them they said they are lab rescues named Lucy and Ethel. And I think about what Isaac just told me on the phone.

The District Attorney's office is not charging James Adolf Aguilar for placing the explosive device in the Adath Tzekek garbage bin—or for anything else. Isaac said there is no evidence that James did anything but talk. And despite the improvised explosive device in the trash can—they've deemed his livestreamed statements about "taking out the Jewish trash" to be merely figurative and protected by the First Amendment.

The guy in the Voltaire t-shirt—who Isaac and I think probably built, planted and detonated the device—hasn't been located. But Isaac said the police are still going through security videos from the Noho Pooch Emporium lot, the alley and Ring videos from the houses and apartments on La Naranja Way.

Isaac also told me not to get my hopes up.

What's also happening, Isaac said, is that James Adolf Aguilar plans to sue him, the rabbi and the six men who kept him inside his overturned car for false imprisonment, assault, and for vandalizing his vehicle. The hitch is that, when James Adolf Aguilar was asked to provide descriptions, he could only say that his attackers were "fucking Jews."

A GoFundMe for Adath Tzedek raised six thousand dollars in the first three days after the explosion. Then an anonymous donor brought the amount to eighteen thousand. Isaac said the rabbi is confident their insurance will cover repairs and a new roof. Until the repairs are completed, the congregation will meet at a Sephardic synagogue in North Hollywood.

I have no proof and I haven't said anything to Isaac—but I'm sure that James's livestream of the explosion brought thousands of new followers to the Order of Christian Manhood's online channel.

For James and his people, this thing was a probably big win.

Does that mean that it was a loss for us?

I can't help wondering if we should have called the police, warned the congregation of Adath Tzedek to stay away—and stopped right there.

Was it right to set a trap? To confront James?

I think about it, but no matter how I look at this, the answer I arrive at is always yes.

When there's a choice, yes, protect the living.

When you have the opportunity to stand up to bullies and liars and assholes, it's always right to do it.

And though we failed, it was right to try to stop James permanently.

Freddie pushes his nose into the hole and sneezes. I pour some water from my bottle into the plastic bowl I keep in my backpack and as he laps it up, the blinking ground squirrel pops his head out of his burrow.

One reason I didn't know about Isaac's traumatic dog bite is that his beard hides the scar. When he finally told me what happened—a neighbor's sweet-until-that-moment German shepherd went for his five-year-old face as he knelt to pet him as he had many times before, I understood his anger when we argued about Linda after finding her next to L.S. Rutledge. And I remembered that there's a dog bite every seventy-five seconds—a fact I didn't share with him.

Why chill the slight warming I've detected in his feelings toward the dogs? But remembering that reminded me that dogs are animals—and animals—like people are unpredictable.

And I haven't formally said yes to Isaac.

But I haven't said no.

Everything I do and say screams yes or has yes in it.

And despite my reciprocal twin heart emojis—I haven't said "I love you." I don't think I have the right to say that until I finish some things and work out some problems—

Solve Linda's dyed fur and made-up eyebrows problem, and figure out when or if or how to tell Isaac who she really is and how she came to be my dog.

I've turned in the other make-up work, and I still have to finish my paper—but I'm close. I'm calling it, "Green Burial and the Jewish Tradition." And I must open the envelope from the dean of my mortuary science program that's still stuck to the refrigerator.

And there's that other unopened envelope from The Eternal Home Of Peace. But I know what it's about. It's past the time when I should have finished organizing my aunt's unveiling, which I still can't face doing or think about attending.

And that huge, impossible promise I made to L.S. Rutledge?

Somehow, I have to fulfill it.

117.

I take Ventura Boulevard back to Life Space. Since my parents' accident—not accident—obliteration—I've avoided freeways when I can. Hydrated and happily tired-out, the dogs eat their post-park liver treats in the back, so the added-on travel-time won't matter much to them.

And driving sometimes helps me think.

I stop across from Casa De Cadillac and wait for the left-turn signal on Beverly Glen to change. The fierce summer light has burned June's fog and clouds away and pools the hot pavement with mirages. Once I finish the footnotes for the paper, I'll be finished with mortuary science until the end of August when the new semester begins.

What item on my Must-Do-Before-Saying-Yes-To-Isaac list should be next?

I look in the rear-view mirror. Freddie gazes out the window from his elevated seat on Linda's haunch. Linda thinks her own thoughts but—as always—feels my gaze and returns it—her mind-reader's eyes knowing and alert.

The light changes. I consider picking up bagels at Hank's, but I never leave the dogs in the car, and even if I did, it's too hot. And Isaac wouldn't be able to share them.

I have to tell Isaac the truth about Linda.

But what if telling the truth means losing him forever?

And what if he's so disgusted with me that he calls the police?

But I can't keep lying to him and performing sneak applications of Linda's fur dye and makeup. This lie weighed me down from the beginning.

Now it's suffocating—and pulling me away from Isaac.

118.

I hear Isaac enter Life Space as I rinse the shampoo out of Linda's fur with the handheld shower.

I turn off the water and Linda does a fast, full-body shake that drenches me.

"It's me," he says. "I stopped at the Moroccan market on the way. The eggplant looked great so I got some. And wine. And those lamb sausages you like."

"I'm giving Linda a bath and she's giving me a shower, so brace yourself—because one of us is going to look fabulous." Do I sound as fake to him as I do to myself?

I hear the paper grocery bag rustle as Isaac empties it.

"You said 'one,'" Isaac says. "How will the other look?"

"I think the right word is 'drowned.'"

I touch the bath-mat and Linda jumps out of the tub and sits on it. She lets me dry her with a towel, then submits to a few minutes of the dryer being waved over her fur. I spray on some of the conditioner /detangler combo stuff I found at the Noho Pooch Emporium when, as a paper-writing break, I drove to La Naranja Way to see if the repairs had begun at Adath Tzekek. They haven't.

"Linda is good," I tell her as I brush the conditioner through her fur. "Linda is beautiful."

And though a big fat liar said it, that's the complete, undiluted truth.

Linda Lieb—as she is known at the vet—is a damp, patient, smart, obliging and beautiful, unchipped, mixed-breed, spayed, mysterious female dog with intelligent eyes, no eyebrow dots, a feathery tail, and a fine, lustrous, all-black coat who—hoping for a post-bath treat and because she goes where I go—is about to follow me into the kitchen and show her true self to the man I hope will not instantly become my former fiancé.

119.

Isaac speed-slices a plump, taut-skinned eggplant with one of his special knives on the special cutting board he brought here last week. A bottle of red stands cork-less on the counter next to two wine glasses. He wears his Hatzalah clothes and the three large rectangle Band Aids that shield his wound are visible under the rolled-up sleeve of his white shirt.

The bruises on the face he raises above the butterflied aubergine have become pale shadows. His nose has returned to being his beautiful nose.

"You look—um—wet. Fabulously wet, though."

My heart is a panicked bird trapped inside my chest—the ghost of the bird that flew into my parents' moving car. "Is one of those glasses for me?"

Isaac fills both glasses, then steps around the counter and delivers mine to me.

"L'chaim."

"To life."

Isaac kisses me.

Linda decides to sit at my feet.

"I took the dogs to that Encino Dog Park and they got dusty. Especially Freddie, who kept sticking his head down a squirrel hole." My voice sounds chirpy. Horribly chirpy.

Freddie's ears perk up when he hears "squirrel."

"What about Freddie's bath?"

"I didn't want to violate my strict one-dog-bath-per day policy—so I just wiped him down with a wet paper towel when we got back. He hated it."

Isaac looks at Freddie for a second. Just a second. Then he

goes back to looking at me. "Are you hungry? I am. I missed lunch."

"What happened?"

"A six-month-old with febrile seizures and a fractured femur after that."

"Sounds tough."

"I stabilized both," Isaac returns to the cutting board. "I just need to salt the eggplant and sauté it with the rosemary and those cherry tomatoes we got at the farmers' market. Then I'll put the sausages under the broiler."

When will Isaac notice that Linda looks different? Not just different—but that her fur is not the color it was this morning when he left?

Isaac lights the broiler with a wooden match, seasons the eggplant, unwraps the butcher paper enclosing the red sausages and puts them in the cast-iron skillet he uses for meat and slides it under the broiler.

"Wait, won't putting the pan in my broiler make it un-kosher?"

"No. Because you cleaned the stove thoroughly so I could use it."

"Not me, the cleaning service before I moved in. But good," I say, refill my wine glass and watch Linda join Freddie on the couch. He sniffs her clean, black fur and seems to approve of it. Wet she was obsidian. Now, that she's drying, the black has softened to an almost-black slate.

I pour more wine into Isaac's glass.

He'll need it.

120.

The smell of roasting sausages warms the kitchen. Isaac sets two plates on the counter, then places a thick, white paper plate on top of each to keep the meal kosher. "The onions need a minute or two more. We're not quite there." Isaac uses a long wooden spoon to move the eggplant, tomatoes, olive oil, garlic and rosemary mixture around in the stainless-steel pan on the stove.

"It looks like we're there to me—but what do I know?" I chirp, then drink more wine and wait for the catastrophe.

"I think you're right." Isaac spoons a little of the eggplant mixture on my plate straight from the pan he holds with a potholder.

"What do you think?"

The eggplant is garlicky and melt-in-my mouth sweet. The slightly charred and collapsed tomatoes have turned into something much better than tomatoes. "I think what I always think when I eat the food you cook—you're the real deal, Isaac. You have a gift."

"Smush some of the eggplant tomato stuff on the lamb when it's done, and eat it with the pita bread." Isaac smiles as he returns the pan to the stove, and bends to open the oven door.

There's a whoosh and a hollow whomp as the oven seethes orange—then vomits heat and flames and smoke.

And the smoke alarm screams.

121.

The Life Space stinks of burnt hair and charred lamb. The stove and hood are blackened. And the alarm keeps cheeping its fiendish, piercing beeps.

The dogs stopped barking long enough to let me to herd them into the bathroom where they share a fresh, dry bath mat behind the closed door. I put another towel at the bottom to mute the sounds and block the smells.

Isaac sits on the stool—his hands around my waist, his head tilted back and his eyes closed. I press a wet washcloth against his short, white-tipped, singed eyelashes and brows. "When will your eyelashes and eyebrow hair grow back?"

"If the follicles are damaged, never. How does my beard look?"

I apply the washcloth to the bottom of Isaac's beard—now a jagged, yellowish white. "Burned. But the rest's okay. No one will notice if you trim it. Should I put something on your brows? Vaseline? Neosporin?"

"No need. Washing is fine."

"I'm so glad you didn't burn your hands."

"Me, too," Isaac says. "But if I had, it would have been my fault. I should have been careful about using a broiler I'm not familiar with."

"For all I know, this is the first time anyone's used it. I never did, so I couldn't warn you about it." I put the washcloth in the sink, then return to Isaac and trace his brows with my finger. "Do your eyelids hurt?"

Isaac raises his head. "Nothing hurts except the migraine that damn alarm is giving me. I've got to stop it. Is the stepstool still in the coat closet?"

122.

While I took the dogs down to the Dog Park—Isaac opened the window—there's only one per Life Space—removed the battery from the smoke alarm, and disposed of the cast-iron pan—his well-seasoned, broken-in, favorite meat one with the carbonized lamb burned into it—in the downstairs Dumpster.

But Life Space reeks, so the AC is set to icy/breezy. The chill doesn't bother the dogs who have seized my side of the bed to sleep off the excitement—Freddie on my aunt's aromatic sweater and Linda with her back pressed against him.

Isaac and I share his side under the quilt I keep in the closet. My head is on his shoulder. His hand rests on the small of my back. My toes touch his toes. His other hand cups my hand. We're not cold, though, because after we both took off our smoke-and-burned-sausage-infused clothes, we kept them off.

"I was thinking—if the eyebrow-moustache-beard thing bothers you, I have an eyebrow pencil you can use to fill in the discolored or missing spots." I kiss the discolored, missing spots in case he's forgotten where they are.

"Makeup on my eyebrows? I don't think so."

"Why not? Lots of men wear make-up. Even dogs wear make-up now." I glance at Linda as a hint.

"Dogs do not wear makeup."

"There are salons just for dyeing and styling dogs' fur. It's a thing. And not just in Beverly Hills."

"People are insane and they don't have enough to do. There's no reason on earth to dye a dog's fur."

I look at Linda again to give Isaac a non-verbal push.

Linda feels my look and opens her eyes.

Isaac closes his as I kiss his neck and wonder if this is the last time I will, then untangle myself from his embrace. "I was using make-up and dye on Linda every day. Until today." I don't sound chirpy now. I sound dead serious.

"I used dye to make her black fur lighter. And make-up to give her eyebrows like Freddie's—so that her face would look different."

Isaac frowns. "Different from what? Honestly, I have no idea what you're talking about.

"Does she have a skin condition? Are you joking?"

When I lean over to turn on the lamp on the bedside table, I knock Isaac's kippah to the floor. So much for being graceful. Isaac watches me get out of bed, pick it up, put it on the table, turn on the lamp, then switch on the overhead light.

"No joke, Isaac. Please. Just look at her. Really look." I'm shivering.

Isaac leans on his elbow and does what I ask. He looks at Linda and keeps looking.

"That bath you gave her did her a lot of good," he says finally. "She looks great. Almost like a brand-new dog."

123.

I sit cross-legged and cocooned under the quilt.

Isaac—wearing only my robe—paces around the too-small Life Space.

"How can you tell me this when I was right there?" Isaac asks from the kitchen. "When I saw the two Animals Services guys subdue that dog?"

"You saw Linda. Linda is that dog. But she wasn't 'subdued" because she was aggressive, she was afraid. And she panicked when they dragged her out."

Isaac paces the few steps it takes to reach the front door, then the few steps required to arrive at the couch. He sits and presses his fingertips into his forehead.

"And Linda is the dog that was taken from the shelter." I use the passive voice. Does that count as lying?

"Who took her?" Isaac looks at me.

I look at Isaac.

"You took her?"

"Yes."

"With help or by yourself?"

"Alone." I haven't finished saying the word when crying comes out—which multiplies the number of embarrassing cries I've had today.

Isaac shakes his head. "You're crying, Ascher? Shouldn't I be the one crying? I'm the guy who just stuck his head in an oven and caught fire. I'm the guy whose girlfriend—I mean —fiancée—decided that now is the perfect time to mess with him and tell him she engineered a jail break for a killer dog."

"I'm not messing with you—I love you." I realize that in a

certain way I've just said yes. "I loved you before you loved me. And I don't want to lie to someone I love as much as I love you. Especially about something like this."

Isaac abandons the couch, tightens the slippery belt around the slippery velour robe that seems to be able to unknot itself at will. My aunt gave it to me. It's a soft, shell pink, or maybe that fancy color they call "blush," and it has a Bloomingdale's label that always scratches the back of my neck. Isaac tugs it down as he marches back into kitchen. "Isn't now a little late to tell me you were lying to me?"

"I was afraid that you'd have Linda euthanized if I told you. And that you'd hate me."

Isaac contracts his discolored, incomplete eyebrows. "You're saying that the dog I've been sharing a bed with night after night was the dog in Mrs. Rutledge's apartment?"

"Yes."

"The dog that mauled her to death?" Isaac's cheeks darken like plums. "That dog?" Isaac points at Linda.

"Yes. And no. Linda didn't maul L.S. Rutledge to death. She didn't maul anyone. Whoever put her in that apartment wanted to make us think she did and is the one who mauled her. I'm sure of it."

124.

I tighten the quilt around me and wait for what I just told Isaac to percolate from his brain into his heart.

The bubbling of the ice maker in the freezer sounds like a flood.

Linda's soft puffs of breath are loud rasps.

And Freddie releases what must be a record-breaking-for-a-small-dog fart.

"And you should do something about his flatulence. It's outrageous." Isaac doesn't raise his voice, but his words are sharply over-enunciated." And don't tell me, Miss Make-Up for Dogs, that they don't manufacture effective canine simethicone. Because they must."

"The vet says it's his age and his meds, but I'll have her check it out again. I'm sorry Freddie has chronic gassiness. And I'm sorry about the whole thing with Linda."

Isaac runs his fingers through his damaged beard.

"—And I know I maybe shouldn't say this because I'm the huge liar here—but you lied to me, too, Isaac."

Isaac ties the wayward belt again, then crosses his arms and watches Linda sleep.

Then he looks at me.

And he keeps looking—as if he's making a decision. "So, regarding this situation. If what you say is factual, and there's nothing else you need to tell me—"

"It's factual. And you know everything you need to know."

"Okay. Then, if this animal—Linda—didn't attack and kill Mrs. Rutledge, and a you say a different dog didn't—then someone, someone human did. A person is the murderer. And that person is still at large?"

Isaac looks at Linda again. "Am I correct, Ascher, that this the situation we find ourselves in?"

125.

We find ourselves back in the kitchen because in a Life Space—except for the bathroom—that's the only other almost-room we can move to.

I wear the robe now.

Isaac wears my Krakens sweatshirt and his new pair of spare black jeans and gnaws on a pita bread from the open bag on the counter.

And I tell Isaac everything. Almost.

And his cheeks turn plum-colored again only when I tell him about the Halligan tool.

I skip the part about the photos I took of L.S. Rutledge when I was a *shomeret* at Mount Of Olives—and skip sneaking a tiny look at their computer.

Would Isaac understand these transgressions? Would they disturb him? Offend him permanently?

He'd understand—but maybe not at first. He'd know why I needed photos of L.S. Rutledge's wounds to compare to the wounds produced by a dog attack and to wounds inflicted by various sharp objects.

He'd know that I had to be one hundred percent sure.

And I am. I am.

But the images of L.S. Rutledge are private. They belong to her and are only for helping me find her murderer.

When that happens—those images will be expunged.

And—except for my fading memory of them—those pictures will never have existed.

126.

The dogs and I walk around the neighborhood. Linda moves freely without her jacket. And her knowing eyes no longer beneath fake eyebrow-dots seem bigger and more expressive.

Before I finish my green burials paper—proof it, check the footnotes, and re-read the conclusion—I slip on the felt-lined, purple plastic gloves, and unfold the two-week-old *L.A. Times* lying in a pile of them in the lobby. I lay the newsprint sheets on the kitchen floor, then spray the inside of the oven and the blackened outside of the door with a guaranteed no-odor oven cleaner that smells the way I imagine napalm smells. I open the Life Space window, turn on the AC fan to MAX while the dogs doze on the couch and the schmutz-eating foam works its "stupendous" magic in the silent darkness of the oven. Then I throw the dirty kitchen towels in the tower washer and start it.

The smoky, lamby sheets and quilt—which might require a trip to a laundromat—are next. Then I read over the conclusion to my paper—

<u>*Green Burials and Jewish Tradition Ascher Lieb MS 102B 6/23*</u>

<u>*Conclusion*</u>

Jewish cemetery-mortuaries offer traditional and innovative ways to inter and memorialize the dead that, unlike many funerary practices, protect the environment. Returning the body to the earth after death has been Jewish practice for thousands of years, and Islam's death practices have been virtually the same. Jewish practice prohibits exposing the body or altering it. The body is never cremated, posed, embalmed or enhanced with cosmetics or protheses. Before interment, members of a chevra kadisha (a Jewish burial society) ritually bathe and sanctify the body (tahara in Hebrew; taharah in Arabic), the body is shrouded, and placed in an untreated, plain wooden casket constructed without nails or metal fastenings. Jewish tradition elevates the privacy and dignity of the body, and views every soul as equal in death. Men and women are dressed in the same fully-covering, white linen shrouds. This shroud and the always-closed casket protecting the body's dignity will biodegrade completely in the earth along with the purified, unadorned body embarking on its return to dust. These practices have been green since ancient times.

But while green burials are gaining popularity, cremation is still the number-one end-of-life choice in America. Though cremations don't pollute with toxic embalming chemicals, cremation retort chambers create millions of tons of $C0_2$ *emissions every year.*

And traditional in-ground-interments also produce greenhouse gases from their cement slabs. A traditional and specifically- green burial being offered by some Jewish and other cemeteries offers families a solution to the pollution problem and, unlike the dispersal and loss of cremains that often accompanies cremation, offer a fixed interment location: Not a grave designated with an individualized marker—but a more economical for both families and the cemetery/ mortuary option— a communal site that functions as a permanent memorial garden or grove that families can visit as they would a gravesite.

Mortuary, burial and interment practices do not only impact the dead. These practices can pollute the planet with toxic chemicals and accelerate global warming with greenhouse gasses, or they can harmonize with the natural processes of decay and renewal. These practices can impose financial burdens or relieve them. They can strengthen survivors' sense of community and continuity or erode them. And they can unite the mortuary/ cemetery and the grieving families they serve in a shared purpose—saving our planet for future generations.

127.

I check the dryer, but the towels are still damp, and as the coffee machine produces another perfect decaf latte, I can't help feeling sort of good. The paper's not up there with the one I wrote for money about the competing theories explaining Edgar Alan Poe's mysterious death. Or the one about Big Foot.

But I wrote this one for free.

And I wrote it for myself.

I attach the file to the email I already composed and saved—and send it.

And as I do, one of the $C0_2$-spewing cement grave-slabs that's been dragging me down detaches itself from my shoulders and tumbles away.

128.

I won't see Isaac until tomorrow. And after his all-night shift, he'll need to sleep. So I decide to organize my notes, print photos, then maybe later do some more digging into my Los Villas del What the You-Know-What possibles.

But first I take the dogs to NoHo Pooch Pavilion and let Linda pick out a new toy—Freddie hates toys—and let Freddie pick a new halter, and pick up some more dried liver snacks for both of them.

Now both dogs sink into their post-shopping sleeps.

The oven cleaner can specifies that the grease-eating foam must left for a minimum of six hours—or "preferably overnight." It's only been three hours, so I locate my blue Chico's pants and go in the bathroom to pin up my hair.

I've decided to do the digging now and organize my notes later.

129.

I style my hair in a tight chignon, but wear my boots with socks inside for comfort, and because April complimented them. And I wear the blue pants because April likes blue. I put on the horizontal-striped blue and white boat-neck top my aunt bought me because she said it would look "smart" that I never wore because—as she said herself after I put it on—the wide, horizontal stripes "don't do me any favors."

The fabric is weird and it looks like the under-uniform for a defunct airline. But it gives me the sort-of-professional, tried-to-seem-put-together, opposite-of-the-real me look I need.

The guard at the Los Villas del Fairfax Village hands over my bright green parking pass and frowns—at me or at my hideous blouse.

I find a parking space near L.S. Rutledge's apartment. The closed blinds are shut eyes, and the step has been cleared of L.S. Rutledge's bright geraniums. The only indication that L.S. Rutledge once lived here are four small nail holes in the door frame where her mezuzah used to hang.

Has the apartment been rented? Or is Los Villas del Murder Village waiting for one of those post-homicide, biohazard cleaning and sanitizing services to remove and dispose of the carpeting, carpet pad and blinds?

I stroll in the shade thrown by the past-their-prime-blooming Jacarandas to the business office where its long window offers its desk workers a view of my least-favorite parking guard.

The lobby walls are succulent green and the doors—marked "Staff Only" and "Private" —are salmon. One wall has a mural telling the story of Los Villas del Fairfax Village. I won't summarize the whole story—but the highlights include tar pools with mastodons about to step in them, members of the Tongva tribe wearing beaded headbands and holding empty, round baskets, with surprised coyotes—not dire wolves—behind them. And Canter's Deli—its neon sign shining—in the lower, right corner.

I locate the iridescent cloudlet of white hair with April underneath it at a desk near the back of the long room. But when I reach her, I see that April's radiance has dimmed.

Instead of the flowy, electrifying blues she wore at L.S. Rutledge's funeral and at the memorial, April wears a camel blazer that seems to make her sit straighter than must be comfortable with an unadorned white blouse underneath. The face regarding me above the papers fanned out on her dark wood desk is subdued. Her foundation is neutral, her penciled eyebrows are light-brown, her eyeshadow is two pearl-gray smudges, and her nude lipstick is almost invisible.

"I'm Evelyn Mandel from the memorial for L.S. Rutledge? Do you remember me?"

"Refresh my memory, please." April takes off her readers and blinks. I notice that her swingy turquoise earrings are absent, too.

"Is this a bad time? Should I have called you first?"

"Wait," April snaps her French-manicured fingers. "The one who brought that awful cake? I remember you."

"I apologize for the cake." I'm still standing. April is still seated. She hasn't asked me to sit in the chair pushed against her desk. "It was raining and I was late and it was the only cake I could find."

"That was the worst cake I ever tasted. A door stop made of plywood."

"I'm sorry."

"Don't be." April laughs. "It was the only funny thing that happened that day. And I really needed something funny."

"May I sit? I want to look at some apartments in Los Villas, and I remembered that you are a rental agent here."

"By all means sit. But not now. Let me take you on the grand Los Villas del Fairfax Village tour first. I know you'll enjoy it.

Eleanor, isn't it?"

April rises and a sequined, brightly-colored wide, A-line skirt rises with her. The skirt is a nonverbal F-you to her bloodless jacket and all the drab business attire being modeled in this room.

"Wow. What a fun skirt."

"It's vintage," April says, smoothing the pleats. "Hand-painted in Mexico in the fifties. I wore it when I folk danced. Now I just collect them.

I follow the swaying skirt's galloping burros, its ring of sequined, snowy mountains and chain of sequined clouds to lobby and then to the Staff door. "Coffee? Tea? Water? The coffee's pretty good and we have to-go cups. There's a big fancy machine."

130.

I sip my Los Villas pretty-good latte and listen to April's spiel about the pool, the gym, the community room—available for private events, even weddings—and Los Villas del Fairfax's incredibly convenient, walkable location as April chooses a brass key with an artificial flower attached to it with a wire from the ring of keys in her skirt pocket and unlocks the Spanish blue door to La Villa de las Flores. The model apartment is a light-drenched, hardwood-floored model staged with a white couch, wicker chairs, little glass tables, vases stuffed with blue dried flowers and mirrors on the soft white walls. The kitchen is the same as the one I glanced into in L.S. Rutledge's apartment except for its granite countertops and stainless-steel appliances.

April pushes the living room's French doors open—another upgrade that L.S. Rutledge didn't have—and indicates the rectangular lawn shared by other units. "You have your own patio for a grill and a table, or chaise longue, and the lawn area is communal. It's an entertainer's dream, Eleanor. Do you entertain a lot? Do you have pets? This indoor-outdoor set-up is a dream for pets."

"Ellen," I say, then "Yes." But the exactly honest answer to the entertaining question is "never." But I say "yes" because Isaac technically counts as a someone I entertain "a lot." April shows me the downstairs bathroom—small, but with a floor of hexagonal black-and-white tiles, then motions me back to the entry and up the stairs.

As I follow the twinkling skirt, I remember that L.S. Rutledge's apartment—though it didn't have the kitchen upgrades, French doors or wood floors—has the same layout as this one.

I realize, too, that after Isaac came upon L.S. Rutledge dead in her recliner—which was right after we got in—we never thought to go up the stairs that L.S. Rutledge couldn't climb to check the bedrooms.

With a swish of her skirt, April grandly opens the door to the first of the two small bedrooms. "And when the Jacaranda trees are blooming like they are right now—all you can see out this window is purple. It's dreamy, isn't it?"

What if L.S. Rutledge's killer got inside her apartment without L.S. Rutledge knowing—while she slept or showered downstairs—then hid upstairs with Linda until L.S. Rutledge—lulled by her pain medications—slept in her chair—then killed her?

What if her killer was still up there when we arrived? Or left while we were in the living room? Or when I was passed out?

We were panicked. Would we have noticed a person silently descending the stairs we couldn't see from the living room? A shadow behind us in the entry? A shadow disappearing out the door?

131.

Los Villas del Fairfax Village has a café, too. April and I sit at one of its outdoor tables while she extols "La Vida Villas." "What with the café, the gym, the pool, holiday events, daily yoga classes right in the community room, the outdoor spaces, a bank and pharmacy right next door—oh and I almost forgot—the food truck nights—Los Villas has everything except a Costco." April bites off the tail of her croissant. "And if you've got Instacart like I do, you never have to leave."

"Los Villas offers a lot more than my apartment building in the Valley."

April wrinkles her nose. "The Valley? A hellhole."

"Yeah," I say. "But I keep remembering the memorial, and how worried and angry people were about Mrs. Rutledge's murder and the homeless encampment."

April sags inside her dull blazer. "New renters have almost evaporated since the murder. Nothing like a homeless camp close by, and a killer dog that probably came from there to drive potential residents away."

I reach the end of my latte but—to appear ladylike—I do not tip the bottom up to get the last drops. "I'm sorry about that," I say, "but it's hard to blame people for being scared."

"Los Villas saved me after my husband died." April's eyes glisten. "I found friends. A job. And when I got sick with COVID, the Amigos Brigade made sure I had food and got my medications. That's why I got involved with the Residents' Association. I wanted to give back."

April taps her nose with her paper napkin. "Los Villas del Fairfax Village is more than meets the eye, Eleanor. It's a world unto itself. And it's safe."

"But the encampment is so close. You're saying that's not a problem?"

"It's much more dangerous for the homeless people than for us." April pats my hand. "There is virtually no crime inside Los Villas. But I'll admit that we have a few rotten apples."

I don't want to seem too interested in the apples rotting in Los Villas del Fairfax Village—so I tip the cup bottom up and let the last, slow trickle of milk and coffee slide into my mouth. Then I watch the Jacarandas beyond the café patio reply to the breeze with a shower of dreamy petals.

"I think I saw one of the apples at the memorial."

"Just between us, Dean is a pill. A pain in the A. Since his wife died, he attends every residents' association meeting—including outreach and parking." April uses her plastic knife to apply a blob of raspberry jam to the remnant of her pastry.

"I'm a widow, so I get it. Dean's grieving and he's lonely. And he probably feels like he's going a little crazy. But he hit on every female in the association, and now he lurks around on food truck nights looking for any females he's missed."

"Did he hit on you?"

"I was the first. Then he zeroed on the others one by one. Including Linda Rutledge."

"How did that go?"

"She told me she shut him down right away—but nicely. Then they had words. Or he had words with her. He even called her names—said she was a bitch. Can you imagine calling Linda of all people a bitch?

I shake my head to indicate that I cannot imagine this.

"When Dean wants 'yes,' he flat-out refuses to take 'no.' He has to have his way or else."

132.

I'm stuck in the late-afternoon crawl that is northbound Laurel Canyon traffic behind a dusty, black compact with a sign on the roof that says, "ASK ME HOW TO GIVE UP TOILET PAPER FOREVER!"

The rain has greened the hillsides and made the nasturtiums manic. I think about what April said and wonder if Dean's rottenness goes beyond being entitled and overbearing. Did the trophy-hunter devise a clever plan to kill the woman who scorned him? A plan that might also force the removal of the homeless camp he hates?

April was right about a lot of things—one being that Los Villas del Fairfax Village looks like pretty great place to live. And—though I will never admit this to Isaac—living on his side of the hill might be good for me and the dogs.

What's left of the old family house and the memories it contains steady me. But the dogs deserve earth beneath their paws—not sidewalk and fake Dog Park plastic turf.

But where would we go?

The Los Villas kitchen is too small for Isaac. And we can't live together in his place, can we? There isn't enough space for Isaac, me and the dogs, and his catering business. And could Isaac handle being around the dogs full-time?

After my aunt died and I moved out of the house in Goleta I shared with Hans, and I ended up being locked-down in my aunt's elder community apartment—I told myself that losing my aunt and losing Hans permitted me to see that I was meant to be alone, and that —if I could only perfect my alone-ness—it would become my greatest strength and the source of my future happiness.

Then an old woman named Rachael jumped off her balcony and died. And Isaac happened. And the way I feel about him happened. And now we're way past the exchanging heart emojis phase.

The No Toilet Paper car turns onto Lookout Mountain Drive without any pedestrians having galloped alongside the window demanding to know how to go paperless. And none of the cars ahead of the Lexus on the turns—three Range Rovers and a matte black Tesla—has interesting signs on its roof.

Perhaps this is because these are Valley-bound drivers traveling back to their hellhole black farmhouses and trophy-master-bath bidets.

After my aunt died, I volunteered with a Jewish burial society, then decided to get a mortuary science degree. It made sense to choose work that does so much good for people, and that did a lot of good for me.

When I helped to bathe, dress and sanctify the dead—I was bathing, dressing and sanctifying my dead parents and my dead aunt. I was giving them what I couldn't after my parents' accident and cremation, and after I arrived at my aunt's deathbed too late.

133.

Before I work on the possibles and open those envelopes—or at least one of them—the dogs and I travel the twilight-lit, still-sun-warmed Valley sidewalk under an ombré sky. I make sure to stop at every lawn and grassy parkway—but gravel, artificial turf and cement offer the dogs enthralling scents, residues and stuff—a glossy crow feather, a fractured Lemon Head candy I removed from Freddie's jaws, a hair clip with red human hair in it, and an oil-stained paper napkin.

Dean is my Los Villas Suspect Número Uno. I decide to work from him and the others at Las Villas outward to the encampment and—if I can't find any murderer-candidates there—to dig into L.S. Rutledge's life before her time at Los Villas del What the Fuck—which I should stop calling it, because when I do, I insult April.

I like her.

And I keep thinking of topics I could have covered in my paper, but didn't—resomation—A.K.A. alkaline hydrolysis, a process that dissolves the body in pressurized hot, alkali water, ocean burials, and recomposition—which is basically composting.

I didn't include resomation though it doesn't pollute the way cremation does, because it's not burial. And I left out "burials at sea" because they're not burials, either.

I know from experience that the ocean isn't a place—it's a vast nowhere.

Ocean ash-scatterings and urn-droppings-at-sea-remind me of the dismal dispersal of my parents' "cremains" —a word that shouldn't ever have become a word. Composting—"soil transformation" —isn't burial, either—it's like resomation, except that it breaks down the body with heat and chemicals that turn it into "soil."

I know I should keep my feelings separate from mortuary science. And if I make it through and earn my degree—I will have to remove my feelings from mortuary work, too. But I'm not there yet.

I keep checking my email to see if my T.A. has read my paper and posted my grade. She hasn't. And though I got an A minus on my make-up anatomy exam, my semester grade depends on Green Burials—nothing else.

134.

With the lone window open, the AC fan on high, and the hood fan chugging, I finished wiping gobs of brown-black, stinking odorless foam from the interior surfaces of the oven and the oven door. I used up two rolls of paper towels and created and destroyed six rags. Then I declared the oven as clean as it would ever be while I inhabited its Life Space.

The ice machine gurgles to remind me of the envelopes held to the refrigerator door with Sunny Morning Elder Care sunflower magnets with the resident emergency extension number in red Comic Sans across the flowers' seeded disks.

I said I'd do it.

I wriggle from the couch without waking Freddie or Linda. I notice a grease and soot smudge on the refrigerator door I missed—but I ignore it and lift one of the magnets, and catch the freed envelope as it falls. The white one with the dark blue mortuary science symbol—a caduceus with angel wings at the top—in the upper left corner above the return address.

Before I read it, I sit on the bed, open my laptop and check my email for my paper grade—nothing yet.

I wripped the white envelope open and unfold it—

Dear Ms. Ascher Lieb,

Among the most important requirements for completion of an Associate's Degree in Funeral Science or a Bachelor's Degree in Mortuary Science, and the subsequent apprenticeship that will lead to a career as a licensed funerary worker or funeral home director are reliability and consistency. Although your grades have been high, your lab and lecture attendance were inconsistent and unreliable toward the end of the semester according to one of your instructors who has expressed her concerns to us.

The bereaved public depends upon mortuary and funeral service providers to show up whenever they are needed—day or night. This is why it is especially important that funeral and mortuary science students attend class and complete the work they're assigned on time.

Reliability and dependability are required in the profession for which you are in training.

Because your grades are strong and there is still work outstanding which instructors will evaluate, we have decided against placing you under Academic probation for the upcoming semester. However, the Dean asked me to caution you that a student with strong academics who exhibits chaotic attendance and tardy completion of assigned coursework would be wise to engage in serious self-examination and reflection regarding the depth and seriousness of their commitment to a demanding field that requires unflagging consistency.

The following semester will include intense seminars dealing with mortuary management, embalming procedures, reconstruction and prosthetics. You will be expected to pursue this coursework with seriousness and commitment, to complete all required work on time, and to attend all labs and all remote lectures. Any absences must be cleared with and filed with the Dean's office for approval prior to the date of non-attendance.

However, if, after serious reflection, you determine that fulfilling the above requirements will not be possible or desirable for you, or that that a career in the funerary and mortuary field is not right for you at this juncture in your life, please know that the Dean wishes you well in all your future endeavors.

Sincerely,

Ms. N. Marylou Skinner
Assistant to Dr. D. Jameson Blade
Dean of Funerary and Mortuary Studies

Fuck.

135.

"Hi." Isaac stands in the doorway.

I sit on the bathroom floor, the contents of the under-the-sink-cupboard scattered around me.

I stop shaking the empty prescription bottle I just found. "Hi."

"Everything okay?"

"Something upsetting happened."

"I'm sorry," Isaac says. "What?"

I look away from the pill bottle and look at Isaac. His eyes are red. His eyelids sag. He's exhausted.

"I fucked up. Again."

Isaac nods.

"Right now I'm looking for Valium."

"Diazepam is not good for you, Ascher. You know that."

"Yes, I do. But would you prefer that I drink? Smoke? Weed depresses me, so I can't do that."

"Self-administering an increasing dose of diazepam over a long period affected your heart rhythms. A lot of alcohol could have the same effect. And smoking causes lung cancer."

"Got it, show-off."

Isaac pushes the Tampax boxes, tissues and band-aids, two bottles of rubbing alcohol, dog shampoo, human shampoo, window cleaner, the hot water bottle and two cans of non-scratch cleanser out of the way with the toe of his clog.

He bends and kisses my forehead—then extends his hand as if he's inviting me to his magic, diamond cloud-castle in the sky. "Come, my love. Let's figure out how to unfuck whatever this is together."

136.

Isaac holds the letter from the Dean in both hands and frowns as he reads it.

The dogs are still on the couch, their eyes moving from Isaac to me.

I'm still in my oven-cleaning clothes—ripped leggings and a Warner Brothers Studios t-shirt my aunt gave me that's mottled with oven-gunk the color motor oil. My hair has escaped the pony-tail that was half-assed to begin with.

I'm the objective correlative of the mess I've made by behaving as though I am somebody capable of accomplishing a big, good thing.

I wait for Isaac to say something, for my nose to gush again, or for a new, involuntary, humiliating stress-tic to manifest itself. How about a horrible nervous laugh? Or a Freddie-level farting jag?

But nothing happens except Isaac re-folds the letter along the folds it already has, slides the paper back into its envelope, puts it on the table, crosses his arms, and smiles.

"I can see why you're upset, but it's really not that bad. They could have put you on academic probation. But they didn't because you're such a good student. I'm sure you'll do great next semester and they'll forget all this ever happened."

"But I won't forget."

"You will. This is just a bump in the road."

"I'm the bump in the road, Isaac, not 'it.' I'm the problem."

Isaac rubs his eyes. "You're not. Tell me why you missed those classes. And why your paper was late. You had very good reasons, right?"

"It was stuff with Linda. And trying to find out who Mrs.

Rutledge's killer is—because I promised someone that I would."

Isaac stops smiling. "I can see wanting to. But promising? That wasn't wise, Ascher. And unfair. Who would demand such an unreasonable promise from you?"

"Me."

My cell phone vibrates on the table.

Isaac picks it up. "Don't you want to see what this is?"

"I set an alert for new emails because I've been waiting for my T.A. to post my grade. But now I don't want to know."

"For the green burials paper? Can I read it?"

"It's totally boring, Isaac. I can see how exhausted you are. Please, take a long shower and go to bed. I'll take the dogs on a long walk and when we get back—though I'm sick of promises—I promise to keep them and myself quiet so you can sleep."

137.

The walk—our second in a few hours—was a blur. Isaac fell asleep instantly, so I didn't hang around changing my clothes or fixing my hair and I spent most of our trek not making eye contact with the people who passed us on the sidewalk.

And refreshing my email feed.

But the dogs were into it, and walked side by side most of the time. Freddie found an exciting, verboten chicken leg bone that I confiscated, then a lollipop with some green pop still stuck to the top of the chewed, white stick—which I also had to take away.

And though it's still morning, when the lobby doors open and the dogs and I enter the elevator, the interior smells not like waffles and bacon—which is what I expected—but like garlic bread. Steak house garlic bread.

And my neighbor, Mark, still in his helmet and with one of the bicycles he keeps in a lower parking level locked storage area—his recumbent—are already inside. The bike is vertical and propped against the back wall. The red flag that sticks up from the back of the seat to make the bike visible to drivers tickles my face.

Mark glances at the dogs, but settles on staring at my filthy clothes, messed-up hair, and the oven-grease splotch on my left, big toe.

"If you heard the smoke alarm—that was an oven fire in my apartment" I say. "I'm really sorry it if the alarm bothered you."

"You should steam all your food in a bamboo steamer like I do" Mark advises. "I'm all about clean eating with a minimum of heat or flame."

"Couldn't the steamer thing burn, though?" I ask. "Bamboo is flammable, right?"

"Maybe, I guess. Yeah. But it's clean. You're nuking food or destroying the nutrients when you cook in that toxic gas oven."

I do not thank Mark for the heads-up because I'm a hundred percent sure that bamboo burns and that a bamboo steamer will absolutely burn if the water evaporates in the pot below it.

The elevator's ascent slows and Freddie farts. And as the doors open, Mark grasps his flagged recumbent bicycle like a life raft and—despite the women etcetera first rule—and he decides to save himself.

138.

A box of Manischewitz kosher matzo stands the counter next to the open carton of kosher eggs. Isaac is not asleep. He's showered, changed into a fresh black t-shirt and jeans, and stirs something in a new pan on the toxic gas stove.

"Good timing, Ascher. I'm making matzo brei," he says. "And Israeli coffee. I think we both need a solid meal before we get to work figuring things out."

"What things?"

"Everything."

I take the dogs' halters and collars off, and give them each a liver treat. "Since when do you make Israeli coffee?"

"Since I bought us Israeli coffee and a copper coffee pot."

"Do you need help? Or can I change out of my scullery clothes and take a quick shower?"

"I'm always good with you taking off your clothes."

The bathroom floor is clean—Isaac has returned the boxes and other stuff back to the cupboard. I peel off my clothes, ball them up and stuff them in the trash receptacle, turn on the water and make it hot, step into the shower and let my humiliation-tears flow.

139.

I lift a forkful of Isaac's caramelized onion, softened matzo and scrambled egg mixture to my mouth. The onion is deep and sweet, the matzo soft and toasty, and the eggs are tender. The dill on top freshens all of it.

"This is so good. Thank you."

"You're welcome."

We eat our eggs. After I've finished the food on my plate, I taste the thrice-boiled, thick dark, sugared coffee. "What's the spice? I love it."

"Cardamom."

"I feel so much better, Isaac. Your matzo brei is better than Valium."

"Good to know," Isaac says. "I'll stash some in my EMS bag."

"You should make some for me every day. Maybe twice a day."

"Once a day, maybe. Twice, no."

My phone sounds. I leave it in my pocket.

"You're not going to find out your grade? Really?

"Really."

I don't give the dogs any of the leftover matzo brei because of the onions. I give them liver treats instead.

Isaac rinses the pan and the wooden spoon and dries them. "I want to know your grade." Isaac wipes his hands on the dishtowel and crosses his arms across his chest. "Then when your school stuff is settled, we can look for Mrs. Rutledge's killer."

I pull my phone from my pocket, open the email from my T.A., and click on the link that takes me to a spreadsheet. I look for the L's, and there it is—

> *Lieb, Ascher. Spring 2023 Funeral and Mortuary Perspectives, A. McMahon MS 102B. 3.667*

"Three point six, six, seven."

"Is that a B or an A?"

"I got an A minus, Isaac. I'm okay."

140.

I scratch Freddie behind his ears, then point to the document open on my laptop. “The column headers are for the suspects I have so far. Dean is first. Then Anthony, Gary, Kris, Jan and ‘others.’”

Isaac nurses his second coffee. “I remember Dean.”

I told Isaac about Dean when I told him about attending the Los Villas memorial for L.S. Rutledge—though I left out the part about saying I was Pauline Mandel A.K.A. Ellen Nadel. “The cells in Dean’s column are ‘hunting,’ ‘anger,’ “felt dissed/rejected by LSR’ ‘encampment rage,” ‘arrogant,’ and sexist.’”

“Okay.”

“The next is Gary—the topiary guy. I don’t have much under his header except ‘garden tools stolen, ‘cutting shears. But I have a weird feeling about him.”

“What kind of feeling? Fear?”

“Not fear. Just that he’s a little bit fake.”

“Now here’s our friend, Anthony. For him we have ‘lying,’ ‘knew her,’ ‘where is he?’, ‘check encampment,’ ‘violent,’ and’ ‘said LSR was allergic to dogs” —how do we check that, Isaac? Aren’t Mrs. Rutledge’s medical records inaccessible. I read that HIPPA protects them for fifty years after death, right?”

“I think so.” Isaac sips his coffee. “But there may be a way. I can ask someone I know for a favor.”

“Which someone?”

“Sarah. You don’t know her.

“What does the Sarah I don’t know do?”

“She’s a mortuary tech at Mount Of Olives. We dated—briefly.”

141.

"I met your Sarah when I was at Mount of Olives for Mrs. Rutledge. I don't want to be rude, but she was kind of bitchy to me."

"She's not 'my' Sarah and she's like that to everyone," Isaac smiles. "She's good at heart—"

Isaac says almost everyone is good at heart.

"—But she's judgmental about a lot of things."

"Like what? I'm curious to know what about you she felt she had to judge."

"Why are we talking about Sarah? Don't tell me you're jealous, Ascher."

"Okay, I won't tell you even though I am. Your Sarah was very proprietary about you. And she made it clear that she looked down on me."

"That's what I mean," Isaac says. "And, since you're so interested—in the middle of our second date, Sarah informed me that I wasn't good enough or Jewish enough for her."

"You?" I laugh out loud. "So why would Sarah do you a favor?"

"Because she likes to feel important. And asking her for information only she can give will feed her ego."

Sarah sounds like she'd be a perfect soulmate for Hans. "When will you ask?"

"In a few hours." Isaac kisses me. "She works the noon to midnight shift. I want to call when she's at Mount of Olives and has the files right there."

"Very smart," I kiss Isaac back. "One of the many things I love about you is that you're the opposite of Hans."

“One of the many things I love about you,” Isaac says, “is that you’re you.”

142.

"I'm making two more columns," I say as I type, "so please stop nuzzling my neck and look." I point to "ENCAMPMENT CONNECTION TO L.S.R.," and "SPOUSES, PARTNERS, ROOMMATES?"

"What does 'encampment connection' mean?"

"It's for the people at the memorial who seemed fixated on the encampment, and who were angry about it before the murder." I say, then type "Did any accompany L.S. Rutledge on her visits? Go on their own?" in the first cell.

"Why would any of them go there on their own? What for? Especially if they were so afraid of it and thought the murderer came from there?"

"I don't know. To look for their stolen stuff?"

"Maybe."

"Or to follow Mrs. Rutledge there—"

"—to see what she was doing?"

"The "OTHERS" column I already had is for people who were angry or upset at the Memorial, or who said things that contradicted what other people said. Kris seemed concerned about L.S. Rutledge and said she was interested in his dog and loved dogs. But Anthony told us she'd said she was allergic to dogs."

"So, this Kris—do you think he was lying?"

"Why would he? He's very into his dog. Very proud of it. That could explain what he said."

"Okay. And who's Jan?"

"She's a tax lawyer who insisted a homeless person killed Mrs. Rutledge. She also said she chatted with L.S. Rutledge every day, but she was really vague about her. And she said she was shy. But, how can a person who visits a homeless encampment by herself be shy? Do you think L.S. Rutledge was shy?"

"No," Isaac says. "She was warm, confident. Not an extrovert, but open and interested in people. I wouldn't describe Mrs. Rutledge as shy."

"Okay. And this cell is for anyone whose beef against the encampment or L.S. Rutledge had to do with a loved one or a friend. So far, the person who might qualify is George, Chris's husband. Though I don't know why—yet." "

"Nice job, Ascher."

"Not really," I say. "Where do we go from here? We can't go door-to-door in Los Villas and interrogate people. I mean who are we to ask anyone questions?"

"I don't know yet. So, let's call Sarah."

143.

Isaac throws me a quick wave before pushing the buzzer, then enters the front entrance to The Mount Of Olives Chapel And Mortuary—Park In Rear. I watch him disappear from my perch in the front of the ambulance he parked in a red zone in front of a new kosher sushi place across Pico Boulevard and I'm worried.

Isaac suggested that the in-person meeting that Sarah demanded would be more productive if I didn't accompany him. But I worry that he's too nice to finagle Sarah into telling him what—if anything—L.S. Rutledge was allergic to, and that he will forget to ask if she was also allergic to cats, feathers, or guinea pigs—whose skin sheds the same dander protein as dogs.

Staring at the impassive exterior of the Mount Of Olives Chapel And Mortuary revives the memory of Sarah's tampon-flushing insinuation and her declaration that all the snacks in the lounge were off limits to me. Those two things and the fact that I don't have any coffee with me doesn't make me less worried. What if Sarah decides she likes Isaac all over again and approves of what he does, and she becomes a Jewish Goldilocks who decides that Isaac is just right after all?

I watch the people entering and leaving the sushi place or stare at the faded-to-orange, blown-up photos of tuna sashimi and salmon rolls in the window.

My phone vibrates.

> sarah wants to say hi just lock the doors come around the back ❤ ❤
>
> please no I dont want to

that is childish im asking u do u want the info sarahs waiting ❤️ ❤️ ❤️

144.

I want the info and I can't refuse my three-heart-emoji fiancé, but I can passive-aggressively make Sarah wait for me.

And when my plodding delivers me to the buzzer, I press it as I am required to do.

Sarah and Isaac appear behind the veil that is the steel security door that now has a sign taped to it that says "NO SUSHI PARKING." "Archer, so good to see you again." Sarah wears peachy lipstick and peachy blush and a dark green pantsuit that sort of matches her eye color. Her mask is pushed down around her neck and she has a manilla envelope tucked under one green armpit.

Isaac wears an N95 and so do I.

I enter the hallway that I remember has a door to the bathroom with iffy plumbing and another marked "Biohazard," and I receive a big welcome hug from Isaac as if I've been lost at sea and a freak wave just spit me out in the rear of this very mortuary. "Ascher."

Sarah drops a professional, "May your dead loved one's memory be a blessing" smile on me. "And Mazel tov. Congratulations on your and Izzie's engagement."

Isn't "your and Izzie's" wrong? Shouldn't it be "your engagement to Isaac"? Or just "your engagement"?

"Thank you," I say. "We're both stoked."

Isaac—who's probably never said "stoked" looks at me, the fiancée who hasn't yet said yes to him out loud.

But that Sarah knows about our engagement—what a formal word—makes it real. And because she knows, our one chance to have made it real with a person or persons we care about has been officially used up.

"Let's go in the lounge," Sarah removes the envelope from her armpit and brandishes it. "It's warmer in there and we can have coffee and munch on snacks while we chat."

Now she invites me to munch on snacks? I resolve to refuse any and all foodstuffs Sarah offers except coffee.

As we follow Sarah to the lounge, we pass the closed door to the decedent's room, and its piercing cold migrates through me.

Is this chill a memory—or a new iciness?

145.

The lounge is warm. I guess the right word is "hot" or "stifling," so Isaac and I remove our masks as Sarah places the envelope on the table and removes her latex gloves and reveals her hands. The fingers that press a kosher Peet's coffee pod into the Keurig machine are freshly-French-manicured, and the fat-around-the-middle marquise diamond embedded in her pavé platinum engagement ring flashes at us like a death star.

"What a beautiful ring." What else can I say? Isn't forcing lavish compliments out of people what jewelry like Sarah's ring is for?

Sarah is all smug smile—a regular Cheshire Cat. "It was my fiancé Zack's great-grandmother's stone, but he had the jeweler design an updated setting."

"Mazel tov," Isaac says. "Zack Zeidenberg?"

"That's my Zack." The machine hums and Sarah watches the stream of scalding brew fill the cardboard cup. "You don't take creamer, right Izzie?"

"I don't usually, but Ascher does."

Sarah places the cup of coffee on the table in front of me, then counts out two Lilliputian caramel-flavored creamers from a Tupperware thing full-to-the top with the no-refrigeration-needed mini-cups. "All we have right now is hazelnut and caramel."

"Thanks," I smile back. "But could I please have three hazelnuts?" I don't care if Sarah judges my excess creamer-use. Maybe I'm hoping that she does.

Sarah gives me the hazelnut creamers, returns the caramels to the airtight container, repeats the ring-dazzling gesture, makes pod coffees for Isaac and for herself, then unlocks a locked cupboard with a key on a jangly keyring and produces a red plastic basket of single-serve packets of *parve* snacks—peanut puffs, popcorn crackers, and vanilla macaroons.

Sarah places the basket in front of Isaac, and as she takes her seat, her corneas glitter like the Zeidenberg Rock. "Zack was recently ordained," Sarah says. "He's been hired as assistant rabbi in a conservative congregation in a new gated golf community with a man-made lake in the west Valley."

"That's wonderful." Isaac rips a pouch of puffs asunder and begins to munch.

I love those peanut puffs, but I won't consume even one in front of Sarah. Sarah doesn't eat, either. She must be slimming down for her dazzling, gated, golf-themed-with-lake, Jewish-enough wedding dress.

"So," Sarah produces that brief death-smile again, then touches the envelope with a perfect finger. "I am doing this for you Izzie, because of our past friendship."

Do two dates equal a friendship? Well, it depends on what happened on those dates, doesn't it?

"And, of course I'm doing this for you, too, Archer, and because the circumstances around Leah's passing were so terrible."

"They were," Isaac says.

"I will never forget the wounds that poor woman suffered," Sarah says.

I won't, either. And I realize that for the rest of my life, I will share this awful knowledge with someone I do not trust and in whom I have so far detected zero empathy. But I don't need Sarah's empathy. If Mrs. Rutledge received it—good. And, though I don't like thinking it, Sarah's heart might be kinder than I thought.

"After the chevra kadisha collected Leah's blood, they gave us four gallon bags of bloody paint chips." Sarah shakes her head.

"So, if sharing a small bit of information might help you in some way—"Sarah's eyes and ring sparkle in Isaac's direction—"I'm happy to. Especially because I know I can completely trust you, Isaac, to be discreet."

146.

Nothing icy passes through me. We sit in warm *parve* light at a table outside the new kosher sushi place across the street from Mount Of Olives as a pot of green tea steams between us.

"We can cross Anthony off the list," Isaac says.

"It's sad that he told the truth, but he's the one on the run."

"No one can do anything about the Order of Christian Manhood until it can be proven that they directly incited violence. The Pico-Robertson attack showed that distributing flyers that inspired someone to shoot two Jewish people wasn't enough to charge them with anything."

"Each time they do something hateful without consequences, they look powerful. And the people they target look weak."

Isaac splits a pair of conjoined chopsticks. "They're cowards. And we're not weak. And after Adath Tzedek, the Order of Christian Manhood knows we're strong. And now we know something for sure—L.S. Rutledge didn't invite a dog or anyone with a dog into her apartment."

The waiter delivers the extra wasabi I asked for with the plates of lox nigiri, tamagoyaki, spicy tuna roll, and kappa maki.

"So, it's Jan and Kris who lied or got things wrong." I dip my tamagoyaki in grated daikon and soy sauce and take a bite. "Kris said L.S. Rutledge loved dogs. And Jan gave the impression that she was shy. I have to find a way to find out why."

"Not on your own." Isaac fills my cup with the perfumy celadon tea, then pops a slice of tuna roll in his mouth. "You're not confronting possible murderers without me."

"I never said 'confront them.' I just have to think of some way to seem to run into them by accident and chat in a friendly way.

If I could think of a good reason to be at Los Villas, I might be able to press them a little. I'm a good bullshitter."

"I've noticed."

I add more wasabi to the soy sauce before dipping my tuna roll slice. "I wasn't born charming like you—so I learned to do the next-best thing."

"I wasn't criticizing. I was stating a fact. And you use your gift for invention for peaceful purposes, right?"

I think of all the plagiarizing I did to prove something to myself and for money I didn't need and wince. "Most of the time. But what about Dean? He's the one I keep going back to––and his guns and his love of hunting. We know Dean's comfortable with blood and violence."

"Leave Dean to me," Isaac says. "Please stay away from him. Promise."

"Okay I promise not to piss him off unless you're with me. Can I ask you something?"

Isaac nods.

"How does Sarah know you're discreet?"

"I have no idea."

"Well, what things does she know you've been discreet about?"

"Stop it, Ascher. If you're asking if we had sex—the answer is no. Now am I supposed to ask you how many times you and Hans had sex? Is that how you want this to go?"

"No. And I regret every minute I spent with Hans. But the way Sarah talks to you drives me nuts."

Isaac reaches across the table and takes my hand. "Sarah will talk the way she wants. And because you intimidate her, she will insinuate things to make you squirm. I wish her and Zack happiness, and I'm grateful for the favor she did for us. But that's it when it comes to me and Sarah. Got it?"

"Got it."

Isaac releases my hand, picks up his chopsticks, lifts an oval of lox nigiri to his mouth and chews it. "Sarah doesn't understand me at all and she didn't try to. She disapproves of everything about me because I'm not a rabbi, a doctor, or a lawyer. She doesn't even like me."

"I like you. And I approve of you, and the more I understand about you, the more I love you."

Isaac leans close to me and kisses my forehead. "Thank you. I'm stoked about you, too, Archer."

147.

Isaac left Life Space after his morning prayers while the dogs still slept and I was barely awake.

There's a lot of stuff to do. The plan is for me to meet him at noon.

I fed the dogs, gave Freddie his meds, brushed Linda—which she loves—and walked the dogs to the Dog Park and around the block before I showered. Then I made a mega-caffeinated latte and deleted Anthony from the possibles list.

Now I smooth the last two unfolded deep blue Blue Matzo t-shirts and sweatshirts into neat, flat squares, and add them to the tidy piles I've already stacked on the Costco table. I straighten Isaac's "Blue Matzo, Kosher New-Mexican Mexican Food" business cards that I've already fanned out and straightened near the shirts. Isaac won't unpack the paper plates, utensils or the samples of roasted corn and jicama and pepita slaw, blue corn, green chile and kosher cotija quesadillas, or the sopapilla batter he has packed in the coolers under the table until later when he'll fry the sopapillas and heat the food on the battery-operated hotplate I set up at the other end of the table.

I can see Isaac's just-washed, shiny ambulance parked along the edge of the long, oval, grassy Jacaranda-shaded lawn behind the Room de Communidad and the Café. I've been watching Isaac at the Hatzalah of L.A. table handing out business cards, taking people's blood pressure and explaining the emergency services Hatzalah provides for the community. Just beyond the Hatzalah table are tables belonging to other community and Los Villas groups—Chabad, City Senior Services, Beit Chai, the Page Museum, the California African American Museum, The

California Science Center, the L.A. Department of Public Health, the L.A. County Museum of Art, L.A. Fire and Rescue, the Los Villas Residents' Association, the Amigos Brigade, Los Villas Yoga Dias and three tables displaying Artes and Craftes for sale.

Children bounce inside an inflated castle at the other end of the lawn and explore a parked police car with its doors flung open. People buy sno-cones, churros, and hot dogs from food trucks while watching the mariachi band play behind a sign marked "STAGE." The festival brochure the sullen parking guard gave me also promises a Villager talent show and a dog beauty contest later on.

Why am I so sure Kris's bow-tied corgi will be the winner?

Linda becomes more beautiful each day. Maybe she likes not wearing clothes or makeup or she feels the absence of my fear that she'd be taken away.

She feels loved and free.

As for Freddie—he's always been beautiful to me.

When I first arrived here at the Los Villas Del Fairfax Villages Fiesta de Communidad—I glimpsed April—clipboard in one hand and a bullhorn in the other—flashing around like a Morpho butterfly in a new, electrifying ensemble. I haven't spoken to her yet because I've been folding and refolding t-shirts and sweatshirts at the Blue Matzo table where I hope to run into or spy Kris, Dean, Gary and other Villagers from the Memorial with whom I want to chat.

And yes, I remember what I promised Isaac. So I man this post as lookout only. Isaac and I agreed that if I encountered any possibles except Dean, I would talk with them in the open where Isaac can see me.

As I scan faces, I think about the paper on the Morpho butterfly I wrote for someone in boarding school. It was my first thrill-plagiarism for money. The butterfly's three-week lifespan, the pairs of open-eye-markings that peer from the dusty, drab surface of its ventral wings, and the shimmer of its splendid, refractive, metallic-blue-scaled outer wings stunned me.

What is the meaning of a life one hundred and fifteen often

airborne and luminescing days short?

What did my aunt's long and my parents' truncated lives mean?

The Hatzalah ambulance's siren wails. I see Isaac sitting inside with three laughing little kids.

Isaac waves.

I wave back.

Being is its own meaning, I guess—and its own mystery.

148.

I was right about something—Kris's corgi won the dog beauty contest and he received the prize of a donated Mid-City Pooch Pavilion gift certificate.

And I was—of course—wrong about something. The Jacarandas are already throwing down long, blue shadows, and I still have not encountered any possibles except the woman with rhubarb-colored braids who had the anti-homeless encampment petition.

And the day I was sure was summery has turned cold.

Now that his Hatzalah shifts are over, Isaac runs the Blue Matzo table where the sopapillas and honey, pepita slaw and the quesadillas are hits. And I am finally free to roam the festival in my new, creased-from-relentless-foldings Blue Matzo sweatshirt. I skip the museum tables, skip the churros, and head for the Artes and Craftes area.

Gary sits behind a table displaying houseplants and succulents growing out of Villager-crafted pots in bright Villas colors. I pick up a pot painted orange and blue that holds a plant with long shiny green and pink-striped leaves. "What kind of plant is this? It's so pretty."

"That's a Stromanthe Triostar, a tri-colored prayer plant."

"It looks delicate. I'm afraid I'd kill it."

"As long as you don't overwater or leave it out in direct sunlight, I don't think you could kill it if you wanted to," Gary smiles. "It looks fancy, but it's almost indestructible."

"Why is it called prayer plant?"

Gary presses his hands together, then bows and raises his head. "It raises and lowers its leaves to follow the light—like praying hands."

"Sold," I say. "How much?"

"Ten bucks. But you can always donate more. All the money goes to Los Villas Amigos Brigade. It's our group that helps neighbors in need."

I give Gary a ten and a five. "Can I pick it up later?"

"Sure," Gary says. "You made a great choice. Just give me your name."

What name should I use? Not mine. Not my aunt's. And certainly not Archer Kahn.

"Sarah Zeidenberg," I say. "You can just write 'Sarah Z.'"

"Sarah Z it is," Gary writes my alias on a piece of masking tape, sticks it on the prayer plant's pot, then adds a sticker that says "SOLD."

"Where I live the tenants barely speak to each other. How do you get your neighbors' Brigade to work?"

"We gather a team of neighbors to visit, pick up prescriptions and provide meals for residents who are sick, experience a loss, or are in crisis. Once they start, people discover that they really enjoy it."

"That's great. And you're in the Brigade?"

"I am," Gary says. "It's been great, though the last neighbor we pitched in for died suddenly. But before she did, a team of three of us were visiting her, getting her medications and bringing food every day. She was in the Brigade herself. Before everything happened of course."

"I'm sorry for your loss."

"We all are," Gary says.

"If I wanted to start a group like this at my own apartment building, how would it work with a neighbor who becomes bedridden? Do you assign someone to stay with them?"

"No. For a lot of reasons we can't ask residents to provide overnight care. We just arrange more frequent visits and give the team keys so they can let themselves in day or night if the resident needs them. That system has worked very well so far."

149.

The last word in Gary's sentence—"far" —hasn't ceased sounding when the fat fingers of a big hand tighten around the hair tie at the top of my pony tail. Then another big hand grabs my arm.

"Is this man conning you into purchasing these grossly overpriced weeds, young lady?" The male voice that belongs to the body whose hands are gripping me booms into the back of my head. "Because if he is, consider yourself rescued."

"Hey, you're pulling my hair. Stop."

"Am I?" The hand squeezing my ponytail relaxes, but not the hand on my arm. "When I see a shapely and beautiful young woman in distress, I immediately snap into action."

"I wasn't in distress until you showed up," I say. "Don't touch me."

"Back off, Dean." Gary says. "She's fine."

"Well, that is delightful news." Dean pulls my arm and the rest of me around until I'm facing him. His big, face is sun-reddened except for pale sunglass-ovals around his eyes. He's dressed in sharply-creased khaki pants and shirt, and a camouflage-fabric, brimmed hat.

I look past the hat at the Blue Matzo table across the lawn hoping to summon Isaac. But he's serving food and chatting with the gaggle of people waiting to be fed and not looking in my direction.

Dean releases my arm. "I'm Dean Stockhauser. And you are?"

"She's not interested, Dean." Gary is up and walking around the table toward us.

"Why don't you go back to the vandalism you call gardening

and steal some more of your own garden tools for attention?"

Gary reddens—especially his forehead. "Sarah, please let me escort you wherever you need to go."

"You're not escorting anyone, Gary. You can't leave all your little plant friends unattended or the Big Bad Blue Witch will put a hex on you. But, thanks for the introduction." Dean reattaches his hand to my arm and pulls me forward. "I'll escort the young lady to the food trucks."

I seize the pot with my paid-for praying hands in it and shove it into the side of Dean's smug, two-toned face.

150.

Ceramic shards, potting soil and the wrecked leaves of the indestructible praying plant litter the grass. Gary's facial redness has deepened. Dean's weird hat is gone and a thin horizontal cut reddens his hairline as Isaac and one of his Hatzalah colleagues––Shmuel, I think his name is—-armpit-drag Dean toward police officers waving next to the police car that had its doors open. As Isaac and Shmuel drag Dean across the lawn, one of Dean's brown leather loafers catches on a sprinkler that muddies his apple red sock. Then the other loafer comes loose.

April has her arm around me as she walks me to a camp chair in front of one of the other Artes and Craftes tables—one laden with dream catchers. "Sit, Ellen. Sit down right here, honey."

I sit down right there and watch Isaac and Shmuel hand-off Dean to the uniformed officers. One of the officers unpins his radio from his shoulder and holds it near his mouth. A siren sounds somewhere and gets louder until a police car with its lights on drives over the curb, onto the grass and advances until its hood is almost touching Dean's grass-stained khakis.

"What's wrong with him?" I ask April.

"Grief, I think," April says. "Dean is a desperately lonely man who's angry that he lost the love of his life."

"He was hurting me. Squeezing my arm and pulling my hair and pushing me. Do you think he killed Linda Rutledge? Because now I'm beginning to. You said he was angry with her."

"I've thought about that a few times, but I don't know." April says. "I've seen him be patient and kind more times than I've seen him be angry or rude. And I saw how he cared for his dying wife."

The police car with Dean in it backs over the lawn and over the curb, fires up its lights and sirens and the officer in the passenger seat waves at Isaac and Shmuel.

Gary shows up with churros on a paper plate, a hot dog wrapped in foil, a paper napkin that a gust of air blows away, and a bottle of water. "Are you okay?"

"I'm fine, thank you. And thanks for the food." I put the food on the table and take a few swallows of the cold water. Then I shiver.

"You're shivering," April says. "You're in shock."

"I'm not in shock. I'm just cold because I'm sitting here out in the cold. If I get up and walk around, I'm sure I'll warm up."

"Just wait. Please. Don't walk anywhere. I promised that nice, handsome man over there—" April points at Isaac who is talking to different uniformed LAPD officer— "that I'd stay with you until he came back. Is he your boyfriend?"

"My fiancé."

"Congratulations, honey. But I have to go get something. And you have to stay put until I do. Please. You have to."

151.

Isaac stands behind the camp chair I'm still sitting in as April requested and he strokes my hair. "Tell me why you're stuck sitting here again?"

"Because I promised April I would. And don't ask me why, but if she calls me Ellen or Eleanor, just play along."

"That other guy called you 'Sarah' and said something about you having a houseplant that prays. I assume I'm not supposed to ask about those things, either?"

"You assumed right." A blue haze emerges from behind the food trucks with a human figure next to it.

"I just want to get out of here as soon as we can. I don't have to talk to the police, do I?"

"That guy who called you Sarah talked to them. And I did too. So, I don't think so—unless you want to press charges."

"I'm not sure. But I'm leaning toward no."

The blue nimbus is April. The person with her is Jan, the tax lawyer. Jan carries something rectangular wrapped in white paper and shiny plastic.

The long gauzy blue sleeves of April's blouse flutter as she arrives. "Thank you for waiting, Ellen. There's something all the members of the Los Villas del Fairfax Village Amigos Brigade want me to tell you, and there's something they want you to have."

Jan pats my arm. "We're all so sorry about what happened with Dean. And we wanted to present you with something as our gift." Jan places the white thing wrapped in plastic on my lap.

"Thank you very much," I say. "But you guys don't need give me anything."

"Oh yes we do," April says. "Dean was horrible. But let's not dwell on that now. Open your gift. It might help you stop shivering."

152.

I pull off the plastic, rip open the white butcher paper and unfold a bright–even–in–the- diminishing-light, white and sparkly blue crocheted blanket with a Star of David in the center—a blanket larger than—but with the same design and made with same metallic-flecked yarn as the Star of David blanket that covered L.S. Rutledge's body bag in the decedent's room at Mount Of Olives Mortuary.

"I'm speechless." I say and try to process the meaning of the object on my lap. "It's incredible. So soft. So beautiful. And so warm. Thank you so, so much."

Jan smiles. Gary smiles. Isaac stands behind the chair, so I can't see what he's doing with his face.

"It is gorgeous, isn't it?" April says. "Jan makes these blankets in different sizes to raise money for a wonderful addiction rehab organization she volunteers with. And after I told her what happened, she was more than happy to present one of them to you."

153.

Isaac holds the ambulance door open for me and I climb in still shivering though I press Jan's blanket close with my free, cold hand. I fasten my seatbelt, put the folded blanket on my lap, and wait to speak until Isaac is belted in and the ambulance has made the turn out of Los Villas del Fairfax Village and is moving up 6th Street.

"I have to talk to Sarah. Now. Can you help me do that?

"What do you mean 'now'"?

"Like right away. Immediately. As soon as possible. In person. You said she works the noon-to-midnight shift, right? So, she should be there, right?."

"She should be there, yes. But I don't get it. Why right now?

"If you're not on board with this, Isaac, just drop me at that corner and I'll take a Lyft."

"What about the dogs?"

"They'll have to wait for a little while longer for me to get back. Especially if you keep stretching this out."

"I'll take you. Should I turn on the heater? You're shivering." Isaac makes the turn that takes us toward Mount of Olives and away from Partridge Place.

"Thanks," I say shivering—not because I'm cold—but because I'm afraid.

"I honestly have no idea what's happening, Ascher."

I look through the passenger window at the darkening blue-corn-blue shadows filling the empty places between sky and ground. "I'm sorry, Isaac. In a little while—if Sarah's in a helpful mood— we'll know everything.

154.

Isaac presses the Mount of Olives buzzer before I can finish telling him why right now isn't a good time for me to explain why the plant guy called me Sarah, April called me Ellen, or why a plant that lifts leaves in prayer throughout the changing light of day belonged to me before I smashed it against Dean Stockhauser's head.

Sarah opens the security door, her N95 around her neck, a blue plastic apron over another pantsuit—mauve, this time—a huge, limp triangle of pizza with a bite where the tip should be in her hand, and a pizza-sauce-colored smear running from the corner of her mouth to the middle of her cheek.

"Come in," Sarah addresses Isaac—not me. "But I don't have a lot of time for you."

"We understand," Isaac looks at me, "This won't take long. Right, Ascher?"

"It shouldn't," I say. "I just need answers to a couple questions. Is there somewhere private where we can talk?"

"Two of my staff are on break in the lounge right now. So, let's use the decedent's room."

155.

The long table upon which L.S. Rutledge rested inside her blanketed body bag is bare, but I can see her there. The awful loveseat is not the thing I want to be sitting with Isaac on, and the death-perfumed, deodorized air is not the air I want to be breathing as I wait for iciness to strike me. So, when Isaac puts his warm, living arm around my shoulder, I'm grateful.

Sarah—sans pizza slice but with the sauce smudge still on her cheek—slides in a wheeled office chair from the morgue next door, closes the door, lowers herself into the chair, smooths her apron, folds her hands in her lap and looks at me.

Her ring doesn't glitter as brightly in here as it did in the lounge. Weird.

"Thanks for doing this, Sarah. We really, really appreciate it," I say. Then I stand, unfold the blanket Jan made with the star facing Sarah. "When I was here with Mrs. Rutledge, a blanket exactly like this one—but smaller—had been placed over her body bag."

Sarah nods.

"Where did Mount of Olives get that blanket, Sarah? Did you buy them from an addiction-support nonprofit? Or somewhere else?"

Isaac's eyes widen under his abridged lashes and incomplete eyebrows.

Sarah is annoyed. "I don't know why something trivial like a blanket is important, Archer—"

"It is important, Sarah, trust me."

"It is," Isaac says.

"All right. I don't know the nonprofit you're talking about.

That blanket was the only one. Someone left it on the back step shortly after we received Mrs. Rutledge's body from the coroner. It was wrapped in white paper and plastic and there was a note."

"Do you still have the note?" Isaac asks.

"I threw it away. But I remember generally what it said." Sarah looks at her ring and touches her cuticle. I guess she's going to make us beg.

"Can you tell us what the note said?"

"For Linda Rutledge. Or For Mrs. Rutledge—I don't remember. Then parts of the *Al Chet* were copied in English underneath her name."

"Copied by hand?" Isaac asks.

"No. The whole thing was typed and printed on regular computer paper." Sarah says. "And then the writer asked that the blanket be placed with Mrs. Rutledge in the *aron.*"

I know that *aron* means casket—but not the rest. "What is the *Al Chet*?" I ask Isaac.

As Sarah pushes a stray hair behind her ear, her finger grazes her cheek and discovers the dry sauce stain, and the irritated smirk she wore since we got here disappears.

"It's a confession of various sins recited during Yom Kippur services," Isaac explains. "'For the sin which we have committed before You under duress or willingly. And for the sin which we have committed before You by hard-heartedness. For the sin which we have committed before You inadvertently. And for the sin which we have committed before You with an utterance of the lips. For the sin which we have committed before You with immorality. And for the sin which we have committed before You openly or secretly. For the sin which we have committed before You with knowledge and with deceit.' And it goes on like that with more sins until the end: 'For all these, God of pardon, pardon us, forgive us, atone for us."

"I'm confused. The person who left this was confessing sins–—but not just his own?"

"Well, the congregation recites this as a group. So, it's 'we,' not 'I,'" Isaac says.

"What did you do with the blanket?"

"It couldn't be placed in the *aron*," Sarah's elbow rests on the desk chair's arm, her hand cupping her chin and her palm covering her cheek. "As you know, nothing is permitted except soil from Jerusalem or a man's tallit. So, when a woman who works here asked if she could take it, I said she could. She has a one-month-old, and it was the perfect for a crib."

156.

From the ambulance parked in the rear of Mount of Olives, Isaac called a friend he used to work with in a kosher hotel who agreed to handle his catering job tonight, a medium-sized birthday party in the Hollywood Hills. The food was prepared, Isaac told him, so all his friend would have to do would be set up, service and break-down.

Then Isaac drove toward Life Space. While he finessed the curves on Mulholland Drive, I explained as briefly and logically as I could why April called me Ellen and Gary called me Sarah.

Isaac nodded once, but otherwise refrained from commenting.

The dogs were okay and overjoyed to see me. Then Linda welcomed Isaac by sitting at his feet and lifting her paw for a handshake.

Isaac lightly touched her head—which she found acceptable. And so did I.

When the dogs and I return from a walk to the Dog Park, the Life Space smells like nutmeg and cinnamon and maple syrup because Isaac is making challah French toast and coffee.

I sit on the couch, scratch Freddie behind his ears and pet Linda's forehead, give both dogs liver treats, then open my laptop.

Isaac delivers plastic silverware, napkins and two plates with paper plates on top of thick, cinnamon-sugared French toast to the coffee table, then returns with mugs of coffee.

"Thank you for going to Mount of Olives, and for understanding about the name thing. And for being a food psychic. Somehow you always know exactly what I need to eat."

"Thank you for saying that, Ascher. And since you did, before we get to work on Jan Hunter, I'd like to bring up something I've been thinking about for a long time."

Isaac looks serious. Sad and stern. What did I do wrong now?

"Shoot," I say, trying sound breezy as I move Freddie closer to Linda so Isaac can sit next to me.

Then Freddie farts.

"That," Isaac says.

"I'm sorry. I haven't had time to take him to the vet. But I'll make an appointment tomorrow."

"The problem, I think, is caused by his diet."

"But the vet switched him to a special diet. A prescription diet for seniors."

"Not his diet, his treats. I think that eating too much liver may be the problem."

"Liver? How can it be a problem? It's Made In USA, vet-recommended, one hundred percent pure, organic dehydrated, humane chicken liver."

"Liver is fatty. And Freddie's old and digestive problems come with age. I probably should have asked you before I did it—but I went to Mid-City Pooch Pavilion the other day and bought some dehydrated chicken breast—made in USA, vet-recommended, pure, organic, humane and dehydrated. I thought if you were okay with it, we could switch to the chicken treats for a week or so, and see what happens."

157.

Jan killed L.S. Rutledge and I think I know how. As a member of the Amigos Brigade, she had a key to L.S. Rutledge's apartment and could enter day or night. She could also park her car in front of L.S. Rutledge's door to unload groceries or medical supplies, or to hustle Linda inside and up the stairs and lock her in the spare bedroom or bathroom so quickly and quietly that L.S. Rutledge—asleep in her recliner, would never know.

That the note accompanying the blanket included a detailed confessional prayer, but was left unsigned also convinces me that someone analytical wrote it. Why it included the joint confession is something I don't understand yet.

Isaac isn't as sure as I am. Leaving the blanket and the unsigned note signifies a deep emotional conflict, he said. But Isaac requires a solid reason for a rational person to commit such a premediated, well-planned and irrational murder.

Emotion is its own logic, I reminded him.

"I know," he said. "I know."

So Isaac purchased an online background and criminal record check that told us that Jan Hunter—tax specialist and crocheter of blankets—is fifty-three years old, has no criminal history, was born in San Diego, earned a B.A. in sociology from UC San Diego, and attended UCLA School of Law, resided in San Diego, West L.A., Malibu and Santa Monica before moving to Los Villas del Praying Plants, and worked at various law firms until settling at the one in Century City she's been with for twenty-six years. None of this was surprising or useful.

My social media and image searches were more interesting.

Young Jan Hunter was beautiful in a negligent, unaware way. Without makeup and with her gently curly hair worn long, Jan surfed, ran, skied, swam, and played tennis. Her college boyfriend—also athletic and good looking—shows up a later as her post-law school husband. Then Jan began attending National Organization of Women and Democratic Women luncheons. Then a swaddled infant appears in her arms. The baby becomes a lanky little boy who looks like Jan——who now dresses in dark suits, heels, with her hair cut short. Then there's one of Jan on one side and her husband on the other side of their son on the bimah at his Bar Mitzvah.

Then come professional photo-shopped group photographs of the law firm, law firm head shots, pictures of Jan in front of women who dress the way she does—professional and put together. Members of the preschool's Gala Dinosaur Night planning committee, then a group shot of a private high school's Annual Fair and Giving committee brunch.

Then the schools disappear—and the son with them. There are no Facebook photos of proud, anxious Jan and her husband moving their son into his dorm on his first day of college. Well, maybe he didn't go to college. But there are no birthdays. No vacations. No son at all.

Then Jan's husband vanishes, too.

But there are more images of Jan—smiles-forced and hair cut even shorter—with her law firm colleagues at a retirement dinner, with the Los Villas del Fairfax Village Residents' Association holiday party, and in a photo captioned "Amigos Brigade" —a group that includes April and Gary and a few other people I recognize.

Isaac and I talked until it was very late, and finally decided that the thing that can't be avoided is that Ellen Nadel—friend of L.S. Rutledge's friend and friend to April—must talk to Jan as soon as possible. And the talk must take place somewhere open with few entrances and exits and places for Isaac to hide.

158.

As soon as the Business Office opens, I call April, and tell her I want to thank Jan in person for the blanket and take her for coffee. April is happy to give me Jan's law office and home numbers, and lets slip that mine is a wonderful idea because "Jan is so terribly lonely." When I call Jan's office and her assistant connects me, she's cordial, gracious and, because her late morning client's plane has been grounded in Cleveland, she accepts my invitation for coffee at the Getty Center—which is about halfway between her office in Century City and my apartment in the Valley, has open spaces, and just one visitor entrance and exit.

We agree to meet at eleven on the steps outside the entrance hall.

Isaac cleans up in the kitchen while I walk the dogs. After we shower, Freddie goes wild barking at the hair dryer I hardly use––but he doesn't pass gas.

I put on the navy pants and the V-necked white blouse, but not the gold chain I wore to L.S. Rutledge's funeral, then pull my hair back in a pony tail. For a moment I wish I hadn't tossed the ballet flats. Then I pull on the tube socks and then the boots.

"You look more business-like than you really are," Isaac says.

"That's because I'm Ellen Nadel—not Ascher Lieb."

Isaac looks at my feet. "Ascher Lieb would wear those boots, but I don't think Ellen Nadel would, do you? She seems a little bit prissy."

I consult the mirror and know Isaac is right. "But all I have are my Converse sneakers and flip-flops."

"Wear the sneakers," Isaac says. "I think they'll look good.

And match your shirt."

"Blouse.

"Isn't a blouse a shirt?"

I smooth on some of my aunt's pressed powder, swirl on some blush, and gloss my lips—my aunt's lipstick is too red for me. "A blouse is a shirt for women. A shirt is a shirt for men. What are you going to wear?"

Isaac opens the drawer where he keeps his spare black jeans, black t-shirt and black socks and peers into it. "Dress shoes, and a tuxedo jacket, I think. And a nice, manly shirt underneath."

159.

Isaac turns into the Getty Center parking structure early—I hope not too early. I made the free but required parking reservation for ten forty-five, but it's only ten-twenty.

The kiosk guard waves us in and Isaac finds a spot for the Lexus on the second level near the elevator. I check my hair and makeup in the visor mirror.

"You look prissy but beautiful, Ellen," Isaac says. "But not as beautiful as this woman I know named Ascher."

"Stop," I say.

Isaac gets out of the Lexus, walks around the trunk and opens the door for me. I feel as though we are going to a funeral—maybe because Isaac is wearing a tan suit and a blue, button-down shirt. And normal shoes. Brown ones that he insists have always been at the bottom of a garment bag that I don't remember seeing in his closet.

"Your phone's completely charged?" Isaac asks again as we wait for the elevator.

"It's going to explode, that's how charged it is."

The elevator doors open and the people already inside—a gray-haired couple, each holding a pair of hiking poles and a man with a goatee—make room for us.

"Good."

The door closes and I notice the absence of the smell of food.

The elevator delivers us to the tram waiting area and we all face the track until a puff of air announces the apparitional approach of a sleek white car—part of a driverless hovertrain system designed by the Otis elevator company—on our right. The doors on the far side of the arriving tram open and discharge the passengers inside. Then the departure doors slide open to admit us.

We step inside with the man with the goatee and the hiking pole couple. I choose a seat that faces east. Isaac sits next to me. The man with the goatee sits at the front. The tram begins the steep ascent along the brush- and chapparal-covered hillside, the tram climbing until we can see the 405 Freeway below and the emerging west-city skyline. The couple with the poles stands near the grab rail, the poles hanging from their wrists.

The woman smiles at me. "I heard the view was spectacular. It is."

"But wait until we reach the top," I say. "You can see the ocean and the mountains from up there."

I want to go over things one more time with Isaac, but I can't. So I watch the solid world drop from sight and the tram windows fill up with sky.

160.

The tram doors whisper open and we step onto an expanse of smoothed, golden-beige travertine. I hold my cell phone to my ear as Isaac, according to plan, strides ahead of me to the entrance. I walk leisurely toward the steps, absorbing the warm light bouncing from stone to stone below the lucid sky.

Isaac pauses before a horizontal bronze nude with one monumental arm outstretched, then smartly ascends the steps, passes under the portico, and melts into the shadows of the Great Hall.

It's a weekday mid-morning so the tram mostly delivers tourists, retirees, teachers and school children wearing name tags on strings of yarn. Most wander the wide plaza, then take their time climbing the steps.

I walk toward the imploring bronze figure until my small head faces her huge, sideways one, consider taking a selfie but don't, take a last look at the entrance, then direct my gaze at the silent, captain-less, float-on-air tram gliding to a stop.

161.

Jan Hunter's graphite cashmere sweater and wool pants are almost the same color as the bronze nude—but Jan is slender, gravity-bound, vertical and advances through space with an aggressive swiftness—the small wine-colored Coach bag across her chest bouncing against her narrow hips.

Jan extends her hand before she's close enough to touch mine. I step toward her and we awkwardly, lightly shake hands. "I'm so glad you could make it on such short notice."

"Serendipity," Jan says. "Sometimes things just come together." We take the stairs shoulder to shoulder, pass through the echoing Great Hall where I don't see Isaac—and step onto the long plaza dotted with benches and metal tables and chairs arranged with views of turquoise pools.

I nod toward a cart selling coffee and pastry. "What would you like? Coffee and a snack or actual lunch in the restaurant upstairs? My treat."

"Coffee is good," Jan says. "I have a late lunch meeting after this."

When I deliver her espresso and my latte and croissant, Jan's waiting at a shaded table near a southward overlook between two buildings. Jan faces the plaza and has thoughtfully left the view-facing chair for me—so I won't be able to see Isaac if he's nearby. Will he see me?

The rectangle of sky contained in the overlook is cloud-striated and mottled like the travertine. Beneath it Jan sips her espresso and smiles. "I forget sometimes that there's a world outside the office. Or even an outside. This was a nice idea, Ellen."

"I wanted to thank you properly for the blanket. I was kind of shook up when you gave it to me. It's beautiful."

"I'm glad you like it."

"I will treasure it," I say. "How do find time to create the blankets with all the work you do?"

"I make time. Crocheting is soothing and simple. All I have to deal with are real loopholes, not legal ones." Jan smiles again.

"April said you donate them to charity." I push a little.

"Addiction Partners. They're a nonprofit that helps users and their loved ones overcome drug dependency."

"That's wonderful."

"It's an unusual group," Jan says. "Instead of enabling addicts, A.P. actually helps them kick their habit."

I decide to return to this enabling thing later. "Do all you blankets have Stars of David? Or do you make them with other designs?"

"I do them with hearts, peace signs, crosses, stars and crescent moons—even smiley faces. Whatever the nonprofit asks me to do. They auction them a couple times a year. April asked if I had a Star of David, and I did, so that's what you got. I hope that's the right design for you."

"It is," I say. "It's perfect. With all you're doing, you probably don't take commissions, do you?"

"Sometimes. Depends on the timing."

"A friend of mine is having a baby," I say. "A boy. I was looking at the blanket you gave me, and thought that a smaller one would make a wonderful crib blanket."

"I can do that. The small blankets don't take as long. When would you need it?"

"Really? That's great. In about three months."

Jan opens her purse and removes a thin leather diary and thin silver pen. "Give me your number and I'll mark you down for a crib blanket to be completed two months from now."

"Two months?"

"I know from experience that babies can arrive ahead of schedule. Which design?"

"Blue on white Star of David, please. With that beautiful sparkly yarn."

162.

We stroll through the plaza and descend the steps to the Garden, pausing under a bougainvillea arbor and Jan asks what I do. I don't say I'm in mortuary science school. I lie that I used to work at Sunny Morning Elder Care and assisted living in the Valley, and that after deciding to leave geriatric care, I'm searching for a new direction.

"I could put in a word for you at A.P."

"A.P.?"

"Addiction Partners. Someone who worked with the elderly would have the patience required for working with people coming out of addiction."

"That's so nice of you. But I don't know much about addiction," I, the person who had a Valium problem, says.

We drift toward the topiary maze at the garden's center. "Actually, they look for people exactly like you. Without preconceptions about drug use and drug rehab."

"Which preconceptions?"

"Most of the do-gooders who think they're helping people with their drug problems enable them."

Jan gazes at the manicured topiary maze at the center of the garden. "Enabling is the opposite of help."

163.

"I'm not sure what you mean by enabling," I say as we climb the steps up to the Plaza and walk toward the Entrance Hall along a wall where the stone is mottled and fossiled with leaves.

"Offering so-called support instead of letting the addict face the reality of his situation."

"What kind of support?"

"Let's say an addict has hit bottom and is homeless. Instead of letting the addict confront this reality, people will soften the situation with food, clothing, money—even tents. So, the addict doesn't seek the help he really needs to end his addiction." Jan pauses her ascent and grips the railing with her hand. "Stopping the drugs is the only thing that saves them."

"I get it," I say.

"I wish other people did. There are too many bleeding hearts out there keeping addicts addicted—and basically murdering them."

164.

I wait for the tram with Jan. When the car arrives, the harried male teacher standing next to us immediately fills the car with a big, boisterous group of cranky six-year-old boys, so we wait. The trams that arrive across the track from us are full of arrivals. But now that the kids have gone, we are the only ones waiting to take the downhill trip.

"How long before the next one?" Jan asks.

"I'm not sure. But I think I read somewhere that it's four minutes."

"I've been having such a nice time that I'm going to be late for my meeting."

"I'm sorry."

"Don't be. I called my assistant from the restroom and gave her a new ETA. Everything's covered."

The snub nose of the white, soundless car emerges around the turn at the bottom of the brown and sage hill, then glides to a stop on the track before us. I look back—no one else hurries to catch the tram. And if Isaac's here—he's invisible.

It's just four minutes, I remind myself and follow Jan inside the car.

I sit where I did on the ride up—in the seat that will afford me the best view of the eastward skyline about to disappear.

The tram moves. Jan stands near the grab pole and gazes out the window.

"I never get tired of this view," I say as, below us the miniature cars and trucks drift southward on the slender gray ribbon that is the 405 Freeway.

Jan pulls her crossbody purse over her head. "My favorite

thing is that the tram is driverless. We might as well be in outer space. That's how disconnected we are from everything and everyone right now."

"I never thought of it that way. But you're right—we're in our own little space ship. Cut off from the world." Four minutes locked in an automated capsule with Jan Hunter seems long now that I'm even more sure she killed L.S, Rutledge. But I can't prove it—not in the time I have left with her.

Jan twists and untwists the long strap of her purse as she stares dreamily out the window at the shrubs and yuccas. "People forget that southern California isn't palm trees and surfers—it's dry brush and rattlesnakes."

This is my last chance, to I decide to prod her. "Sort of like the bleeding hearts you talked about? Like Linda Rutledge and all her good deeds at the homeless camp?

Jan keeps her eyes on the window. "Fuck Linda Rutledge. Who was she to meddle in people's lives? To appoint herself savior of people she could never save? People she ended up hurting."

I'm feeling my way, but keep going. "Did Linda hurt someone you cared about?"

"Linda Rutledge murdered my son, Ellen. Or is it Sarah?"

Jan no longer stands near the pole. She's leaning over me, the twisted purse strap in her hand. She shoves my head down, loops the strap behind my neck, then crosses and tightens it so hard that I gag and my head hits the window. I kick her calves and try to push her hands away—but Jan is strong and strangles me with all her strength.

Through the pinhole I look through, I see Jan's eyes widened by exertion, then the Northern lights and exploding fireworks that have no sound.

And as the hole closes, I remember my promise to Isaac.

To Isaac.

165.

My throat hurts. My head aches. And there's a face behind the fog. "Isaac?"

"I'm right here, Ascher."

"It's hard to talk."

"That's an oxygen mask. Don't worry about it."

My eyes close without my permission and I see flashes—the tram car, Jan, the twisted purse strap.

Isaac encloses my hand in his.

"Jan—"

"—tried to strangle you," he says "I know. Everyone knows. The police took her and she's gone. And we're together, Ascher.

166.

I had trouble swallowing for a few weeks, but Isaac made me delicious smoothies. What Isaac called petechiae—a spatter of red spots under my eyebrows and in my ears—faded after about five days. But when I worked up the nerve to look at myself in the bathroom mirror this morning, my eyes were still bloodshot, my eyelids were still swollen and the ugly bruise around my neck was still there. And sometimes I still get hoarse.

My biggest problem is falling and staying asleep. But, Freddie––who hardly farts now—and Linda, and Isaac are helping me with that.

Isaac wanted me to stay at his place after the attack. I brought the dogs with me for a test-night, and it went okay. So, the four of us have been here at Partridge Place for the last five weeks and it's been good. Freddie and Linda enjoy their walks around the new neighborhood, and I take them to Los Villas for grass-time every day and to visit April.

Linda follows Isaac around. Isaac and Freddie are distant, but seem cool with one another. And once a week, Isaac and I have shakshuka breakfasts at Pacific Kosher in North Hollywood—so I don't get homesick for the Valley.

What happened with Jan and my understanding of everything else has fleshed out. Isaac was right behind the pillar near the plaza-level tram stop when Jan and I entered the car. Isaac said that Jan seemed relaxed, and I seemed relaxed, so he made the split-second decision to wait for the next car so that Jan could talk to me without a stranger present.

We were both thinking the same thing in that moment. But Isaac has apologized a thousand times for what he calls his "fatal and unforgiveable mistake." And I've told him a thousand times that it was my choice to get in that car with Jan—not his.

It's true. I could have ducked into the restroom. I could have pretended to receive a call. And I could have come up with a lie that would have taken me inside the Great Hall. But I didn't.

After Jan's arrest, the police executed a search of Jan's apartment and her computer. They didn't find one of those insane shrines that they always find in psycho-killer movies, but they found computer searches for photographs of dog-bite wounds. And they found Gary's missing garden tools—a pair of mean-looking shears and a hand rake with sharp, pointed tines that the police canine aggression expert the district attorney's office consulted declared could have produced wounds that mimicked dog bites and the wounds visible on L.S. Rutledge's arms and neck in the initial crime scene photos.

And yesterday Isaac told me that both tools had minute flecks of human blood on them.

I feel good that I fulfilled my promise to L.S. Rutledge. And I got rid of the photos—so maybe she can finally be at peace.

But I don't feel good that grief and guilt that she couldn't save her son pushed Jan to murder someone generous and lovely who I really wish I'd known.

It was nagging at me, so I asked Isaac if he could ask someone in Shomrim to find out from their LAPD contacts if Jan ever told them where she got Linda. But I'm not counting on finding out.

When the world thought she was a monster, Linda mattered.

Now, she's just a dog.

167.

I stand on the fragrant grass covering the burial plot next to hers that my aunt purchased as a surprise, parting gift to me. Should I find out if the plot next to mine is available for Isaac? I push the thought away.

Cemeteries are about life—not death. And life is why I'm here.

I don't wear my aunt's pearls because my neck is still sore. But I've circled one of her scarves—the red and white chiffon polka-dot one that she thought went so nicely with her lipstick—over my throat and my new silk Anthropologie blouse. The scarf covers the bruises and, like incense, faintly broadcasts my aunt's fading Arpège scent.

I look around to make sure no one is close and that Isaac—who's been a little clingy since the thing with Jan—didn't decide to arrive early.

I'm alone except for the gardener mowing the lawn way down the hill and the squirrel resting on a sun-warmed marker two rows over. If I squint, I can see the studios and the new condos where my aunt's house used to be. And the overpass above the 134 Freeway where members of The Order of Christian Manhood hung a banner two weeks ago that said that "Pedophile Kikes In Hollywood Start All The Wars."

I send a silent fuck you in the direction of the overpass then–-though I know my voice sounds scratchy—I begin.

"Everything that's happened taught me that I've left too many things unsaid. So, I wanted to come early for some Auntie E and Ascher time and say some things I should have said already.

Thank you for mothering and fathering me, for loving me when I wasn't loveable—which was pretty much the whole time you knew me, I guess. Thank you for finding me when I couldn't find myself. And for believing in me when I didn't believe in anything or anyone. Not even you.

I want you to know how sorry I am. For being wrapped up in myself and for being afraid. But what really kills me is that I wasn't there to help when you were sick. And I wasn't with you when you died. I know you were trying to keep from burdening me, but I needed to be with you.

And you needed to be with me.

All the love you poured into me wasn't wasted—any goodness I have inside me is from you. And I know that after all you did for me and for the other people in your life, you probably just want to get the hell out of Dodge and have some solitude and peace. But there's one last, huge favor I need to ask—

I know today is an ending. And that unveiling your marker will make everything real. And final.

But I need you not to end now.

So, please don't go.

I've tried for months to prepare myself for your final departure–but I'm not ready. So, if you have any say in this, or any pull—can't whatever's left of you put off checking out?

I have a new dog I want you to meet. And I know it's hard to believe, but she's Freddie's best friend. And there's a man named Isaac Kahn. He's a chef and an emergency medical technician, and he's thinking of becoming a P.A.—a physician assistant. And I think he should because he'd be a great one. He's smart like you and has the same gift you had for lighting things up and for connecting with people.

You'd love him and I know he'd love you.

And for some reason he loves me and thinks I'm beautiful and that I should wear my hair pushed away from my face. And he wants us to get married. And I said yes. His parents and his sister are flying in from Rochester in three weeks to meet me. I'm nervous—but he keeps telling me that they already love me.

But I don't know how to get married without you with me. Doing it without you would be doing the most important thing in my life without breathing.

You were my oxygen after my parents died. You were why I could keep going. So, if you can stick around for a while after we do the unveiling today, I'd be grateful.

And, Auntie E, if you can't, I'll still be grateful and I'll always love you.

And maybe—if Isaac helps me—I'll figure how to marry Isaac without you there."

I lift a corner of my aunt's scarf to my eyes and blot my tears with it. Then I remove the three crappy pieces of white Lieb house gravel and the mandarin orange-sized chunk of granite I pilfered from below the Hollywood sign my aunt loved more than anything in L.A. and that Isaac and I hiked to last week from the pockets of my nice, navy Chico's pants.

I arrange the stones on the grass below the veiled marker.

Then I look around.

The squirrel has gone. The guy keeps mowing the endless grass at the bottom of the hill among the rows of rectangular bronze markers that undulate over the gentle slopes.

I kneel and pull back the linen cloth. And before I return it to her marker, I recite the words I had engraved on it so my aunt–—if she is listening—can hear them:

Evelyn Pauline "Paulie" Nadel
1942-2022
Loving, Beloved, Bright-Souled, Magnificent
Aunt, Sister, Sister-in-law, Friend and Blessing to All
"…invisible gift, purest, sweet necessity–my air"

The End

Acknowledgments

Immense thanks to canine aggression and veterinary forensic expert James L. Crosby M.S. (Retired), Ph.D. for generously sharing his knowledge and expertise with me, and to the kind and patient Mystery Loves Georgia auction winners whose names I used in this book.

Chris McVeigh, the lighthouse-souled genius of the independent Fahrenheit Press always has my admiration and gratitude.

And I am deeply grateful to my son, chaplain and soon-to be-rabbi, Ian Perry, for his sharpness and guidance, and thankful to my husband, Thomas Perry, for everything.

About the author

Jo Perry earned a PhD in English, taught college literature and writing, produced and wrote episodic television, and has published articles, book reviews, and poetry. She lives in Los Angeles with her husband, novelist Thomas Perry. They have two adult children. Their two cats and two dogs are rescues.

Also by Jo Perry

- *Dead is Better*
- *Dead is Best*
- *Dead Is Good*
- *Dead Is Beautiful*
- *Everything Happens*
- *Pure*

More books from Fahrenheit Press

Pure by Jo Perry

Caught in a pincer movement between the sudden death of Evelyn (her favourite aunt) and the Corona virus, Ascher Lieb finds herself unexpectedly locked down in her aunt's retirement community with only Evelyn's grief–stricken dog Freddie for company.

As the world tumbles down into a pandemic shaped rabbit–hole Ascher is wracked with guilt that her aunt was buried without the Jewish burial rights of purification.

In order to atone for this dereliction of familial duty, Ascher – in her own words 'a profane, unobservant, atheist Jew, frequent liar and grieving loser' –volunteers to become the newest member of Valley Haverim chevra kadisha, a Jewish burial society on–call twenty–four–seven during lockdown and performing Mitzvot at no cost to the bereaved.

What follows is a journey through the insanity of lockdown in Los Angeles as Ascher attempts to bring peace to a troubled soul, and perhaps in the end redemption for herself.

This novel is everything.

In the hands of a lesser–writer a novel set in the time of covid could lead to a cliché ridden trope–fest, but instead with the skill and grace we've come to expect from Jo Perry she has delivered a book that is wise and beautiful and uplifting.

In our opinion with *Pure*, Jo Perry has surpassed even her own high–bar and written the finest novel of her career to date – but don't take our word for it – here's what some of her fellow writers say…

"Faultlessly imagined and beautifully written, this is one of the best novels I've read all year." –Timothy Hallinan, author of the acclaimed Simeon Grist series

"Pure is an immersive, twisting and turning metaphysical murder mystery set in the L.A. of 2020 with its Covid lockdowns, conspiracy theories and

ethnic hatreds. Highly recommended." –Seth Lynch, author of the 3rd Republic mysteries.

"Perry's mysteries never fail to mesmerize...With Pure she's outdone herself..." –Jeffrey Siger, author of the celebrated Chief Inspector Andreas Kaldis novels

The Beloved Children

Three young women; Chrysanthemum, Rose & Orage are thrown together performing as The Three Graces on the stage of Fankes' Theatre during the closing days of the Second World War.

It's there they come under the spell of wardrobe mistresses Dolores and Janna – a chance encounter that will guide and change all of their fates forever.

Set in the dying days of vaudeville theatre and laced with mysticism, fortune tellers, ghosts, and evocative descriptions of the closing days of the War – The Beloved Children will literally make you laugh out loud and perhaps even shed the odd tear.

The Beloved Children is wise, funny, heart–breaking, joyous, poignant, and entirely entirely enthralling.

Tina Jackson has conjured characters that you will fall unapologetically in love with and placed them in a world that you won't want to leave.

This book genuinely weaves a spell around the reader and once you make friends with Janna, Dolores, and The Three Graces you'll never want to be without them in your life again.

"This gloriously offbeat tale has shades of Angela Carter, with its beguiling characters weaving a magical spell."

– Kitty Marlow, The Mail On Sunday

Black Moss by David Nolan

In April 1990, as rioters took over Strangeways prison in Manchester, someone killed a little boy at Black Moss.

And no one cared.

No one except Danny Johnston, an inexperienced radio reporter trying to make a name for himself.

More than a quarter of a century later, Danny returns to his home city to revisit the murder that's always haunted him.

If Danny can find out what really happened to the boy, maybe he can cure the emptiness he's felt inside since he too was a child.

But finding out the truth might just be the worst idea Danny Johnston has ever had.

"As one would expect from a writer with the skill and experience of David Nolan, this haunting book deals with very difficult issues in an incredibly sympathetic manner while at the same time throwing a light onto one of the most complicated and shaming areas of our society – the failure to protect those who are the most vulnerable."

The Perception of Dolls by Anthony Croix

"It's almost as if history is trying to erase the whole affair." – Anthony Croix

The triple murder and failed suicide that took place at 37 Fantoccini Street in 2001, raised little media interest at the time. In a week heavy with global news, a 'domestic tragedy' warranted few column inches. The case was open and shut, the inquest was brief and the 'Doll Murders' – little more than a footnote in the ledgers of Britain's true crime enthusiasts – were largely forgotten.

Nevertheless, investigations were made, police files generated, testimonies recorded, and conclusions reached. The reports are there, a matter of public record, for those with a mind to look.

The details of what took place in Fantoccini Street in the years that followed are less accessible. The people involved in the field trips to number 37 are often unwilling, or unable, to talk about what they witnessed. The hours of audio recordings, video tapes, written accounts, photographs, drawings, and even online postings are elusive, almost furtive.

In fact, were it not for a chance encounter between the late Anthony Croix and an obsessive collector of Gothic dolls, the Fantoccini Street Reports might well have been lost forever.

<u>Cash Rules Everything Around Me by Rob Gittins</u>

Morrissey Jarrett is fresh out of prison and back on the streets of his hometown Cardiff.

During his enforced absence the city has been re–developed to within an inch of its life and a disoriented Morrissey falls back into old habits as he scams, schemes, and steals whatever he needs to survive.

Morrissey has big dreams though. Dreams of making one last huge score, dreams of leaving his life of crime behind, dreams of reuniting with the love of his life and dreams of walking off into the sunset with her. Happy. Ever. After.

All he needs is a plan.

Luckily, the circles Morrissey frequents provide ample opportunities for ill–gotten gains and soon the perfect job literally falls into his hands.

And so, along with a hastily assembled crew of misfits, Morrissey embarks on planning the perfect heist. With all their eyes fixed steadily on a payday that could change their stars forever – all they have to do is keep their heads down, play it cool, and follow the plan to the letter.

What could possibly go wrong?

www.ingramcontent.com/pod-product-compliance
Lightning Source LLC
Chambersburg PA
CBHW020338310726
48979CB00015B/2417/J

* 9 7 8 1 9 1 4 4 7 5 6 9 6 *